BETWEEN TWO WORLDS

Jenny St. Germain was a white woman from a white world—but that seemed so long ago. The Navajos had saved her, the Navajos had taught her their ways, the Navajos were her people, she vowed, now and forever.

Daniel Strongbow was a Navajo—but that, too, was long ago. For he had fled his tribe, he had given his allegiance to the U.S. Army, and his devotion to the man whom Jenny once had so passionately adored, Colonel Jessie Norwood.

Jenny and Daniel. They could not fall in love, for that would mean betraying all they were, and all they chose to be.

They could not fall in love—until, in a wave of desire they could not control, and a flood-tide of fulfillment they could not forget, they did. . . .

DEVILWIND

DEVILWIND

Jenny's Story

by
Aola Vandergriff

A SIGNET BOOK

NEW AMERICAN LIBRARY

PUBLISHER'S NOTE

This novel is a work of fiction. Names, characters, places, and incidents either are the product of the author's imagination or are used fictitiously, and any resemblance to actual persons, living or dead, events, or locales is entirely coincidental.

Copyright © 1986 by Aola Vandergriff

All rights reserved

SIGNET TRADEMARK REG. U.S. PAT. OFF. AND FOREIGN COUNTRIES
REGISTERED TRADEMARK—MARCA REGISTRADA
HECHO EN CHICAGO, U.S.A.

SIGNET, SIGNET CLASSIC, MENTOR, ONYX, PLUME, MERIDIAN and NAL BOOKS are published by New American Library, 1633 Broadway, New York, New York 10019

First Printing, December, 1986

1 2 3 4 5 6 7 8 9

PRINTED IN THE UNITED STATES OF AMERICA

for
Jagdev Indar Singh, M.D.,
a prince among men

PROLOGUE

The two of them, Jenny and her guardian, didn't realize they were so near their destination. They had spent the night on a high, unprotected plateau; the grizzled man lying far enough from the girl to control his desires but close enough to protect her.

This morning they arrived, after a brief ride, at the ranch house they had been searching for. It had come at them out of the early fog like a surprise. For a moment it held a sort of spurious beauty. Though the structure was gray and unpainted, the dawning sun touched it with watery blue and rose, hiding the fact that it was little more than a shack.

Jenny Johansson dismounted and tied her horse to the rickety rail fence that surrounded the seemingly deserted structure. Then she paused to look up at the man accompanying her, with great, swimming eyes that betrayed her nervousness.

"Thank you, kindly, Mr. Washburn. I can manage by myself now. You get back to your children. I feel terrible making you come so far out of your way."

He gave her a crooked grin. "Whoa up, girl. I volunteered, remember? And we're not even sure this is the right place. I promised your ma I'd see you here safely, and I'm gonna do it, hell or high water!" At the sight of her downcast expression he looked at her with amused understanding and relented.

"I *am* worried about my kids. I'll just wait here. When your man comes to the door, gimme a wave and I'll take off."

Though this was the moment she had waited for, planned for, Jenny was suddenly reluctant to have Washburn leave.

"Maybe," she said shakily, "you'd like to come in for a cup of coffee and meet Jesse?"

He grinned again and shook his head. He didn't intend to spoil her reunion. Besides, it would hurt him too much to watch. Though he had loved his wife, he had grown fond of this pretty, coltish girl who cared for his motherless children after Lizbet's death.

Too fond, perhaps.

"No," he said, "I think not. Run along. And . . . Jenny?"

She turned to look at him, and he said, lamely, "I wish you well."

"I know that," she said. Impulsively she threw him a kiss. "And thank you. You've been very kind."

Then she flew up the winding path toward the wind-scoured building, her dark hair hanging down her back; a lovely, half-wild child.

She doesn't belong here, Washburn thought, watching her. She didn't belong in this high country with its wind-tortured cedars and pinion; this harsh land studded with bunch grass and greasewood. There was none of the lush softness of Sweethome, where she had lived with her mother and stepfather, Inga and Theron St. Germain.

For a moment he felt a twinge of anger at the two people who had let this girl go off into the unknown.

At least they had sent her off in the company of a family. They had no way of knowing that Lizbet would die along the trail or that this kind of life in the wilderness awaited their daughter.

He wondered now if it would be too late to ask Jenny to return with him, to tend the little ones he'd left in the care of a housemaid at the Exchange Hotel in Santa Fe; to come back home with them to Memphis.

For he was going back there. He had seen enough of this godforsaken place. The journey west had been for Lizbet's health. And Lizbet was dead. Now he had nothing left but his children and a memory.

Jenny Johansson had already forgotten Ed Washburn. She hurried toward the forlorn gray house. There was no room in her thoughts for anything but Jesse; Jesse Norwood, the Southern boy her stepfather had referred to as "poor white trash." She had fallen in love with him, and he had gone away, promising to send for her. But in Jesse's last letter he said it might be better to forget him and find someone else.

At first Jenny panicked. Then she decided he had to have a reason. Maybe things hadn't worked out for him in the New Mexico Territory, and he didn't want her to know. Jesse had his pride.

She kept his real message to herself and lied

to her mother, saying that Jesse had sent for her to come to him.

Now she was trembling like a frightened deer.

What if he had meant what he said? What if he didn't really want her? She couldn't bear it if he didn't. Surely he would be glad to see her. Please, God, he had to be!

She stood on tiptoe to reach the knocker: a leather thong that held a rusted horseshoe. And then she waited, her heart beating much too fast, for someone to answer the door.

—— **PART I** ——

1

At Sweethome, Inga St. Germain walked to the small arched bridge over the river that she had always thought of as her special place.

She stood, gazing down into the tawny water, her blue eyes clouded with worry.

Lately she had felt very lonely—and afraid. She missed her daughters, especially little Jenny. She hadn't wanted Jenny to leave home, but it seemed willed by fate.

Ed Washburn, a friend of Theron's, had arrived just when Jenny received a letter from Jesse, asking her to come to him in the New Mexico Territory. Ed and his family were headed west, for the health of his wife, Lizbet. They desperately needed someone to help with their children. It was a heaven-sent solution for both Jenny and the Washburns.

But Inga's real reason for allowing Jenny to go was the health of her own husband, Theron St. Germain. Theron was unwell. He had grown crochety, irrational at times, and was prone to fits of temper in which he fought the battle of the North and South all over again.

Inga wanted him to see a doctor, but Theron

insisted he wasn't ill. So she tried to cope with his moodiness, hiding his unusual behavior from Jenny and the black tenants of Sweethome. She had hoped Theron's problems would go away.

Jenny had gone before Inga noticed his ... difference. But now she had to face up to the fact that the situation was more serious than she had guessed.

Last night had been the worst of all. At times Theron didn't recognize his own wife. He railed out at her, calling her an intruder, as he did years before when he'd returned from a Northern prison camp to find three strange women in his house. Inga and her two daughters had taken over Theron's ruined plantation, assuming that it had been abandoned permanently.

Theron knew Inga once more, a few minutes after he had gone back in time. But he insisted she call for old Caleb, a former slave, dead since before their marriage. His eyes had been wild, his forehead burning to the touch. Inga was certain he was feverish.

He had to see a physician. The problem was, how to get him to do it?

"Inga?"

She raised her eyes from the amber waters below the bridge.

Theron was coming toward her. He had dressed for the first time in several days and was wearing a faded blue shirt, open at the throat, with belled sleeves. One sleeve was folded to cover the stump of his missing arm. His black hair was rumpled, his skin golden under the sun of an autumn afternoon. He appeared to be his old self.

"I thought you were napping," she said.

He shook his head and grinned. "What is this?"

he asked. "Are you trying to get rid of me? Maybe you're meeting someone out here! A romantic tryst?"

Inga laughed. "Come to think of it, I am. I'm meeting my husband."

Theron put his arm around her and drew her close.

Together they stood listening to the sound of black voices calling to their horses and to one another as they worked at the fall plowing. Inga thought of how it had been her idea to give them food, housing, and a share of what they raised in return for their help. She had created a permanent group of hands to keep Sweethome solvent. Now she had the best of all possible worlds.

If only Theron would always be like he was today!

As if he knew what she was thinking, Theron interrupted her stream of thought. "Sweetheart" —his voice was casual but strained—"I want to ask you something. Did I . . . say or do anything last night that didn't seem . . . natural?"

When she failed to answer immediately, he said, "I did, didn't I?"

He sounded so lost, so deep in his own suffering, that she turned, burying her head against his shoulder. "I know you didn't mean anything you said."

"It's just that I have trouble remembering sometimes," he said painfully. "I'm afraid I was mixed up."

"It's all right, Theron."

"No, it isn't. I haven't been asleep this afternoon. I've just been lying there. I think I ought to go see that doctor in Memphis again. My arm's been bothering me a lot lately."

Inga put her hand on the spot where his sleeve was folded to cover the stump of his severed arm. The flesh was pulsing and feverishly hot.

It must have been the fever! In spite of her concern, she couldn't help feeling a vast relief. There was nothing terribly wrong with Theron's mind. He had been a little delirious last night, that was all.

She smiled up at him, her eyes suffused with deep affection. God, how she loved this man!

That night there was no recurrence of his illness. Theron made love to her as he had in the early days of their marriage. Tracing her fine-boned features with loving fingers, he touched her kiss-bruised mouth, her slender body.

I do not deserve him, she thought later, when she was certain he was asleep. *I do not deserve him!*

She thought of her first marriage. She had been little more than a child when she married Olaf Johansson. She had borne him two children; one, a replica of herself, Kirsten, as blond as the sun . . .

And Jenny, a dark little changeling.

Olaf hadn't accepted the second child as his. Jenny had the dark complexion and high cheekbones of an Indian; she was small and slight. Inga's husband had accused her of infidelity with a passing Sioux. Finally Olaf laid violent hands on Jenny, intending to sell her to a drinking friend. Inga struck him down. Certain that she had killed him, she took her daughters and fled.

Only then did Inga learn that her mother, Birgitta, not she, had brought Indian blood into the family through an illicit relationship. Inga herself was part Indian, though her features belied her heritage.

What had made her think of Olaf after all this time? When she confessed her past to Theron, she had felt cleansed, absolved, but now the memory of that night returned. She could remember it all so clearly: the terrible thudding sound when she struck Olaf; the way he turned to look at her in amazement, taking a few staggering steps before he fell—

Inga shivered.

"What's the matter, sweetheart?"

"Theron," she said with a gasp, "I thought you were asleep."

"How could I be? I was thinking how wonderful you are. Ah, Inga, we have so little time!"

She gave herself up to his lovemaking once again. And it was sweeter than ever.

Later, when he was really, truly asleep, Inga pondered what he had said.

"We have so little time."

It sounded like an omen.

The next morning Inga and Theron set off for Memphis. They filled the journey with laughter and love; it was almost like a second honeymoon. The road leading into town was smoother than when Inga had first come this way. Now it was well traveled, and occasional inns had been built along the way to take in a weary traveler.

Reaching Memphis at last, they debated whether to call on the doctor first, or upon Inga's old friend, Miz Fannie. The woman was the proprietress of a house of rather dubious repute, but Inga maintained that she was still an innocent in spite of her business.

Theron settled the matter with the flip of a coin.

"The doctor," he said gloomily. "Hell!"

Inga assured him that she would have a better visit with her concerns about his health off her mind.

"Let's get it over with," she coaxed.

Inga sat outside in the waiting room of an office that smelled of alcohol and chloroform. She twisted a handkerchief to shreds as she waited for Theron's return. And finally he came out of the room, stumbling a little, his face gray and stunned.

The doctor came to the door behind him.

"Mrs. St. Germain, would you mind stepping in for a moment?"

She entered, and he closed the door.

When she emerged from his office, she looked even worse than Theron. He studied her face and tried to smile.

"Well, are we off to Miz Fannie's now?"

"No, Theron, I just want to go home."

The trip back to Sweethome was a silent one. At night, in the great, high bed at the inn, Theron turned to Inga in desperation, holding her, loving her as if each moment would be their last together.

Still, they could not discuss what was on both their minds.

When they reached their plantation, Theron was reeling with exhaustion. Their black housekeeper, Dinah, clucked over him. His bed was turned down, ready and waiting for him; she would bring him a cup of tea.

Inga interrupted. "It isn't necessary. I'll take care of him."

Dinah raised startled brows but left the room. She was busily engaged in making bread when her mistress came down. She had left Theron reluctantly, at his insistence.

Dinah would have to know.

Inga made several false starts, trying to broach the subject, and finally Dinah took the initiative.

"Well, Miz Inga, you gonna tell me what that doctor say?"

Inga burst into tears, and Dinah gathered her to her massive bosom, heedless of her dough-covered hands, while she sobbed out what they had learned in Memphis.

A bone infection had settled in the stump of Theron's arm and was rapidly moving through the rest of his body. His mind, afflicted by his illness, the rigors of the war, and a year in a Yankee prison camp, was beginning to go.

The doctor's verdict amounted to a death sentence: a terrible death.

Dinah was silent for a moment. "Massa Theron know this?"

"All except the—part about his mind."

"Now look, missie, you bettah send for Miss Kirsten and Jenny. You gotta have somebody."

"No."

Inga raised her head proudly. She had two lovely girls. Kirsten had chosen to go off on her own, and Inga set Jenny free to find her own happiness, though it cost her a great deal of pain.

When Inga married Theron, she had assumed responsibility for her husband in sickness and in health. Now Theron was her responsibility, and he was hers alone.

2

In New Orleans, Inga's daughter Kirsten was still in bed. Nick had just kissed her and had gone downstairs to set up for the evening of gambling.

"Don't be long, sweetheart," he warned. "Remember, you're my biggest drawing card!"

Kirsten stretched luxuriously between the satin sheets. This life they lived was a topsy-turvy one. Sleep all day. Play all night. But she loved it.

She had especially loved making the place over. Gilt mirrors, crystal chandeliers, and walls of blue watered silk. Nick's Card Parlor was drawing a whole new clientele now: wealthy men who could afford to lose tens of thousands.

As she thought of that, Kirsten remembered the necklace one of the big spenders had given her the night before. He was a dashing fellow named Slim Morley who owned The French Rose, a brothel down the street. It was supposed to be one of the most glittering spots in New Orleans, more plush even than this gaming house. She would give her soul to get a look inside.

And she could, if Nick would only come to his

senses. Morley wanted Nick to go into partnership with him. But so far, Nick had refused, saying he didn't approve of Slim Morley's business.

Kirsten tossed her head frowning. How much difference *was* there between a gambler and a pimp? Her grandfather, Pastor Lindstrom, back in North Dakota, would say they were both doomed to hell. But he was a pompous old fuddy-duddy who had brought his narrow-minded ideas with him from Sweden.

If only she had some money to spend, she would darn sure invest it in The French Rose! Maybe if she talked with Nick and convinced him that she wasn't happy—

With a shock it came to Kirsten that she wasn't happy. In spite of the grandeur she had created to surround her and the fact that Nick was handsome and amusing and gave her everything she wanted—well, almost everything—something was missing. For one thing, she needed some money of her own.

Rising, she searched for the necklace Morley gave her. It was only a small strand of tiny rose-pink pearls, but Lydia, the fox-faced, carrot-haired girl who was with him, had looked daggers at her. Kirsten smiled to herself at the memory of Lydia's jealous eyes. She held the pearls to the light. They would go well with her azure taffeta gown. And Morley might come in again tonight.

She brushed her silken hair, donned several rustling petticoats, then slipped the dress over her head. When she clasped the pearls at her throat, she drew in a quick breath of wonder at her own beauty. It was cut short by a voice from behind her.

"Where did those come from?"

Nick had returned. He lounged against the door frame, one dark, satanic brow quirked in a question.

If he knew they had come from Morley, he would never forgive her. "They're not real. I—I won them," she lied.

The brow remained quirked, but Nick spoke in a reasonable tone. "Just remember what I told you. If you take gifts from the customers, they'll expect something in return."

"Dammit, I told you! I won these!"

Nick sighed. He was usually able to detect whether Kirsten was telling the truth. But this was not one of those times. He was none too sure about that story she had shown up with when she'd first come to New Orleans; that she had become pregnant by him and lost the baby. . . .

But, hell! It could have happened that way. And what if it wasn't true? Though Kirsten wouldn't marry him, she came to his bed willingly. He didn't think she would cheat on him. Not unless there was an enormous profit in it, he amended wryly.

And he loved her, not as he had loved her mother but differently. He had met Inga on the riverboat, leaving St. Paul, and had held her in his arms one wonderful night when they almost were run down by a blazing ship that lit the Mississippi with the fires of hell. Inga had been so afraid that she had clung to him like a child.

He was certain then, that he'd found the love of his life, and he had left Inga in Memphis, promising to return. When he went back, he couldn't find her. Inga and her daughters seemed to have disappeared from the face of the earth.

Then, on another journey, at another time, he had held Inga's daughter in the same way. He remembered how he had buried his face in her soft blond hair, and murmured Inga's name.

He would not make that mistake again.

He looked at Kirsten, feeling a faint stirring of passion. He knew it would grow to be tumultuous before the night was over; that he needed to take her now. He moved toward her, his face growing hot, his lips thickening.

"Kirsten," he said hoarsely. "Kirsten—"

"Don't!" she said a little sharply, "you'll muss my dress!" Then, in a placating, little-girl tone, "I want you, too, sweetheart. But wait. There isn't time."

She was right. He heard the laughter of early arrivals below as the barman, Pete, let them in. They came at this hour for one reason; to watch Kirsten make her entrance. She wouldn't disappoint them. Nick smiled indulgently.

"Ah, darling, how you love to make me wait," he said in a teasing voice. Then he hurried down the carpeted stairs to greet his customers. A few minutes later there was a sudden hush, broken only by the rising strains of a violin. Nick followed the example of the other men in the beautifully appointed, glittering room. He lifted his eyes to see Kirsten at the top of the curving steps, poised and lovely in the azure gown that matched her eyes, her creamy skin accentuated by a string of rose-pink pearls.

He was struck dumb by the fact that this was his woman. Kirsten belonged to him.

The pros, or would-be pros, usually took their places at Nick's table, certain that they could outwit his dexterity with the cards. Even then, they could hardly keep their attention on the game or their eyes from the lovely lady at another table where infatuated players didn't care if they won or lost.

Music played softly; French wines flowed freely. And, as the hours passed, Kirsten grew more flirtatious, more seductive, more beautiful than ever. This was her kind of life. She wouldn't trade it for anything in the world. . . .

Unless, of course, it was a place like Morley's French Rose.

As if he had heard her thoughts, Slim Morley appeared in the doorway. And the jealous little cat who usually accompanied him wasn't with him tonight. Kirsten smiled at Morley, and ignoring Nick Tremont's frown, the brothel operator made his way toward Kirsten's table where he glared at an effeminate young merchant until he relinquished his chair at Kirsten's table.

Then, casually, Morley tossed a large sum of money into the pot. Recognizing a challenge, Kirsten met his bid. She won, raking the money in. Finally, toward dawn, the other players dropped out. Morley put his hand over Kirsten's as she started to deal.

"I did not come here to play," he said in his softly accented voice, "but to make you a proposition. I've been trying to deal with Nick Tremont, but the man isn't smart enough to recognize an opportunity when he sees it. I would much prefer to deal with you."

At first Kirsten was too stunned to answer. Her mind whirled as she envisioned herself as

proprietress of The French Rose; purchasing
gowns even more beautiful than those she now
wore. She would be the queen of New Orleans
with the city's men at her feet.

Then she came down to earth. Her face reddened. "I have no money of my own," she confessed. "Nick just gives me a little for expenses."

"But you handle the receipts." Morley's eyes
held hers in a hypnotic stare as she fumbled for
an answer.

"Yes, but—"

"You can invest those receipts and return the
profits you make to cover them. Nick won't even
realize they're gone."

"No," she whispered. "I couldn't—"

Morley shrugged. "Think it over. Now deal.
Double or nothing."

She dealt, and he won easily. He picked up
the money left on the table, a silky smile on his
face. "Remember what I said about that little
investment. You might want to look the place
over. Come by—anytime."

She watched him go. If it weren't for Nick,
she told herself, she might find Morley attractive. He was too tall, too thin, but he had an
interesting face. A pencil-thin mustache concealed
a cruel mouth, and his black eyes undressed a
woman and made her feel seductive.

But there was Nick, who was a good and gen-
erous man, whom she had to admit she loved
after a fashion. And she also knew that Morley
wasn't exactly the most ethical man she had
ever met.

She was still thinking about Slim Morley and
his proposition when the gaming closed at dawn,
and she followed Nick Tremont upstairs to bed.

She removed her gown and sat, clad only in her chemise, while she used imported cream to remove the cosmetics with which she had painted her face.

Nick stood behind her, watching, thinking that she didn't need the makeup. She was lovely without it. Then, noticing that she wore the pearls, he stepped forward and unfastened them for her. They still held the warmth of her body, and he cradled them in his hand for a moment, feeling the life in them.

These were certainly not spurious pearls. And watching Slim Morley tonight, he had an idea where they had come from. But he would be damned if he'd ask again or make an accusation he couldn't prove.

Kirsten turned to face him, and he saw her perfect features, innocent in her shining face. Nick's heart banged in his chest, as if it would escape.

"Remember," he said quickly, "you promised. . . ."

In answer she went into his arms, pressing her body along his hard length, moving just a little from side to side until he groaned raggedly.

"My God! What you're doing to me!"

Kirsten backed away, looking up at him with impish eyes. "What am I doing?"

His hands were shaking as he tore at the fragile chemise she was wearing. "You little devil," he growled. "If you knew how much I need you!"

"I know," she said smugly.

Damn her, he thought. Oh, damn her! She was so sure of herself; so sure of him! He tried to return her roguish grin, but his heart was pounding and the best he could manage was a quick smile. His eyes were glazed with desire.

Carrying her to their bed, Nick placed her on blue satin sheets that brought out the blue of her eyes. He intended to control himself; to touch her tenderly, lovingly. But Kirsten did not share his mood. Her body came to life, all its nerve endings lit with passion, burning into him like a branding iron. She was begging him to hurry, to bring their passion to fulfillment.

"Just a little," she said, moaning. "Just a little more."

Her words destroyed his good intentions, and he made love to her forcefully, almost cruelly, as if he had the power to destroy her. And when he had finished, he lifted himself from her, appalled. He had been little more than an animal.

"Are you all right?" he asked urgently. "Kirsten?"

She was quiet—too quiet. "Kirsten?" Her name rang out with a sound of fear.

Kirsten opened one blue eye, then the other, raising a languid hand to caress her lover's brow. To tell the truth, she had enjoyed the whole episode tremendously. But she knew that if she handled Nick correctly, he would buy her another piece of jewelry to assuage his guilt.

"It was ... nice," she said in a small, unsteady voice, looking up at him pitifully.

He buried his face against her breast, murmuring apologies. He had no idea that she wasn't even listening.

She was thinking about her first lover, Matt Weldon, who lived across the road from Sweethome. He had been the father of the child she had told Nick was his. But Matt's lovemaking had been nothing like this.

She couldn't help wondering, however, if it could be better still; how it would be to lie with Slim Morley. . . .

And how it would feel to be co-owner of a brothel called The French Rose.

Nick's Girl

...
had been nothing like this.
She couldn't help wondering, how...
...could be better with him, it would be...

3

As Kirsten had expected, the very next day Nick purchased the ring she had been admiring. It was a star sapphire surrounded by diamonds, and it cost the moon. It took her mind away, temporarily, from Slim Morley's proposal. But not for long.

Kirsten managed to stave off temptation for a whole day. The following night, queening it at her table, she waited and watched for Slim Morley to come in. When he didn't, her attention wandered and her playing suffered. She excused herself, finally, leaving the regulars at her table to wonder at her odd behavior.

"Maybe," one of them offered, "she's found herself another guy."

Every man at the table grinned, each smug expression a testimony to Kirsten's skillful maneuvering where men were concerned. They all knew the object of her affections, and knew him very well.

But Kirsten had met her match, and she knew it. For the first time, sinking into her blue satin bed, she failed to savor its luxury. Morley would not be back. She knew that instinctively. Any move at this point would be up to her.

But how far did she want to go?

She shivered, thinking of the man's cruel, black eyes, the slash of his red lips beneath the pencil-thin mustache. No one knew anything about him, though it was said that he was descended from one of the pirates who served Laffite; that any man who crossed him disappeared from the face of the earth. There was an air of mystery about him that appealed to her. She thought of his slender, long-fingered brown hands, and imagined them touching her. . . .

What nonsense! She had no interest in Morley, none whatsoever, only in the brothel he operated, The French Rose.

And he had invited her. "Come by anytime," he had said. She had heard so much about the place. Though how it could be any more beautiful than this . . .

She cast her eyes about the room, seeing the lovely shades of gauzy blue and green. She had decorated the whole establishment in her favorite colors. And someone had the nerve to say it was *almost* the plushest place in town, second only to Morley's.

She had to see his place for herself!

"Sweetheart?"

Nick entered, interrupting her train of thought. "Yes?" She answered, more crossly than she had intended.

"I missed you downstairs and wondered if you were ill—"

"I have a headache," she said, lying.

"Is there anything I can do?"

"No," she said bravely, "but—thank you."

And at that moment she made up her mind. She wouldn't have anything to do with Morley, of course, nor with any business proposition he might have to offer. But it would do no harm to pay him a friendly visit, to see his place of business.

When Nick came to bed at dawn, she had turned away, her back to him. He leaned over and touched her forehead, and she moaned convincingly.

"Poor baby," he whispered. Then, in deference to her headache, he went into his study where he could sleep through the daylight hours.

Immediately Kirsten bounced up, her eyes sparkling. Now she could go where she wanted to go, do what she wanted to do, and Nick would never know!

She raised her shade so that the sun would strike her eyes at about ten in the morning. Then, with a smile on her face, she drifted into a dreamless sleep.

When Kirsten woke, she dressed hurriedly but carefully, in a rose-pink gown, cut low to reveal her creamy bosom. Then she donned a hat of a deeper shade, decorated with egret feathers. She chose a matching parasol. When she had finished, she studied her reflection in the mirror.

The outfit might be a little too fancy for morning wear, but she certainly looked grand!

She hastened down the stairs.

"Miz Kirsten?"

She froze at the sound of a man's voice. She had forgotten about Pete, the bartender. Last night had been a busy one, and Pete's helper had been out sick. Pete had stayed to wash glasses and do a general cleanup.

"You goin' someplace?"

"Just out for a walk," Kirsten said. "I have a headache and I need some fresh air. It's such a lovely morning!"

The old man looked at her strangely, and she realized she had been babbling. *I didn't even have to answer him*, she thought. *It's none of his business.* Then she stepped outside to find an overcast sky. It wasn't such a lovely day after all.

The French Rose was a magnificent old building at the other end of the French Quarter. It was stuccoed pink, and climbing ivy managed to maintain a foothold between the narrow street and the building. It covered the wrought-iron balconies beneath arched windows, framing the structure in lush greenery.

Kirsten lifted the knocker and let it fall.

After a wait that seemed interminable the door opened. It revealed a sleepy, scowling face, framed by a frowsy mop of orange-red hair. Lydia.

Kirsten squared her shoulders and lifted her nose in the air. "I wish to see Mr. Morley."

"He's in bed," the girl said sourly. And who should know better than she, since she had been there with him only minutes before?

Kirsten was still standing there indecisively when she heard a deep voice ask, "Who is it, Lydia?" Then, "Well, hello!" Slim Morley, clad in a crimson velvet robe, dismissed Lydia with a wave of his hand and drew Kirsten inside.

At first she was stunned. The floors were marble and covered with Oriental rugs. The walls were stark white, but everything else was crimson: crimson velvet drapes, deep scarlet chairs accented with black. Mirrors reflected the color that was in turn reflected from other mirrors. It was breathtaking.

As if he knew what she had come for, Morley led her from room to room, pointing out items of interest. That chandelier, with its shimmering teardrop prisms, had been created especially for The French Rose, back in the old days when it had been the home of a prominent figure.

Kirsten realized that the house was sleeping now, during the day. At night it would come alive with light and laughter.

"We have something for everyone," Morley told her. "Here's where we bring the voyeurs."

Kirsten stood on tiptoe to peer through the peephole at nothing—and blushed. It did not help to see Morley's sardonic smile at her discomfort.

"The girls' rooms are all above," Morley said, continuing the talk. They were equally sumptuous. "Now here's a place I especially want you to see." He smiled mischievously.

He led her into an office that was almost spartan in its appointments and slid a piece of paneling aside. Kirsten caught her breath.

Behind the panel was a spacious room, fit for a king. It held, on a raised dais, a round bed with a velvet spread. A rain of silken netting in the same shade of crimson swept from the ceiling. Above the bed, mirrors reflected the color of the spread. It was easy to guess at the reason for those mirrors; to imagine the translucent reflection of flesh meeting flesh in the act of love.

"T-this is . . . your room?" Kirsten stammered.

"It will be. I am waiting for the right woman to share it with."

Kirsten backed away from the room, hating herself for sounding so flustered. But she couldn't help it. As sure of herself as she usually was, she had never met a man quite like Slim Morley. And her intuition told her he was too much for her to handle.

She quickly made her excuses and left, and Morley did not try to stop her. He merely looked at her with a half smile that said he knew she would be back—and soon.

She was glad she had seen the house; it was beautiful. But it had frightened her. Right now all she wanted was to get home to Nick.

And for some obscure reason, Kirsten thought of her mother, Inga. She would give a lot, right this minute, to be a little girl again. She remembered herself as a child, holding fast to her mother's hand, while Jenny—adventurous little Jenny, who would never be as pretty as she was, Kirsten thought smugly—ran on ahead.

4

At the moment Jenny might have traded places with Kirsten. She had never felt less venturesome in her life. She had lied to her mother by saying that Jesse sent for her. Now would come the moment of truth.

As Jenny waited for someone to answer the door she looked up at the roof of the veranda; it stood out against the sky like a greasy thumbprint. Perhaps this was why Jesse hadn't wanted her to come to the New Mexico Territory. He was embarrassed by the obvious poverty of this place. It was certainly a far cry from the shack Jesse had lived in when she first met him. Though that was poorly built, it was very neat and well-kept.

This house could definitely use some cleaning up. There were traps stacked on the porch in a tangle of old boots and saddle blankets that smelled of horses.

Jenny thought of the softly scented gardens of Sweethome; its tall, white columns and painted exterior. Then she banished the memory. She would live with Jesse anywhere!

She closed her eyes for a moment, recalling

Jesse's solid frame; his gray, level gaze from beneath a shock of yellow hair; his bronzed, naked shoulders as he plowed, shirtless, in the sun.

She could remember every word he said when he left her. He said he was heading west to New Mexico, to work on the ranch of Sam Whitman, a friend from his stint with the Confederate Army. He told her that when he could give her the kind of life she deserved—the kind of life she lived at Sweethome—he would send for her. His pride would not allow him to be a lesser man than Theron St. Germain.

She set her hand again to the makeshift knocker, then heard footsteps approaching the door. The die was cast. Jesse might be happy to see her, and he might not be.

She braced herself as the door creaked open. Stunned, she gazed into the dark eyes of an Indian girl. Were they lost? Had they come to the wrong house? Jenny half turned toward Ed Washburn, who watched from beyond the fence, waiting until she went inside.

Finally she summoned her voice.

"I'm looking for Mr. Jesse Norwood."

"He is not here." The girl folded her arms decisively.

"T-then Mr. Whitman?" Jenny asked, faltering. "Sam Whitman?"

"He is sleeping."

The woman's words amounted to a dismissal. Jenny's cheeks grew hot with outrage. Here in this godforsaken place in the mountains, more than a hundred miles from Santa Fe, there could not be more than a visitor or two a year. And she was being treated like an interloper.

Well, perhaps she was one! But she had waited a long time and come a long way. She deserved some answers, and this girl's identity, her relationship to Jesse, were not the least of them!

She stiffened, glaring back at the Indian girl. "Then you will please wake him!"

"Who is it, Tsis'na?"

The voice came from behind the girl; she stepped aside to reveal a tall man in wrinkled garments who looked as if he had slept in his clothes. His hair was standing on end, his blue eyes were bloodshot, and his features were homely but congenial. Remembering her own father—not Theron St. Germain, but her true one—Jenny realized this man had been sleeping off the effects of a bottle.

"I-I'm Jenny," she said, stammering. "Jenny Johansson."

Sam looked surprised but he seemed delighted. "Well, what do you know! Jesse didn't tell me you were such a beauty!"

Jesse! She clung to his name as if to a lifeline. "Where is he?"

"He's gone on a little trip," Sam Whitman said, not quite meeting her eyes. "Got some business to tend to." Then, moving back, he said, "Come in! Come in! We'll give old Jesse a surprise! I'm Sam Whitman, by the way."

She hesitated, not quite sure of his expression as he looked her up and down, admiringly. Then she remembered that he was Jesse's friend and therefore to be trusted. Turning, she cast one desperate look at Mr. Washburn, her last tie with home, then raised a hand in farewell.

He saluted her and cantered away.

"And who was that?" Sam Whitman asked.

"A—friend. He brought me here."

"He's from Santa Fe?"

"No, he's from home. He was taking his wife west for her health, but she died. Now he's going back to Tennessee."

Sam's eyes glinted. "Good riddance. Now I'll have you all to myself—until Jesse comes back," he added hastily.

"But . . . where is Jesse?"

"Don't you worry your pretty little head about him. Right now you come in this house and let me give you a proper welcome!"

He ushered her inside, leaving a large hand on her arm a trifle too long.

"You and me's gonna get along just fine," he said exuberantly. "Just fine. Tsis'na"—he turned to the Indian girl—"take Miss Jenny to Jesse's room. Heat some water in case she wants to freshen up a bit."

The misgivings Jenny felt were intensified at the sight of Jesse's room. A row of hooks along the wall was empty, as was a homemade chest of drawers. Toward the door that led into the main room—where Sam evidently slept, judging from a rumpled bed that occupied one wall—there was a pile of harnesses, a worn saddle, whiskey bottles, and other cast-off debris. The objects had evidently been thrown there for want of storage space. They were now covered with dust.

Jesse either owned no possessions—or he had taken them all with him. Was it possible that he didn't intend to return?

Jenny washed her face and stood for a moment, hand on the doorknob to the other room, feeling a strange need to remain where she was. But she couldn't hide in here forever.

She pushed the door open.

- Sam stood near the fire, his arm draped familiarly around Tsis'na's waist. Jenny closed the door quickly, feeling a rush of blood to her face. So that was how it was!

At least, she thought with relief, the girl was Sam's—and not Jesse's. But she was certainly an intruder here. No wonder the girl had resented her coming!

What had she gotten herself into?

As he rode back toward Santa Fe, Ed Washburn mulled Jenny's welcome over in his mind. The homely, rather ragged-appearing man who had let Jenny into the house was not a figure to inspire undying love. He wondered if he had done the right thing, leaving her there.

When Jenny finally forced herself to come out of the bedroom, she found Sam Whitman to be an entertaining companion. Whitman had shaved and donned clean clothing. Though he was still evasive about Jesse, he proved to be a genial host, quoting from books and plays, filling her in on the history of the New Mexico Territory. She soon forgot her awkwardness as she listened to him ramble on.

Jenny remembered what Jesse had said. Sam was a kind of country lawyer who would rather talk than work. She warmed toward the homely man who had taught her dear Jesse to read and write and who had helped him make something of himself.

She didn't realize how often she mentioned

Jesse's name until Sam looked at her, his lips quirked in amusement.

"Jesse, Jesse, Jesse! Is that all you can say?"

She flushed, horrified. "I'm sorry. I didn't mean to be rude."

"Just remember, I'm here. I'm good-looking and charming too."

He was teasing. She laughed in relief but was careful to avoid dwelling on Jesse's name.

Finally, following a pleasant dinner, she excused herself and went to her room. She would sleep in the same bed where Jesse had slept. He would be home soon and all would be well. But first she would write a letter addressed to Sweethome. Finding a pencil and paper among the scanty possessions she had brought with her, she began.

Dear Mama . . .

Then, pencil to her lips, she paused. What could she say? That she had come here to find Jesse gone? That she was sleeping in a strange house, with a strange man in the next room, with only an Indian girl as chaperon? That Sam Whitman was very vague about when Jesse would return?

Surely, she thought, tomorrow she would know something more. For now she was too tired to write. And, admittedly, a little scared. If her mama read anything she had written in this state, surely she would know the truth of the situation: that Jesse wasn't here.

Finally Jenny put the paper away. She would wait for Jesse to return. Besides, she had already written her mother from Santa Fe.

Sam Whitman, in the next room, was just as wakeful as Jenny. Maybe he should have been honest with the girl, but the minute he saw her, he had fallen for her like a ton of bricks. Hell, Jesse hadn't even bothered to tell the girl the truth. Why should he?

He would just wait awhile, play it by ear. Maybe when Jenny found out that Jesse wouldn't be coming back, she might decide old Sam looked pretty good. Resting his head on his folded arms, he grinned at the ceiling.

He would give her a little more time, he told himself confidently. And then, by God, she was going to be his!

5

The weather changed, bringing an early snow to the high mountain area. Tsis'na awoke in the log shed that had become her sleeping place since Jenny's arrival and found her blankets dusted with white. She had grown unused to the cold these last years, but she couldn't help feeling grateful to Jenny, whose coming had sent her from Sam's bed.

Jenny woke, touching her bare feet to a cold floor that reminded her of the farmhouse in which she'd grown up in Minnesota. She went to look out the window at the drifts of snow beneath the ledge.

There was a great thumping and bumping from the kitchen, and Jenny dressed hurriedly. She found Sam carrying in firewood; the stove sent out a glow of heat. He grinned at her.

"Looks like we're snowed in. Maybe for the winter."

"But what about Jesse? Will he be able to get home?"

Sam groaned humorously. "There's that name again! Can't you forget Jesse for a minute? This weather gives us a chance to get acquainted, and you don't seem to appreciate it like I do."

"Oh, but I do." She laughed. "And to prove it, if you'll show me where things are, I'll get breakfast."

"The hell you will! What do you think I keep that Injun for." He went to the door. "Tsis'na, get your lazy butt in here."

The Indian girl entered stoically. Though her hair was frosted with snow and her lips blue with cold, she did not shiver but went straight to work.

Sam's attitude toward Tsis'na bothered Jenny. When she asked why the girl slept outside, he laughed lustily. "Don't know Injuns, do you? They're like animals. Curl up anywhere and sleep like dogs!"

Sam's attitude reminded Jenny of the abuses heaped upon her by her father, Olaf Johansson. Olaf had been convinced that Jenny was half Indian. Her dark skin and high cheekbones were a constant accusation that Inga had betrayed her husband, though Inga denied it. Tsis'na's slight shoulders stiffened, and Jenny knew that Sam's remark had hurt her just as she, Jenny, had been hurt in that long ago time. From that moment she determined to make the Indian girl her friend.

That was easier said than done. Despite Jenny's friendly overtures, Tsis'na remained aloof. "Have you worked for Mr. Whitman a long time?" Jenny asked uncomfortably.

"Many moons. I am a slave."

Jenny went cold all over. She thought again of her own background; her Indian blood was the result of her grandmother Birgitta's brief affair. The Indian features had bypassed her mother, Inga, and her sister, Kirsten, only to show up when Jenny was born. But maybe this was why Jesse no longer wished to marry her—maybe being an Indian made her automatically a slave.

She finally gave up trying to start a conversation with the girl.

Luckily Sam was voluble and amusing, so she wasn't too lonely. Jenny was amazed at his vocabulary, amused by his wry twists of humor. But she continued to question him about Jesse. Was there something he wasn't telling her? Was Jesse hurt somewhere, or sick?

"Of course not," he said defensively. "Why would I hide something like that? No, sir! Jesse's up there in Santa Fe, snug as a bug in a rug! He'll come back when he's ready, I guess."

"Santa Fe!" She was looking at him strangely. "Sam, I was there! And I could have gone back with Ed Washburn, if you'd only told me!"

"Then we wouldn't have had time to get acquainted," he said hastily. His smile was so charming, it was impossible to remain upset with him.

"Besides," he added impishly, his head cocked to one side, "the longer the wait, the sweeter the reunion."

He laughed as Jenny blushed.

As the days passed, Jenny read and reread Jesse's last letter. Why had he written it, and why was he still in Santa Fe? Had Sam actually sent a message to him, and was Jesse staying away deliberately?

Jenny didn't know what to believe.

She didn't realize how lonely she was until Sam began to go on mysterious errands. At first she was overjoyed, certain that he had gone to get Jesse. But he always returned alone. Once, when Sam had been gone for several days and she summoned the courage to ask where he had been, he stared at her for a moment. Then he burst into a roar of laughter.

"You missed me! By God, you missed me! And I didn't know you cared!"

He reached for her with intimate, searching hands, and with a shock Jenny realized that he was a little drunk. She drew back her hand and planted a stinging slap on his stubbled cheek. Then she trembled as he scowled at her ferociously, his fist upraised.

Finally he lowered it and began to laugh. But after Jenny had gone to bed Sam sat up drinking far into the night. Jenny lay shivering beneath her blanket, finally admitting to herself that Sam was not the man he pretended to be, and that she was afraid.

She managed to be civil to him after that, but she prayed that Jesse would soon return. The thought of the long, cold winter stretching before her in the company of a silent Indian girl and a surly, drinking man, was more than she could bear.

On a night when the wind blew wildly around the house, whistling through every nook and cranny, a new sound intruded. Jenny sat up in bed, thinking that perhaps it was a loose board banging in the gale.

Then she heard the approach of booted feet and rough male voices.

Could it be Jesse coming home?

Jenny hadn't been feeling well lately; she was a little feverish and dizzy. But she leapt from bed expectantly, wrapping a woven Indian blanket around her flannel nightgown. Her face was shining as she opened the bedroom door. Her smile soon faded.

At the front door stood a grizzled army captain, backed by several of his troops and an Indian guide, handsome in a military scout's uniform. The captain shot Jenny a contemptuous look. Then he turned his angry gaze back to Sam.

"Dammit, don't try to deny it! We've got proof! You've been dealing with a band of renegades, selling likker and guns to the Injuns. We're not going to prosecute this time, for Colonel Norwood's sake. But if it happens again, we'll lock you up and throw away the key!"

Nobody heard Jenny gasp with surprise. Colonel Norwood? Surely they weren't speaking of Jesse! But Whitman's next words made it clear that they were.

"That damned Jesse! I figured he wouldn't keep his mouth shut! He cooked this up, him and that dirty Injun!" Whitman pointed at the scout. "Jesse's a damn Injun lover! Him and old Jesse are buddies. You going to take his word against that of a white man?"

Jenny was struck dumb by the mention of Jesse's name. Now Sam was railing out against the man he claimed was his friend. None of this made any sense. Then suddenly it did: Sam had lied to her. He'd been lying to her all along.

She stepped forward.

"Excuse me," she said in a small voice. "If you know Jesse Norwood, will you take me to him? I have been waiting for him. My name is—"

The captain stared at her in confusion, his face turning a dull red.

"Jesse's no squaw man," he said deliberately. "If you're trying to cause the colonel any trouble, you're talking to the wrong man. He's a friend of mine, and so's his—"

"She don't go to be familiar, cap'n," Sam interrupted. "She's a little tetched in the head." He tapped his forehead. "And she belongs to me."

Jenny's wide eyes went blank with shock as the captain continued his tirade.

"Tetched or not, she probably knows how Jesse feels about using the Indians as slaves! I hear you've still got the one you bought in sixty-two and lent to that son of a bitch Kreuger while you were off to the war. This 'un makes two! For God's sake, man, why do you persist in breaking the law!"

The captain glared for a moment; then, in a tired voice, he delivered his final words.

"I'll be back. You've been warned about the whiskey and guns. Next time it'll be the stockade. I also suggest you get your personal life and your women straightened out."

He rode away, the scout following more slowly. Jenny caught the fringed sleeve of the Indian guide's jacket. "Wait, it's not like you think!"

The Indian's dark eyes held both pity and shame for Jenny. He shrugged off her hand, turned, and was gone. Jenny turned shocked eyes to Sam Whitman.

"Sam! Why did you let them think—"

She stopped, realizing he was drunk; he grinned at her—a loose, sloppy grin.

"If you don't want to be treated like a damned squaw, try not to look like one."

He put an arm around her, and she pulled

free, hurrying to her room. Then she stared into the wavy, dusty mirror. The blanket she had snatched up was woven in an Indian pattern. Above it, her dark eyes sparked with anger. Her feverish cheeks were stained a dusky rose, and black hair tumbled in a cascade down her back.

She looked more like an Indian than Tsis'na!

Jenny remade her rumpled bed and crept between the blankets. Finally she slept. She dreamed that Jesse, in a spruce uniform, was ignoring her as he issued orders. She caught at his arm and pulled him close. "Hey, there, little one" came Sam's slurred voice. "Easy does it. We've got plenty of time."

Jenny awoke with a start. It was Sam! Smelling of stale sweat and whiskey, he was in her bed.

She desperately tried to fight back, emitting a thin scream that he closed off with a hamlike hand. The sheer weight of him was too much for her. "Shh, shh, it's all right." He fumbled at her clothing, trying to calm her with drunken endearments.

With a tremendous effort Jenny managed to twist free, only to be caught in that bearlike grip again; her head slammed back against the pillow with stunning force.

Finally she lay still. She was unable to breathe, her mouth and nose smothered beneath the damp flesh of Sam's bared torso. *I'm going to die*, she thought as the room grew dark around her.

6

Jenny saw the sudden shadow that appeared behind Sam, and the flash of silver as Tsis'na held her knife to his throat. Jenny drew a shuddering breath and shut her eyes.

Sam's eyes rolled up into his head and fell forward.

Tsis'na pulled his heavy body from the bed and leaned over Jenny. "Are you all right?"

"Yes," Jenny said chokingly. Then she belied her own words; she leaned over the edge of the bed and was sick. "Is he—is he dead?" she asked when she could speak.

"He just passed out," the Indian girl said curtly. "Here, let me help you wash your face."

She tended to Jenny, then half dragged, half walked Sam Whitman to his bed in the other room, refusing Jenny's offer of help.

"I have done this many times," she said. "He will not disturb you again tonight. Sam will be sorry in the morning."

Jenny was wakeful through most of the remaining night. The sound of Sam's snoring penetrated the walls, an indication of his inebriated state. As long as he snored, it meant she was safe. But she knew she would have to leave this house as soon as possible.

It was all she could do to drag herself out of bed in the morning and face Sam. As Tsis'na had predicted, Sam was contrite. When Jenny entered the kitchen, he kept his eyes glued to his coffee cup.

"Tsis'na tells me I made a fool of myself last night," he mumbled. "Guess I was drunk." She turned her face away, and he looked at her pathetically. "Forgive me," he said. "I'll do anything to make it up to you, Jenny."

"Then you will take me to Santa Fe," Jenny said sternly, "to find Jesse!"

As she had thought, he immediately began to hedge. "Listen, honey, Jesse Norwood ain't the man you think he is. Believe me!"

Her anger began to rise. "You will take me to Santa Fe!"

He spread his hands placatingly. "Wait until it's warmer. Right now there's a freezing rain out there."

But Jenny's expression didn't change. Finally Sam began to grin. "You bet. If that's what you want—"

"It is." She would not allow him to forget his promise.

Within the hour, bundled against a sleeting rain, Sam and Jenny set out for Santa Fe. It would be three or four days of hard riding, with stops at line shacks and adobe inns along the way. Sam was at his solicitous best. He seemed to feel that when this trip was over, he would come out the winner.

By the time they finally reached Santa Fe, Jenny's chest was congested. It was hard to breathe, but she was certain that her fever had broken. Her face was now cold and clammy to the touch, her vision blurred.

"Why don't we go over to the Exchange Hotel?" Sam asked in a consoling tone. "We can get a good night's sleep, then go look up Jesse tomorrow."

Jenny was sorely tempted. Her mouth was so dry, her throat so swollen. The nights on the trail had been gruelling. Her red dress was soiled and she needed a bath.

She thought of the hotel with nostalgic longing. Standing at the southwest corner of the plaza, the Exchange was almost luxurious compared with the rest of the grim Sante Fe trail. When Mr. Washburn rented rooms there for Jenny and his children, it had almost seemed like home.

But Jenny knew she wouldn't rest until she saw Jesse. "We'll find Jesse now," she said hastily.

"Suit yourself." Sam shrugged.

They rode along the hard-packed streets, finally reaching an area of great new homes built of adobe, in Spanish fashion, with wrought-iron balconies and red-tile roofs. Sam paused before one of them, his eyes glistening with malice.

"This is it." His eyes dared her to go to the door.

Jenny waited outside the mammoth portal, the Indian blanket still shielding her from the cold rain. She heard the sound of high heels clicking toward the door. It opened to reveal the face of a beautiful Spanish woman. Jenny's voice caught in her throat.

"*Si?*" the woman asked coolly.

"I'm looking for Jesse," Jenny whispered. "Jesse Norwood?"

The woman's face grew haughty, and her creamy forehead creased in a frown. "My husband is not home at the moment. Did you have a message for him?"

Jenny's mouth went dry. *Husband?* She backed away, unable to speak, her dark eyes huge in a white, frozen face.

"If you are hungry," the woman called after her, "Conchita has orders to feed your people at the rear door."

Jenny shook her head and walked back toward Sam. She went carefully, as if she were barefoot and treading on broken glass. Sam was slapping his knees and chortling. "Thought you was an Injun, by God! Figured she would!"

His laughter stopped, and he reached to catch Jenny as she stumbled. Suddenly aware of her pallor, he realized she was a very sick girl.

Damn! He'd never been around anyone who was sick, and Jenny's condition scared the hell out of him. He had to get her back to the ranch. Tsis'na would take care of her there.

He lifted Jenny to the front of his saddle and, leading her horse, began the long and laborious journey home. He made the ride straight through without stopping. He damn sure didn't want Jenny dying on him.

The sleet burned his face, coating the blanket Jenny was wrapped in until it was stiff. Her eyes were closed, her mouth and eyelids blue. He had to keep checking to make sure she was still alive. Each time he paused, he tipped a bottle to his lips and then went on.

Finally he reached his ranch, where he turned

the unconscious girl over to Tsis'na. He told the
Indian girl he was riding over to Kreuger's place
and would be back in a week or two.

Then he rode off into the slant of freezing
rain.

All night Tsis'na sat at Jenny's bedside. By
the next afternoon, it was clear that the girl's
condition had worsened. Tsis'na left her and
went out into the yard where she built a small
fire. Then she took her own blanket to cover it
from time to time, causing it to emit small puffs
of smoke.

She prayed to her gods that she had not forgotten the art of smoke writing. And that someone would see her signals.

Soon there was an answer from the sky.

Late that evening some of Tsis'na's own people appeared. Greeting their kinswoman, they
were doubtful that their efforts would help a
white woman. Perhaps she would not even want
their help.

Tsis'na stood straight, looking them in the
eye.

"She is my sister," she said.

It was enough. They bowed in assent and went
to work setting out the materials for the singer
to use in his healing ceremony.

They brought pigment in colors of red, brown,
and ocher, made from small bits of sandstone
that had been ground into fine powder. There
was also clay, pollen, and charcoal, placed on
trays of bark, one color to each tray.

And the ceremony began.

A sand painting was made upon the floor; the
maker completed it one segment at a time, picking up a pinch of color and spilling it carefully

between his index finger and his thumb. As each segment was finished, the artist backed away carefully to start anew, until it was finished to his satisfaction. The elements of the border never fully encircled the picture, leaving it open to the east.

When the sand painting was finished, they carried Jenny from her bed and propped her up in the manner indicated by the singer, who rubbed sand from parts of the painting upon specific parts of the girl's body.

And it was done.

Jenny was placed, once again, upon her bed. All the sand was gathered into a pile at the center of the room, put into a basket, and taken outside to the east of the ranch house. There it was given, ceremoniously, back to the Earth Mother. Equally ceremoniously, the Indians took their leave.

"The woman may live. She may die. But we will come for you, Daughter, when the time is right. The fat cattle you have told us about will be our reward. We will not forget."

Tsis'na watched impassively as her people faded into the night. Then she went indoors to watch over Jenny.

She had done all she could do; it would have to suffice.

7

Kirsten knew nothing about Theron's illness or how close her sister Jenny was to death. She sat in her silken bedroom, surrounded by the mystic colors of the sea, preoccupied by her own troubles.

It was one thing to be faithful to Nick, but what if she never had a chance to become wealthy in her own right? She couldn't help comparing Nick to Slim Morley.

Because of his connections in the shady underside of the city at the time of Reconstruction, Slim was a very powerful man. But Nick would never amount to much more than a cardsharp. Kirsten looked around, her pretty face marred by lines of discontent as her imagination put the stamp of poverty on the luxurious room.

As she studied her surroundings Nick entered the room. He had bathed and shaved and wore only a towel wrapped around his waist.

Kirsten thought of Slim in his crimson velvet robe, smelling of some exotic lotion. By comparison, Nick seemed too strongly masculine, a bit uncouth. "For heaven's sake," she said tartly, "go put some clothes on!"

Nick raised his wicked black brows and grinned. "You never complained before." He dropped the towel, revealing the hardness of his well-muscled body. Its dark beauty hinted at his Creole ancestry.

"Come here," he said softly. "I know you want to, sweetheart." And she found that she was drawn to him, in spite of herself.

It was only later, lying satiated in Nick's arms, that Kirsten remembered the new dreariness of her surroundings. Now would be a good time to bring up the subject. She traced the smooth lines of his torso with lingering fingers, stopping only when he became aroused beneath her touch.

"Nick, I've got to talk to you."

He sighed and smiled at her indulgently. "Talk away."

"I think we ought to redecorate. Don't you find all this blue . . . depressing?"

"Hardly!" He looked down at the pretty girl; her golden hair was spread over a satin pillow. "It's the exact color of your eyes. Besides, it cost a fortune to have this done. To do it over in less than a year would be ridiculous!"

"But red is so cheerful, more plush. We could do all the rooms in red, with gilt mirrors and everything to match. I think the customers would like it better, don't you?"

Nick's mouth set in a straight line. He had frequented The French Rose shortly before Kirsten joined him: a lonely man's way of finding companionship. And it was the only establishment he knew that was done solely in those colors. Kirsten must have been in that house.

Seeing Nick's tortured eyes, Kirsten quickly

changed the subject. "We can talk about all this later. It's not really important, darling. For now, let's take up where we left off." She began walking her fingers up and down his body again, this time to no avail.

He rose abruptly and forced a weak smile. "I've got some business in town, sweetheart. I had better go take care of it now."

Later that afternoon Kirsten was at work in Nick's study, counting the take from the previous night. Pete, the bartender, arrived with a visitor. It was Lydia.

She wore a too ornate gown with earrings that dangled to her shoulders and a feather boa. She entered, nose in the air, hips swishing, walking like an angry cat. Kirsten sensed her bad mood and rose to face her.

"What can I do for you?"

Lydia stared at her with a hard expression, betraying her nervousness only by picking at her glove. "You," she said in a shrill voice, "can stay away from my man!"

Kirsten's eyes went round with shock, then they narrowed. "I don't know what you're talking about," she said crisply.

"I'm talking about Slim Morley!"

Kirsten smiled with cold amusement. "I don't recall ... pursuing Mr. Morley, but I'll tell you this! If I want him, I'll go after him! And I can promise you, I'll win."

"You won't," the girl screeched. "You won't! I'll see you in hell first!"

She rounded the desk and grabbed Kirsten by the throat. Her nails left bleeding scratches as Kirsten tore her hands away and clutched a handful of Lydia's orange-red hair. Lydia, in turn, snatched up a letter opener from the desk, and Kirsten bent backward. She gripped the girl's upraised arm to keep her from stabbing downward.

"What the devil!"

Suddenly Nick was between them, separating the two struggling women. When he had hold of each, at arm's length, he glared at Kirsten.

"What the hell's this all about?"

"It's her fault," shrilled Lydia. "I came to tell her to lay off of Slim and—"

"And?" Nick asked in a dangerous voice.

"And I told her I wasn't interested," Kirsten said with deceptive coolness, "but that she had no business telling me what to do!"

"Is this true?" Nick looked at Lydia.

Lydia looked unsure of herself. "I guess. But it didn't sound quite like that."

Nick shrugged, glaring at her. "I suggest you get out of here before I throw you out," he said firmly.

Lydia scuttled away. When she had gone, Nick began to clean the scratches she had inflicted on Kirsten, carefully applying salve and bandages. Then he held Kirsten away from him, looking into her eyes.

"I'm not going to ask whether Lydia's version, or yours, is the right one. But in the future, if you have anything to do with Slim Morley"—he paused, gritting his teeth in anger—"I will kill you myself. Now, have you got that straight?"

His fingers were digging into her collarbone, but Kirsten managed a painful nod. He let her go with an angry shove and went downstairs.

Kirsten's hands went to her throat. It hurt.

Lydia had tried to kill her. Coming out of her
state of shock and fear, she felt a more devastating emotion: fury.

Fury at Lydia for thinking she was chasing
Slim. Of course, she hadn't been, she told herself. The nerve of the girl!

And then Nick's nerve: the way he'd actually
threatened her. She rubbed at the bruises he
had left when he held her shoulders so tightly.
Who were they to order her around like that?

A few days later Kirsten donned a gown with
a froth of lace at the throat to cover her injuries.
Taking the receipts from the previous week in
her handbag, as she usually did, she started
toward the bank. Then she altered her route.

When she reached The French Rose, she approached Slim Morley, facing him across his
desk. She tried not to think of the round bed
with its mirrored ceiling just beyond the panel.
Kirsten dumped the contents of her bag on his
desk.

"I have," she said, smiling nervously, "come
to invest."

"You won't be sorry," Slim told her smoothly.
And she certainly hoped he was right. Kirsten
already had begun to feel a little bit sorry.

8

As Kirsten made her weekly trip to Slim Morley's, she was unaware that she was being watched.

Pete, the gaunt, gray-haired bartender at Nick's Card Parlor, was more than just an employee. He was a man Nick Tremont had fished out of the gutter when he was down, and he loved Nick as a father would love a son.

It had been Pete's job to take the receipts to the bank before Kirsten had come to live with Nick. Perhaps that was why he didn't particularly like her, Kirsten had deprived him of one small thing he could do for his friend.

And it was Pete who saw Kirsten start for the bank each week, then change direction. At first he only wondered. Then he followed her. To his amazement Kirsten went into The French Rose.

Pete debated going to Nick with his suspicions. But when he went to the bank and discovered that Nick's account was empty, he was afraid not to. Instead of the explosion of temper Pete expected, Nick turned white and dismissed him, saying that he was sure there was a logical explanation. He would take care of it himself.

That night Nick could not keep his mind on his cards. In the early dawn, after a night of steady losing, he climbed the stairs. Reaching the room he shared with Kirsten, he paused for a moment outside the door, thinking.

Then he entered.

It had been a slow night; Kirsten had come up several hours earlier. And now she slept, looking like an angel that had fallen from heaven and into his bed. He woke her, gently. She opened her beautiful blue eyes ever so slightly. Then she made love to him with a sweetness he was certain he shared with no one else.

With a dull ache Nick realized he could never really trust her; he must never believe every word she said. But he couldn't bring himself to accuse her of wrongdoing, not yet.

"Kirsten," he said, smoothing her hair back from her love-dewed forehead with a tender hand. "I've been thinking. You're right about redoing this place. I think I have just about enough in the bank to swing it—"

She was deathly still, like a small, frightened animal in his arms.

"I've changed my mind—"

"But I haven't," he said implacably. "I want you to withdraw all our cash tomorrow. Unless, of course, there's a reason why you can't?"

He knows, she thought.

"There's no reason," she said, struggling to keep her voice calm. "No reason at all."

"That's good," he said. "I don't know what I'd do if I couldn't trust you."

He wanted to make love again, and Kirsten did it by rote, going through all the motions while her mind was spinning with worry. She was trapped. Someone must have told him about her business venture. Lydia?

She would scratch out Lydia's eyes, she thought wrathfully.

But it was no time to be angry. Nick would only have to make a visit to the bank and she would be condemned.

What was it he had said? "If you have anything to do with Slim Morley, I'll kill you myself!"

Later that morning, while Nick slept, Kirsten put on her most seductive gown and left the card parlor. Morley had warned her that she would only receive returns on her investment quarterly, and to hold back enough so that she could cover herself if Nick requested cash for any reason. But she hadn't done it, and now she was in trouble. Slim would have to help out. But she had a feeling he would want to be paid for his help, and she could well imagine what form that payment would take.

She blushed, noticing that her hands were trembling as she teetered between excitement and fear.

She didn't knock at the door of The French Rose. Morley had told her long ago that she was now a partner and should just walk in. He was not in his study, and she didn't want to wake him. She could wait.

The interior of the room was dim and shadowy, the shades drawn against the light outside. She settled into a deep leather chair. Slim would be here presently. Luckily this was her day to drop by, and he was expecting her.

Kirsten was half drowsing when a furtive figure entered the room. She sat up straight as she recognized the newcomer: it was the girl she hated. Lydia.

Kirsten leaned forward. What was Lydia doing here?

She caught her breath as she saw what the girl was up to. She had a key to Slim's desk, and she opened a drawer, taking out an immense wad of money.

As Kirsten watched, enthralled, she slipped a few bills from the stack and thrust them into the bosom of her gown. Then she pushed the drawer to, hastily.

Kirsten did not hear the lock catch.

As soon as Lydia left, Kirsten sprang into action. A slight jerk reopened the drawer. She removed the remaining money and stuffed it into her handbag, then pushed the drawer shut.

This time it closed with a click.

Kirsten returned to her chair.

Slim Morley entered the room. "What can I do for you, my dear?" he asked.

Kirsten shrugged and made her voice sound plaintive. "I was just lonely. I wanted to see you."

Slim came toward her, smiling, and she held up her hands, palms outward.

"Wait!"

He paused, and she looked up at him anxiously. "I don't like to say this, but I've been wondering about Lydia. Can you trust her?"

"With my life." He laughed. "Now come here."

She skipped back nimbly. "Let me tell you what I saw—"

She spun quite a tale. Lydia hadn't seen her sitting in the room, she had unlocked the desk and taken its contents, but surely there was some explanation.

Slim's face grew as bleak as winter.

He checked the drawer and found it locked. Then he opened it and discovered the money missing, just as Kirsten had said. Swearing under his breath, he left the room. Kirsten could hear him loudly asking where Lydia was. His voice filled with rage when he learned that she had gone shopping.

By God, he would find her soon!

Kirsten left the building unnoticed, and hurried back to the card parlor. Nick saw her come in, and his face turned pale. She went to him, resting her golden head against his shoulder.

"I picked up the money, as you said," she whispered. "But I really don't think we should repaint."

She opened her handbag, just enough so that he could see its contents. Nick looked dazed.

"But Pete said—"

So there was the spy! Kirsten looked at the floor. "Nick, I've been meaning to talk to you. Pete is jealous of—of anyone you care for. He's been trying to make trouble for me lately. I think he's sick, and he scares me."

"He told me once that he's saved enough to retire," Nick said reflectively. "Maybe he ought to be put out to pasture. If he's bothering you, darling—"

"I suppose so," Kirsten said, feigning reluctance. Then, "Oh, Nick, I love you so!"

That night Nick lost heavily again. All his attention was focused on the angelic beauty who once again joined in at the gaming table. He couldn't know the reason behind her Mona Lisa smile. Above the blue satin gown baring her creamy shoulders, Kirsten smiled, because her investment was still safe and secure.

And because soon, old Pete would not be around to spy on her any longer. And she had a feeling she wouldn't have to worry about Lydia too much longer, either.

9

Though the winter hung on with a death grip in the New Mexico Territory, an early spring touched Sweethome. Once again, Inga stood at the center of the little bridge on Sweethome's perimeter. She hugged herself with folded arms as she gazed down into the amber waters of the small creek. It was a protective gesture, to keep away the troubles that weighed so heavily on her soul.

She must go back in soon; she didn't dare stay away from Theron's side for too long. At times he reverted to the spoiled young scion of Sweethome, ordering the ex-slaves about unmercifully.

Luckily the staff understood that he was not himself. They took his harassment good-naturedly, assuming that he would one day return to his normal behavior.

Inga dashed tears from her eyes. She knew Theron would never be normal again. He had lost weight, becoming a shadow of his former self, harsh lines of pain bracketing his mouth. And then there were his mental lapses. Day after day she had watched him fail—it was only a matter of time.

Her head bent over the railing, Inga didn't hear the approach of Matthew Weldon from Eden Plantation across the way. He coughed to announce his presence, and she whirled with an expression of fear that faded as she recognized him.

He stopped at the edge of the bridge; he hadn't crossed it in several years. "I've heard your husband is ill," he said quietly. "Is there anything I can do? Perhaps bring a physician from Memphis?"

"No," she said simply. The hopelessness in her voice brought a look of understanding to his eyes. She saw that he was already aware of the situation at Sweethome, possibly through the servants' grapevine that existed between the two plantations. She felt like clutching his shirtfront in a cry for help. But Weldon had been her husband's enemy, and whether Theron was right or wrong in his opinion about the man, accepting his sympathy now would be a kind of betrayal.

"Thank you, but we need no aid," she said stiffly.

He grinned boyishly. "I'd rather hoped you would," he confessed. "My wife is expecting a baby, and I thought maybe we could help each other."

"Inga," Theron called, "Who are you talking to! If it's that damn Yankee—"

"I'm sorry," she said hurriedly, "it's out of the question." Then she practically ran to meet her husband.

She knew how much the sight of Weldon had upset Theron. His face was red with an unreasonable anger, his eyes unfocused. He looked almost the way he had the night he returned to Sweethome: a hating remnant of a Union prison camp.

"I asked you," he said, snarling as she approached, "was that Matthew Weldon? I thought I told you he wasn't welcome here!"

"He heard you were ill. He just wanted to help."

Theron's voice rose to a dangerous pitch. "I don't need help! Especially not from his kind!"

Inga managed to calm him down and get him into the house and into bed. When she went down to the kitchen to help Dinah, the woman was disturbed by the tension in her mistress's face. "Massa Theron givin' you a hard time again? What you s'pose set him off now?"

Inga told her about Weldon's visit, and Dinah frowned. "That man's in for a heap of trouble. I hear the Klan's out to git him. He's already got a warnin'."

"But—he hasn't done anything!"

"He's a Nawthener, ain't he? Come down here, builded hissef a house on Southern folkses land. We don' take kinely to strangers."

"Dinah! You're as bad as Theron! Weldon's just a human being, and his wife's expecting a baby."

"Can't he'p that." Dinah shrugged and went back to her work. Inga stared after her, wondering.

What was this about the Klan? How valid was Dinah's information? It was true that the servants seemed to get hold of scraps of rumor before anyone else. She really should warn Matthew Weldon that he might be in danger.

But would he believe her?

Before he became ill, Theron had explained to her why the Klan was formed. It was a group of men who claimed that their aim was to keep the South from being exploited by scalawags and carpetbaggers; to protect its property and its womanhood from roving bands of renegades, both black and white. But lately the Klan seemed to be getting out of hand. A number of Southerners had moved back to the area since the war. They had called to pay their respects to Theron—young hotheads spilling out their bitterness over their defeat. Some of them brought horror stories they had gathered from others; tales of blacks raping decent Southern ladies, Yankee soldiers cheering them on; of babies dying at the points of bayonets; of old people being tortured to death.

The stories grew, expanding greatly, Inga was sure, in the telling. The defeated Southerners, many of them prisoners of the North, were filled with a need for vengeance. But surely the Klan wouldn't take its revenge on an innocent young man with a pregnant wife.

Just then, Dinah answered the door and ushered in a second visitor. All thoughts of Matthew Weldon's plight left Inga's mind.

"Mr. Washburn! Oh, Lord, I'm glad to see you!

He smiled. "And I, you, ma'am, Dinah told me—" he stumbled over the words—"that Theron is pretty sick. I'm sorry to hear it."

Inga looked suddenly old, then her face cleared. There was no use in dwelling on her problems. As Dinah said, what would be, would be. "Theron is ill, but we pray he will recover," she said. "But tell me, did you leave Jenny with Jesse?

What are you doing here? And how is your wife's health?"

It was Ed Washburn's turn to age before her eyes. He swallowed hard, then explained that he had lost his wife before they reached Santa Fe. He had decided to bring his children home and rear them in familiar surroundings.

"I just dropped by to see if there was any salable land in the area, and to bring word of Jenny. I delivered her right to her young fella's door, and I reckon she's happy."

A cloud crossed his face as he recalled the condition of the house where he had left Jenny, and the appearance of the man who came to its door. But there was no point in worrying this fine woman. And there was no accounting for love, else his Lizbet would not have married him.

"Jenny hasn't been writing," Inga said softly. "I had only one letter, right after she reached Santa Fe."

"I was with her when she went it. But maybe, after she got together with her man, she just kind of forgot."

A faint sense of unrest flickered inside him. He didn't really believe what he was saying, but it might be true. Sometimes young people thought only of their own pleasure. And Jenny was very much in love.

Inga did not answer him. Surely Jenny would have written of her happiness. But it was enough to know that Washburn had left her safe and well. She was silent as he droned on about the difficulties of getting mail out of a remote area in the New Mexico Territory, knowing he was trying to reassure her.

"Would you like to see Theron?" Inga asked suddenly. "He's asleep but I will wake him."

Washburn wouldn't hear of it. Inga offered him lodging for the night, and he shook his head.

"Thank you kindly. But I have to be going. I left my children at an inn along the road to Memphis and promised I'd be there tonight. Give my best to Theron. And if you hear of any property at a reasonable price . . ."

"I'll let you know," she said softly.

Inga watched Ed Washburn leave, thinking that he, like Theron, was a product of the South. He, too, had fought in the war. But he was a fair-minded man and had taken his defeat gracefully. She wished that Ed Washburn could have been her neighbor, rather than the Northerner that Theron hated so.

Then Inga forgot the man as she steeled herself to face the terrible monotony of waiting; waiting for her husband to die in a long and terrible way.

She had no idea that an event was to take place that very night, which would change the course of her whole life, or that she would accept it willingly.

10

It was almost dark when Inga went out to bring in the laundry, trying to save Dinah a trip. She was still worried about Jenny, but she had managed to overcome her worst fears. Jenny was bright and intelligent, and she was a good girl. Although Inga hadn't had an opportunity to become well acquainted with Jesse Norwood, the fact that Jenny loved him was enough.

Right now her main concern was for Theron. Taking in the sheets that smelled sweet with a scent of almost spring, she paused to say a little prayer.

Please, God, don't take his mind away any more. I love him so.

"Miz Inga!" Dinah came bustling toward her. "They's trouble!"

"Theron?" Inga gasped, dropping the clothespins she held. "Oh, dear God!"

"T'ain't Massa Theron," Dinah assured her. "It's Miz Weldon, 'crost the road. Her time done come on her a mite early. She needs some h'ep. Her husban's waitin' for you on the porch."

Inga started to run, then stopped, remembering her loyalty to Theron. "I can't go, Dinah. You take care of it. Get your birthing things."

"No, ma'am!" The old black woman said sullenly, "That woman, she high-toney, for sure. Don' like niggers. Won't have 'em in the house. And, mahse'f, I don' like Yankees."

"Dinah!"

"I got the stuff laid out. You go 'long. Massa Theron's sleepin'. I'll look in on 'im."

There was no arguing with her. Inga went into the back door of the house and through to the front, snatching up Dinah's birthing gear as she went. Matthew Weldon was waiting on the front steps, his soft brown hair disheveled, his blue eyes red-rimmed as if he had been crying.

They lit up at sight of her. "You don't know how I appreciate this, Mrs. St. Germain. Martha—Martha has a horror of being tended by the Negro servants. I had thought to take her to Memphis for her lying in, but there isn't time—"

"Don't worry," she said, a little tartly. "I can manage quite well."

She hurried over the small, arched bridge that led to Weldon's plantation. Reaching the house she faltered for a minute at the doorway. Then she heard a distant cry; the cry of a woman in labor. And she hurried on, followed by a frantic young father-to-be, who was still explaining the circumstances.

"Martha's been after me to take her back home to have the baby, since she's been unable to make any friends here. But her folks died in a fire last year. She has no other relatives. The house she grew up in was burned. Really, she has no place to go. But she hates it here."

His expression was a mixture of fear and guilt. Inga decided she did not like this Martha she had never met; this woman who had burdened her husband with her obvious unhappiness.

"She will survive," she said. "Most women do. Having a child isn't too unusual, wherever it's done."

A wave of red swept up from his collar. "I know," he said humbly. "But Martha is ... delicate."

Martha Weldon appeared to be anything but delicate. Her tumbled dark hair framed a face that was petulant and plump with self-indulgence. Inga and Matthew hurried up to her room where they were greeted with fury.

"Where have you been?" Martha exclaimed in dismay.

Matthew started to tell her he had gone for help, but his explanation went unheard as his wife began to shriek with pain. Seeing the misery in Weldon's eyes, Inga sent him from the room while she performed a quick examination.

Everything was in order. The child was on the way. But the contractions were still far apart. It was going to be a long night.

Inga drew up a chair beside the bed where she could observe the woman, who now slept peacefully, and sighed. Theron might be more rational tonight and might want her in his bed. The times he knew her as his wife were now few and far between. How she savored the sweet moments when they clung together desperately in the night: she, out of love and grief; he, in need of reassurance.

But tonight Inga knew she must wait out this woman's travail, no matter how long it took. It wasn't for her sake, she told herself, but for the sake of the man downstairs. As she waited for the birthing to begin, she thought about Matthew Weldon. Before she left, she would have to tell him the gossip filtering through the quarters. The threat of the Klan was growing. And from what Dinah told her, Weldon's life was in danger.

Inga shivered. And then Martha woke, caught in the grip of another wave of pain.

The baby was born at three in the morning. Although the woman screeched and clawed like a wildcat, it was an easy birth. Inga cleaned up mother and child, then descended the stairs, the baby in her arms.

"It's a girl," she told Matthew Weldon, turning back the edge of the blanket to reveal a tiny face like a rosebud and small starlike hands waving in the air. She tried to place the child in Weldon's hands, but he drew away.

"What about Martha?" he said distractedly. "How is my wife?"

Inga, still bleeding from scratches the woman inflicted, had had enough. "She is just fine," she said. "And don't let her try to tell you otherwise! She had an easy time of it! But she refuses to have anything to do with this baby. She goes into hysterics every time I try to show it to her, saying she doesn't want it. If you have any ideas on how to handle the situation . . ."

Weldon reddened again, his eyes cast down to the floor. "I know. I figured she'd be this way. I wonder if—if one of your people might be able to serve as wet nurse?"

Inga felt her face turn crimson. Such things weren't discussed in mixed circles. After all, she hardly knew this man!

"Zada," she said stiffly. "Her youngest is about three weeks old. I'll send her over."

"I wonder if I might impose to an even greater

extent?" he asked in a low voice. "Martha—
Martha is not herself. Would you mind keeping
the child until she comes to terms with being
a—a mother? I would gladly pay you."

"Of course I will" burst from Inga's lips. "And
I don't want to be paid! If you think that I—"

"It will just be for a month or so," Matthew
said hurriedly. "I'll try to talk to Martha—"

A month or so! Inga stared at him, aghast.

"*Matthew*!"

Martha was screaming from her bed upstairs.
Weldon looked at Inga apologetically and hurried toward the staircase. Inga was left standing
in the foyer, a baby in her arms.

The consequences of what she had just done
struck her.

Here she stood, a woman with a dying husband who consumed every moment of her time,
and now she had taken on the care of an unwanted child. She couldn't do it! She wouldn't
do it!

"Mrs. St. Germain?"

Inga lifted her head to see Johnson, Weldon's
old friend and valet. He had been the one to
bring hysterical Kirsten home after her long
disappearance. Like Martha, she had been pregnant with a child she didn't want. But that
baby had been born dead. Inga's eyes misted as
she recalled the still birth of her little grand-
daughter, the child Kirsten insisted was Nick
Tremont's.

"Yes?" she said, answering Johnson.

"Please take the child and go." He sounded as
if he had been crying. "It would be better for
everyone."

Then Inga found herself outside as the sun rose to announce the birth of a new day.

How to tell Theron of this newcomer into their lives? It would be best not to let him know. And how to feed and care for the baby? Would Dinah see her as an infant—or a Yankee?

She walked home through the scented morning, holding the soft little bundle close.

This was the child she and Theron would never have, the grandchild that might have been.

And soon she would have to let it go.

Thoughts of what she had intended to tell Matthew Weldon—that his life might be in danger—had faded from Inga's mind. All she could think of was the little one as she carried her into the house where Dinah sat waiting for her mistress's return.

She knew she needn't have worried as Dinah came toward her, reaching out to the child with loving arms.

Inga wished they could keep her forever.

11

Jenny woke from a strange dream, a dream of light and color, of a landscape in which crudely drawn masked figures danced and capered. It was impossible, but she felt she was part of that scene. She opened her mouth to ask Tsis'na, who stood over her, but the Indian girl touched her fingers to her lips and hushed her.

"You must rest."

She slept again. This time she came fully awake, only to learn that she had been seriously ill for a matter of weeks. Sam was away; he had gone to see a friend.

Jenny didn't mention Jesse Norwood, nor did Tsis'na. But Jenny could tell that Tsis'na knew what had happened in Santa Fe. The normally tactiturn girl kept talking, as if to avoid mention of Jesse's name.

Jenny only half listened. Most of the time she was wishing she could die. For these last few years of her young womanhood her heart and her mind had been set on one goal: that of becoming Jesse's wife.

And now that had been taken away from her.

In addition, most of her other options had

78

been destroyed. She had lied to her mother. How could she go home and confess that Jesse hadn't sent for her at all? And she couldn't stay here. She had to go before Sam came back. But where?

She suddenly realized that Tsis'na was telling a story—her own story. Long ago her people had been herded onto a reservation at Bosque Redondo. Tsis'na had not accompanied them. She had been sold as a slave to Sam Whitman and eventually loaned to an unscrupulous outlaw friend of his, who abused her.

But she had survived.

Many of her people had starved before they were released to begin their long walk home. They left Bosque Redondo in a column ten miles long, so long that it took seven days from the time the leaders crossed the Rio Grande until the last straggler reached it safely.

And people cheated them. People like Sam Whitman, who after returning from the war, received a contract to furnish the Indians with meat. He did not fulfill that contract but drove the fat cattle to Silver City, selling them to members of the mining community.

To the Indian went the dead and the dying.

The girl's voice was filled with torment. And suddenly Jenny's heartbreak seemed very small. Impulsively Jenny reached for the red gown she had worn to meet Jesse in Santa Fe—the garment Tsis'na had just washed and returned to her room. It meant nothing to her now.

"You admired this dress. Would you like to have it?"

Tsis'na's solemn features glowed with sudden pleasure. "Thank you, my sister," she said. "Tsis'na thanks you."

When Tsis'na left the room, Jenny closed her eyes. She summoned Jesse's face with its mop of sun-bleached hair above his steady gray gaze. She had cared for him. And he had loved her but not enough. It was over. Now she was free.

Within a few days Jenny was no longer bed-ridden. She could sit in a chair, her blanket under her chin. She watched Tsis'na shape tor-tillas with her small, agile hands, and listened, fascinated by tales of her ancestors.

"The people," Tsis'na said, mixing a lump of malleable masa in a huge pottery bowl, "were once not human. They lived in the first world, which was red in color. Day and night were shown by light: white in the east at dawn; blue in the south for full day; yellow in the west at evening; and black in the north for night."

Tsis'na busily patted a tortilla into shape and went on to explain how the people had bickered and quarreled until the chief to the east called them disobedient and told them they must go to some other place.

After four nights they were surrounded by wa-ter. To keep from drowning, they went in circles until they reached the sky, where someone with a blue head called down to them, "In here, to the east, there is a hole—"

"Excuse me, Tsis'na," Jenny interjected, "how do you do that?"

Interrupted in her tale, Tsis'na was confused for a moment.

"Oh," she said. "You are speaking of this—"

Tsis'na held out a hand filled with the golden masa. "It is not difficult. Do you wish to try?"

Jenny did, and then she wished she hadn't. Her creation was a lumpy mass, compared to

Tsis'na's paper-thin tortillas. "I'd better just practice for a while," she said.

Tsis'na smiled, then went on with her story.

"Did I tell you they went to a second world? A blue world inhabited by swallows. They explored this place, and all they found was the world's edge, a great cliff rising from a bottomless arroyo. And they lived with the swallows, who treated them as relatives, for twenty-four days, until one of them made free with the wife of a swallow chief.

Then they were told they could stay no longer."

Tsis'na frowned at a black fleck in the masa dough, carrying it to the light to ascertain its origin, then went back to her story.

"Led by the white face of Hiltsi, the wind, they flew through a slit in the sky to a third and yellow world, inhabited by grasshopper people. Again, on the twenty-fourth day, the same crime was committed, and they were expelled. They flew through a twisted passage made by the wind, and then arrived in the fourth world that was black and white.

"Couriers found no life to the east," Tsis'na went on dreamily. "There were deer and turkey tracks to the south. And to the west humans, who lived in houses in the ground and cultivated fields; Pueblos, who treated the people well and fed them, though they had the teeth, feet, and claws of beasts and insects, and smelled bad since they were unclean."

She paused, placing a tortilla carefully on a hot stone to one side of the fireplace. When it began to puff, she flipped it over deftly and removed it after a few seconds.

"There came four strange and miraculous

beings, called Yei, who told them to wash themselves; the men to dry with yellow cornmeal, the women with white. They came again, in twelve days, and made magic with buckskins, feathers, and ears of corn, all placed a certan way. And when they had completed their ceremony, a man and a woman lay there instead of the ears of corn. These were First Man and First Woman."

"Adam and Eve," Jenny said. "Adam and Eve!"

The dreaming light went out of Tsis'na's face. "They had no other names," she said. "I am tiring you. Sam will not be pleased."

"No," Jenny pleaded. "Please go on."

"There is much to tell," Tsis'na said curtly. "But the tortillas are made, and I have other work to do. Sam would not wish me to waste my time in talking. Now you must rest."

Jenny did not sleep for a long time. Bizarre as Tsis'na's story of creation was, she felt a strange kind of understanding—as though she had known all this before, perhaps in a dream. And when she slept at last, she dreamed again. This time, of the creation of First Man and First Woman.

She was the woman.

The man was not Jesse.

Jenny could only see him through a haze. He was dark and somber, yet there was something familiar about him. She forgot all about her dream when she awoke, for Sam was home.

Finding Jenny much improved, Sam was his old, ebullient self. Smugly he took full credit for Jenny's recovery. As soon as she was fully recovered, he intended to collect what she owed him. With her mind off that no-good Jesse Norwood, Jenny could spare a little loving for him.

Sam rode out early the next morning. Curious, Tsis'na followed him. She returned, her eyes shining like stars. He had gone to a hidden coulee to meet with others of his kind. The coulee was filled with fat cattle the men had stolen. Sam would give them whiskey and guns to trade with the Indians. They were altering brands.

Tsis'na built a fire and sent puffs of smoke into the sky for other eyes to see. Then she rolled some dried meat with some fresh tortillas inside her blanket.

She would be ready when they came.

That evening, Sam was truculent. It was obvious that he had been drinking throughout the day. He approached Jenny warily, and brought up the subject of romance as though he knew he would be refused and was already angry.

Jenny flushed. "I'm sorry," she began.

"Sorry!" He shouted, jumping to his feet and overturning his chair. "How the hell long do you expect me to wait? Or has that Injun been filling you with lies about me?"

He took a threatening step toward Tsis'na, who was frying tortillas at the fireplace. "Don't look at me that way, you Injun bitch!" he roared. "I'm gonna sell you off first chance I get. That is, if I don't kill you first!"

Then he struck her and slammed out of the house.

Tsis'na's eye was blackened. A trickle of blood ran down from one corner of her mouth. "It is well," she told Jenny, trying to smile. "It is a good thing to remember."

She left the house. Jenny was afraid to go to bed, afraid Sam would return in his drunken fury. It was better to remain awake and fully dressed and to find something to do.

The image of home rose before her eyes; Sweethome, with its peace and beauty. She was homesick for the love those walls contained. She wanted to cry in Inga's arms, to be comforted.

She couldn't do that. But at least she could write her mother and try to keep her from worrying.

She found some paper, some ink Sam had made from berry juice, and sat down to write.

Dear Mama,
As you may have heard from Mr. Washburn, I am here, safe and well, staying at the home of Jesse's friend, Mr. Whitman. Since Jesse is gone on an errand, he has engaged a girl as chaperone for me. I only wait for Jesse's return.

She paused, recalling something Inga told her long ago. A little prevarication often led to a bigger lie. How true that was.

"I be damned!"

Sam stood behind her, swaying, bottle in hand. He dropped the bottle and snatched up the letter, ripping it in half and throwing it to the floor. "Yer not gonna write that bastard!"

He thought she was writing to Jesse. "Sam—"

He struck her across the cheek. There was a roaring in her ears. "Listen to me, now, Jesse ain't coming back! He don't want you! And you're gonna be nice to me, all right? You been moping around long enough!"

"No, please—"

He shook her until she hung in his arms, hair swinging as she fought him. Then he scooped her into his arms and carried her to his whiskey-scented bed, ripping her bodice as he buried his stubbled face in her throat.

"You little wildcat, I'll show you what a real man's like!"

His hands encircled her slender neck, clamping down and choking her into submission. The world around her dimmed, and she slipped into merciful darkness. She did not see Tsis'na enter the room or lift a clay water bottle above her head and bring it down with a resounding crash.

Tsis'na stepped outside. A mournful bird call issued from her lips. With a rustling like the wind, her people came.

Tsis'na was the daughter of a great chief who died at Bosque Redondo. Her people, no longer trusting the word of the white man, had been hiding in the wilderness, biding their time. They had been busy acquiring weapons, stealing horses, preparing to head for lower Arizona to join others like themselves. They had seen Tsis'na's smoke.

For these last hours they had been awaiting nightfall and Tsis'na's signal that the strangers had gone; that Washburn was alone; that fat cattle awaited them in the coulee; that all was well.

Tsis'na led her people into the house as soon as they arrived, pointing to the unconscious Jenny and Sam.

"That is the man," she said. "Do with him what you will. But do not harm the woman. She is my sister."

12

Jenny remembered the next several days as a series of images. There was the sight of a blood-spattered room when she closed her eyes; a room that held the remains of a human body. And there was an almost invisible trail that climbed toward the sky as Tsis'na's people led them into even higher mountains.

Jenny's legs ached as they climbed; she had been inactive all winter because of her illness. Now she trudged at the rear of the winding column. The Apache men ignored her presence; the women were silent and imperturbable.

"I don't think they like me," she whispered to Tsis'na.

"We are not a demonstrative people," Tsis'na said. "And we must put distance between ourselves and those who will follow, seeking retribution."

"But Sam Whitman was not a good man. He bought you, held you prisoner, cheated your people. Perhaps, if you took this to a court of law, you would all be exonerated—"

Tsis'na laughed mirthlessly. "You forget. We are Indian. We are not people. Less than five years ago thousands of us were slaves. Did you know orders were given to shoot down our men like dogs? No, white man's justice is for his own kind. Even their ministers preach that we have no souls. That we are not human."

Jenny looked down at her own brown, briar-scratched legs. *Nor am I*, she thought. Tsis'na, in the faded red dress Jesse had so loved, looked more civilized than she.

They climbed still higher. The air grew thin and invigorating. Jenny finally found her stride, walking as straight and as far as any of the others. She felt a tremendous swell of pride.

And finally they dropped into a valley of hot springs that filled the air with steam. Having negotiated the trail, the Apaches began to laugh and joke with each other as they set up camp, herding the cattle they had taken from Sam's place into a natural stockade.

"We will rest here awhile," Tsis'na said.

The days spent in this place were truly idyllic. Jenny smiled at the sight of the smooth-skinned red-brown children at play, she and Tsis'na occasionally joining in. According to Tsis'na, the boys were encouraged to simulate the Warrior Twins; the girls, Turquoise Woman. They were seldom naughty, for their Navajo parents threatened disobedient children with being cooked and eaten by evil Yei.

Tsis'na and Jenny often went into the woods for berries. These were dried and added to the supplies being gathered for their long trek. Soon they would be going into Arizona to join Cochise and throw themselves on his mercy; they would ask to be made a part of the Chiricahua band.

As they worked, stripping the vines and filling

the baskets the Indian women supplied, Tsis'na instructed Jenny in Indian lore.

One must never kill a snake, or else the hatred of the snake would be directed forever toward the individual. One must never eat the flesh of a bear; he is a friend. Neither must one eat the flesh of any water creature—eels, frogs, crabs, snails, water turtles, and clams—or they will reap the vengeance of the water monster who lives in the sea but has control of all earthbound water.

"Oh, Tsis'na." Jenny groaned. "I cannot remember all this."

She tossed a berry, mischievously, striking her friend. And soon they were involved in a merry battle that left them laughing and berry-stained.

A week went by, and another. Tsis'na's happy disposition began to fade. The girl seemed preoccupied, withdrawn, and Jenny began to wonder what she had done wrong.

Then she woke one morning to find Tsis'na's blankets empty. Jenny struggled to her feet and looked about in panic.

One of her new friends, a grandmother named Tsi'dii, or Bird, saw her fright and raised a hand to gesture toward the distant horizon.

Jenny saw Tsis'na then. She stood on a high pinnacle, her arms outstretched, her red skirts blowing in the wind. Jenny watched, heart in her throat, as the girl came back down the dangerous way she had gone up. Reaching Jenny, Tsis'na said calmly, "I made a prayer to the gods. Perhaps they will answer it. Perhaps not."

Her face was pale and drawn as Jenny asked, "What did you pray for?"

"Our safety," she said curtly. "I am afraid. The white man's power is greater than ours, and this place is known to them. As soon as one remembers, they will come."

"Then why don't we leave?"

Tsis'na shrugged.

"Chief Nes'iah is old. His body pains him, and the water here is healing. He is tired, and there is a feeling of peace. He does not feel the devilwind that comes, sweeping us before it like dead leaves—"

"Perhaps if you talked to him?"

"We are not like your people. I am only a woman and unmarried, therefore worthless. I must prove myself before I can become a warrior woman with influence. At this time I have none. There are only the gods to hear me. And I do not think they are listening."

13

Tsis'na did not mention her fears to Jenny again, though it was obvious they were still with her. She seemed to be her old self again, except for repeated references to the gods. Though the religious names of the Navajo were woven in with tales Jenny found difficult to believe, they seemed to bring a new serenity to Tsis'na.

The camp was a busy place at all times. Though the cattle were fattening on spring grass, the warriors hunted wild meat to supplement their diet. The women dried the meat of these animals over a slow fire.

The jerky they created, mingled with dried fruit, would be their staple until they reached Cochise in Arizona. "If," Tsis'na said mournfully, her eyes darkening with premonition, "the gods allow us to live that long." Jenny tried to laugh her worries away, and soon everything was back to normal.

Tsi'dii, the grandmother, had brought along a bolt of calico trade goods. She had woven a rug, taken it to the trading post, and received the cloth in return. It was something she treasured.

She wanted Jenny to have it as a gift.

With great ceremony the old women of the tribe tore a dress from the material, making it up for Jenny in one night of prayer and singing.

"They know you now," Tsis'na said, putting her arms around her. "And they love you!"

Looking down at the gaudy, gypsylike creation, Jenny had to admit that it suited her. It seemed to erase the last vestige of her old life; to assuage the pangs of homesickness and the pain of losing Jesse. She seemed to be someone new.

That night, as she lay with her blankets spread near Tsis'na, she looked at the dark sky with its myriad of stars. She felt a srange yearning along with a stirring of memory.

"Tsis'na," she murmured drowsily, "did you see the men who came to Sam's door last winter? There was an Indian scout; Sam said he was a friend of Jesse's—"

"Daniel Strongbow," Tsis'na told her. "His mother and father were killed when he was a boy. He was taken in by a white family. He thinks in the white way."

Was that good or bad? Jenny wondered. But at least she knew his name. Not that it mattered. But he had borne a marked resemblance to the First Man of her dream.

Within a few weeks strife developed in the camp. The young warriors were eager to be off, to fight at the side of Cochise. Some of the women were worried, certain that their camp would be found.

But Nes'iah, chief of the tribe, who had intended to pause here very briefly, felt secure. He did not want to move on. Evidently they had not been followed from the Whitman ranch. They had been careful to remove all evidence of In-

dian attack when they fired the house. Probably
the white eyes believed the house had burned,
that the man had died in the flaming building.

Still, to quiet the nagging of his young wife,
who had been urging him to move on, and for
the sake of Tsis'na, who felt the chill of the
devilwind in her bones, he felt compelled to
make concessions.

To avoid argument, he tightened camp secu-
rity and urged the women to make haste with
the making of moccasins and the preparation of
food for their journey. He also initiated a few
desultory attempts at digging in to fight, should
they be attacked.

These efforts soon ceased with the excitement
of the hunt. There were still berries to be found
and dried. It had been a long time since the
tribe had seen such riches—or felt so safe.

Only the grandmother, Tsi'dii, listened to
Tsis'na's warning, nodding her head wisely.
Nes'iah was a careless old fool.

Tsi'dii had been a warrior wife in her time.

Jenny began to avoid their company. She felt
depressed enough without their dark moods. She
took to the woods, gathering berries by herself,
needing to be alone with her thoughts.

And her memories of Jesse—memories that
were fading faster than she cared to think.

She forced herself to picture him as she first
saw him: a Confederate soldier on the burned-
out plantation of Belle Terrain. She had slipped
through a fringe of trees like her Indian ances-
tor, to see a shirtless, broad-shouldered man at
the handles of a plow, drawn by an ox. His
yellow hair was flying in the wind. And she
loved him even before she saw his face.

She didn't meet him then, but only after a group of ragtag renegade soldiers attacked Sweethome and Jenny narrowly escaped with her life. She'd gone one day to spy on Jesse, wondering if he, too, was a dangerous man. He had caught her and carried her to his shack to silence her screaming.

And there she felt as if she belonged. She knew that someday she would be Jesse's wife—a hope that had been dashed forever.

Her basket was filled with berries, but still Jenny did not want to go back to the camp. As she sought to remember Jesse she saw another face. A face with copper-colored skin and black, black eyes. A face that haunted her for no reason at all. Determinedly she shoved it from her mind and returned to thoughts of Jesse.

There was a spanging sound, and a bit of bark flew from the closest tree. Something stung her cheek, and she put a hand to her face, feeling a trickle of blood. From beyond the strip of trees that hid her came a fusillade of shots, followed by the screams of the dying. It was the chant of a death song.

Jenny drew in her breath on a sob. Tsis'na had been right! The devilwind had come. Please let Tsis'na be safe. Oh, please . . .

And Jenny began to run, her eyes streaming tears. She prayed, not to Tsis'na's gods but to her own.

And no one was listening.

14

Jenny burst from the woods without a thought for her own safety. Then she stopped, appalled by the scene ahead of her. The fresh, clear atmosphere had become a swirling mass of choking dust, punctuated by flashes of fire. She was overcome by the metallic scent of gunpowder.

In the midst of the melee rode a group of whiskered men, laughing and shouting as Indians fell around them, dying, just as Tsis'na had predicted.

The devilwind!

Gathering her skirts, Jenny ran into camp where she paused, disoriented.

The brush arbor she shared with Tsis'na had been set ablaze and was now a smoldering ruin. Jenny strangled on the smoke from it and rubbed at her streaming eyes to clear them. She was intent only upon finding her friend.

"Tsis'na!"

Her voice was lost among the dying screams of Tsis'na's people and the triumphant yells of those who attacked them.

She saw Chief Nes'iah, and started toward him, her arms outstretched in a plea for help.

Then she saw that he stood like a statue, in
proud acceptance of what was to come; straight
and unmoving, his blanket wrapped around him,
as one of the invaders rode him down.

"That'll l'arn ye, ye red-skinned bastard," the
rider yelled.

He fired a shot into the Indian chief's body.
His horse reared at the smell of blood and gunpowder, narrowly missing Jenny as it came down
with flailing hooves. The man on its back had
spotted another victim, thus missed seeing Jenny
in the haze of dust. He turned the animal in a
spin and was gone.

Jenny began to tremble. She knew she had to
leave this place and quickly—if she were to leave
it alive.

And then she saw Tsis'na.

The Navajo girl lay facedown, her dark hair
swirled around her body. Jenny knelt and turned
her gently. A bullet had entered her back, exit-
ing from her chest where it left a gaping hole.
The girl's bright color had bled away, and she
wore the gray pallor of death.

Jenny shook Tsis'na until her head lolled back
on her shoulders. She dropped the limp body
and began to shudder, unable to stop shivering.
Tsis'na was dead! And Jenny had not been with
her. She had been lost in a daydream in the
woods.

A rifle exploded, almost in Jenny's ear. The
body of an Indian fell across her, slamming her
down against Tsis'na. She lay there for a moment, unable to move. Involuntarily her fingers
closed over something that came off in her hand.
She clutched it tightly as she scrambled up,
dazed and shaken.

There was fighting everywhere she turned. A horse reared, screaming, as it felt the shaft of an Indian lance drive beneath its ribs. It unseated the bearded man who rode it, sending him crashing to the ground.

Jenny stared at him, conscious for the first time that this was no cavalryman.

These were not military people avenging the death of Sam Whitman.

These were murderers. And they would not hesitate to give her the same treatment.

The man on the ground blinked, focusing on Jenny at last. With a bull roar he reached out with a bloodstained hand and grabbed at her ankle.

She pulled away and ran for her life.

Blind with fear, Jenny crashed into a pile of brush at the camp's perimter and fell into an unfinished dugout; one of Chief Nes'iah's aborted attempts to fortify the place. It was barely wide enough for her slim body. She peered fearfully over the edge, certain that her heart was beating loudly enough to be heard over the commotion of war.

She heard the sound of a woman weeping; an Indian woman she had known as Falling Star.

She was pleading for the life of her child.

The noise was abruptly cut off.

"Oh, God," Jenny whispered. "Oh, God."

She was suddenly conscious that her hand pained her. She had been clutching something tightly. Too tightly. A stone?

She pried her fingers open and looked at the article she held with brimming eyes.

It was a button. A covered button from the dress she had given Tsis'na. She stared at it, then began to tremble again; this time not with fear or sorrow but with anger. If she survived this day, she would carry this button with her forever. She would carry it until she evened the score for Tsis'na. The men who mounted up now, preparing to leave, had attacked without reason. Except to kill. Jenny tried to memorize each face, red-limned as if with the fires of hell from the glow of the burning shelters. They had killed Tsis'na, her sister, and someday she would avenge her death.

In a few short, bloodstained moments, little Jenny Johansson had grown up.

The invaders discovered the cattle, grazing in their natural corral. Whooping with delight, they hazed them out, driving the animals through the center of the camp. The cattle were bawling and wheeling, their eyes red and rolling with terror. Bodies were squashed like ripe melons beneath their trampling feet.

When the dust finally cleared, the bearded killers were gone. They left nothing behind but a place of smoldering ashes and bits and pieces of what had once been human.

Jenny did not move. She was frozen with rage, sick at the carnage she saw before her. Alone with the dead, with the sickening smell of dust and blood borne on the wind.

No, not alone!

Jenny shrank at the sound of stealthy steps, wishing she had a gun or a knife. But it was a very small figure that issued from the trees, moving onto the battlefield, going from one crushed body to another.

Jenny drew in a harsh breath.

The child who appeared in the devastated

campground was one of Chief Nes'iah's many children. A little girl named Bit'so.

Jenny left her hiding place and began to run. But she was too late. The child had already seen the trampled body of her father and stood staring down at him.

"Bit'so!"

The little girl came toward her, her face without expression.

"They are all dead," she said stolidly.

Jenny knelt to hug her, wishing the child would break down and cry. Anything but this tragic acceptance. "Oh, Bit'so, I'm sorry," she whispered. "So sorry!"

The child shrugged. It was a forlorn and lonely gesture. "We must go now."

"But they should be buried!"

The haunted, dark eyes lifted to Jenny's. "There is no time for burial rites. The others wait."

Then others lived, if only Tsis'na had been one of them!

But there was no time to weep for her now. That would come later. Jenny took Bit'so's hand and followed her into the trees.

15

Bit'so explained what had happened as they made their way through the trees. Half a dozen warriors, led by D'zili, had been gone from camp on a hunting expedition.

They had survived.

Somehow, old Tsi'dii, the grandmother, managed to rescue Bit'so's little sister, So'tso, who fell during the flight and suffered a broken leg.

And then there was Ugly Woman, the girl with a foot like a deer, who had been gone to the spring for water. She had taken the baby, Ee'yah, whom she'd been looking after, with her. He, too, was safe.

One warrior, who had stayed behind to tend his ailing horse, had survived the attack. He took a bullet in his shoulder but escaped to warn the others. They had all met among the trees. Bit'so had gone to see if anyone still lived, while the others conferred. Their own small band was gone, wiped out of existence. It was necessary that the few warriors who remained travel fast and join forces with Cochise, their cousin and friend, in Arizona, as soon as possible.

According to Bit'so, the aged, the children, the lame, all would be left behind.

Seeing the shock on Jenny's face, Bit'so said hastily, "You are young and strong. Perhaps the men will take you with them—"

And leave Tsi'dii? Ugly Woman with her club foot? The two little girls, one injured, and the baby?

"I would rather die," Jenny said hotly.

Bit'so nodded solemnly.

Soon they came upon a secluded glade where the warriors stood and argued, their copper-colored bodies dappled with leaf shadows.

Within moments the men had come to a decision. They could not be hampered on their journey. But they were willing to make a concession. First Tsi'dii, who had the gift of healing, would remove the bullet from Young Bear's shoulder.

Then they would take the women and children to a place they knew of: the Place of the Old Ones. They would leave them where they would be safe, returning for them on a later day.

Tsi'dii began a low keening, her eyes glazed and inward-looking.

"We cannot go to that place. It is bad luck. There are ghosts and witches there. If you do this bad-luck thing, you will not live to see Cochise.

"Nor will I!"

"We do not have to listen to your doomsaying, old woman!"

Tsi'dii drew herself up proudly. "Tsis'na and I foretold the coming of the devilwind."

D'zili, the new leader of the group, looked nervous. "Nes'iah was careless. We will not be."

"It makes no difference," Tsi'dii said wearily. "The sun of the Navajo is setting. I will remove the bullet from your warrior's shoulder. Then let us go."

Grim-faced, she set about her task, building a small smokeless fire over which to sterilize her knife. Then she carefully probed, finding the bullet and cutting it, expertly, from the bloody flesh.

Young Bear rose from the ground, and fell into his appointed place in line, his teeth clenched. He would walk. If he fell by the way, he would merely rest awhile, then try to make his way alone.

There was no time to set small So'tso's leg. But she was not a warrior, and therefore not essential to their survival. D'zili scooped So'tso into his arms. The child's face was white with pain. Small Bit'so took her place beside Jenny as they plunged into the trees.

Jenny started at the sight of her. The little girl had hacked off her long, lovely hair with a dull knife she carried in the fold of her moccasin.

"She mourns her people," Tsi'dii said sorrowfully.

"So do I," Jenny said, fists clenched against her heart.

They walked onward, through night and day. Jenny had to put her anger and sorrows aside. There was no time for that now. No time for anything but the gruelling pace led by the warriors as they made their way deep into the mountains of the Gila wilderness.

And finally they came to the place of which D'zili had spoken.

It was a cliff dwelling, apparently rooted in

the beginnings of history. It was not the usual red-rock dwelling, simmering in the sun, but was built on a wooded green hillside beneath an overhang.

The ancient structure looked down into a narrow mountain defile that rose steeply into grass and trees, keeping it always in leafy shadow.

"You do not have to stay," came the sound of D'zili's voice.

Jenny, who had been staring in fascination at the structure above, turned to face him.

"I do not understand."

"You may come with us," D'zili said.

Jenny's face lit with a smile; the first smile since Tsis'na's death.

"All of us must go!"

D'zili looked away from her. "That would not be possible," he said stiffly. "But my squaw is dead. I have need of another. . . ."

Jenny's face was red, her eyes blazing.

"And that would not be possible," she said. "I will stay with the others!"

D'zili turned away from her in silence. He carried So'tso up a steep, curving path and set her outside the half-walled enclosure. Then he led the other warriors away, Young Bear limping far to the rear.

They did not look back.

"They, too, are afraid," Tsi'dii said.

"What is this all about? What's to be afraid of?"

Tsi'dii looked at the ancient ruin looming above them, her voice taking on a prophetic depth.

"This place is taboo to the Navajo."

"I don't understand."

"It belongs to the old ones. We do not know

when they died, nor how they died. It is believed their spirits still linger here, where they once lived. It is not certain they are friendly to the Navajo.

"We do not say their name."

"I do not believe it," Jenny whispered.

Tsi'dii only looked at her for a long moment, then turned away.

First they made So'tso comfortable, setting the broken limb with a number of straight peeled sticks. Tsi'dii was not hopeful for a full recovery. It had been too long between the breaking of the leg and the setting of it. The child would probably always be lame.

Afterward Tsi'dii and Ugly Woman went foraging for roots and herbs to make a healing tea. Giving the baby a piece of jerky to chew on, Jenny left him in Bit'so's hands while she inspected the place that would be her home for a while.

There were a number of small rooms, indicated by half walls built of small, almost symmetrical stones. There was also a large, cylindrical space that evidently was used as food storage.

At its base was a quantity of great speckled beans, perfectly preserved from a past long ago.

Jenny had a strange sense of having been a part of that past. Then she shook her head to clear it. Instead of daydreaming she had better start thinking about those beans. If she planted them, would they grow?

She had no idea how long she would be here with a club-footed girl who was too shy to speak; an aged woman, half crazed with fear of this place; two small girls; and a baby.

Someone was going to have to take care of them all.

Then she thought of Inga, her mother, and how she had led them on foot to Sweethome. Through Inga's efforts somehow they had endured. They had survived.

That was what Jenny intended to do now, and for the same reason.

For the sake of the children.

16

Jesse Norwood dismounted stiffly and heaved a sigh, partly out of relief to be home at last and partly out of sorrow that his mission had uncovered tragic news.

He had visited a small reservation for which he had held high hopes, only to discover that corruption still existed. No matter how close a watch he kept, nor how often he contacted Washington about the Sam Whitmans of this world, getting something done seemed to be an exercise in futility. Whenever there was a profit to be made, there was always someone who won out and someone who lost.

And in this case the losers were the Indians.

Their blankets and food had been confiscated by unscrupulous agents. Many of them had died of cold or starvation during the winter. Spring came, and they could no longer believe in the white man's promises. They left the designated areas, heading for their old homes in the west.

Colonel Jesse Norwood felt responsible.

Sergeant Wood, a grizzled veteran of the Indian Wars, listened to Jesse's concerns and shook his head.

"Hell, Jesse, you can't expect to change things over night. And I don't figger your Injun friends thought you could. People is people. Leastways, it wasn't as bad as last year."

That was little consolation. "I promised them," Jesse said gloomily.

Sergeant Wood waved his words away, as if promises meant nothing in this cruel land. "One good man can't do much when there's a hundred on the take. You want my advice? Go home to that purty little woman of yours and forgit about what can't be helped."

Jesse's heart lifted at the thought of Elena. She would be waiting for him, with shining eyes. She would summon a little maid to pull off his boots; another to prepare a hearty meal for the returning traveler. All signs of her love—though she would never think of doing any of those tasks herself.

Not as Jenny would have done.

Now, where had that traitorous thought come from? Lately he had managed to put the memory of Jenny from his mind. That was another promise that he had broken. And it did no good to look back.

Marriage to Elena had brought him everything he wanted. The young Spanish girl had seen him and instantly wanted him. He grinned a little. Whatever Elena wanted, Elena got! Her distinguished father, descended from Spanish royalty, had a great deal of influence in Washington. Jesse's marriage brought him money, influence, self-respect, and a congressional commission that gave him the chance to help a downtrodden, oppressed people.

The last was his real reason for marrying. But

he had to admit that Elena was beautiful and intriguing; the marriage of convenience certainly hadn't been hard to take.

And Jenny, after all, had been a first love. He would have been cheating her if he actually had kept his promise and gone back for her. She would have come to live on a barren ranch with a poverty-striken husband and his drunken outlaw friend. She would have grown old and faded, working all the days of her life.

Instead he had set her free. St. Germain would see to it that she married among her own kind: a Southern aristocrat, a gentleman born.

And though he still loved Jenny and would always love her, through Elena he had made something of himself. And despite what Sergeant Wood said, Jesse knew he was slowly but surely turning the tide for the Indian.

Best of all, no one, not even St. Germain, would ever call him poor white trash again.

Jesse felt a light touch on his shoulder and turned to see the face of Daniel Strongbow: scout, interpreter, and good friend. Jesse had left him behind on this jaunt because of a flap over some-one selling whiskey and arms to the Indians. Daniel would get to the bottom of that, if any-one could.

Jesse clapped him on the back. "Dan'l! How goes it?"

Daniel shrugged; the light of joy at seeing Jesse quickly left his face. Jesse spoke with sudden intuition.

"The skunk dealing in whiskey and arms, was it my old friend Sam? Then, by damn, go get him! Bring him in to face the music."

"Sam Whitman did this thing. But he is dead."

"Dead!" Jesse's voice was flat with shock. "When? How?"

"Apache," Daniel told him. He went on to tell how Sam's body was found by a trader of rather unsavory reputation named Dutch Kreuger. The fellow was so certain that Sam's death had presaged an Indian uprising that he had hotfooted it to Santa Fe with the news. Captain Melton was now getting a troop together to check his story out, and Daniel was going along to look for evidence.

Jesse put a hand on the Indian's shoulder. "I am going too."

"Your wife will not like this."

Jesse sighed heavily. "That can't be helped. I owe this much to Sam for what—what he used to be. And I don't want the Indians who did this to be killed. They should be brought in to face justice, like any white man."

He asked when the troop would be leaving, told Daniel to saddle a fresh horse for him, and made his way home.

When he reached the Spanish-style town house that had become his when he married Elena, Jesse paused briefly to reflect on his impossibly good luck. Jesse was the youngest of the Norwoods, son of a father and mother who could neither read nor write, who kept tally of their crops as the slaves did, with sticks, laid in rows.

If it had not been for Sam, he would have been in a similar situation. He owed Sam a lot.

He felt a pang of sadness as he remembered the man Sam had been once: a friendly, talkative fellow spinning yarns of his ranch in the New Mexico Territory, exaggerating everything. He was a man who could discuss books and plays, who seemed to have come from a good family; a man who thrived on battle and excitement.

A man who, when the war ended, turned to drink and illegal activities.

"Jesse!"

Elena had seen him. She came flying down the walk like a crimson leaf in her red dress, her black hair streaming behind her. Her dark eyes were huge and sparkling, her full, red lips ready to be kissed.

He held out his arms and caught her as she flew into them. She was as bright and beautiful as a lovely butterfly.

After a warm embrace she smiled up at him and led him toward the house. "Maria," she called, "come to remove your master's boots! Juana, prepare refreshment. Rosa, take a message to my father's house. Tell all the Ruiz family that there is to be a fiesta this night, in honor of my husband's safe return."

"No, Elena."

She raised puzzled eyes to his guilty face. "My love! What is wrong?"

"I have to leave within the hour. Sam has been killed."

"I am sorry." It was a perfunctory statement; Jesse knew she couldn't care less. Elena had never liked Sam—and she liked him even less dead than alive. In her mind Sam was taking Jesse away from her. She leaned against him.

"You do not really have to go."

"I'm afraid I do. Not just for Sam's sake. The Indians who killed him—"

"Indians!" There was a tinge of disgust in her

voice as she pouted. "Are they always more important than I am?"

Juana had brought in a tray of hot and steaming delectable foods. Jesse looked at it with regret. It had been some time since he had eaten.

But he knew what he had to do.

He lifted Elena in his arms and carried her, laughing, up the stairs. He still had the better part of an hour.

There would be time.

He dropped her on the bed with its scarlet coverlet and stood looking down at her.

She was beautiful! One of the most beautiful women he had ever seen. And this woman made of fire was his; the wife of a redneck dirt farmer from Tennessee. It still did not seem real.

She lay in a swirl of velvet skirts, her dark hair spread around her face like the petals of a black rose; her lashes lowered in mock submission.

A choking knot of passion welled up in his throat as he reached out to her.

He took her with a kind of anger, eliciting delighted little cries of pain.

Why did he feel this need to punish her?

"It was good, my darling," she whispered, licking her lips with a small pink tongue. It seemed almost as if she purred as she repeated "*Bueno* . . ."

But was this the way love was supposed to be? Violent, exhausting?

He tried to make up for it by being gentle now: kissing her closed lids, her pouting mouth. And finally she slept.

He rose, sighing, and went downstairs. Maria brought his boots, and Juana looked despairingly at the tray of food she had prepared. Now it was cold—the ensalada wilted, a coating of grease forming on the tortillas.

"You did not eat it! And now it is spoiled!"

It was obvious that the girl's feelings were hurt. She was proud of her efforts. He tried to smile.

"Thank you, Juana. There wasn't time."

"*Si, señor.*"

He could tell by her flat tone that she understood but didn't approve. To Juana there was nothing more important in a man's life than food. And Jesse had to admit that he would have enjoyed her cooking, but he knew his demanding little wife.

Elena never would have forgiven him.

He took a cold tortilla to placate the little maid. Then a knock at the door announced the presence of the Indian scout, and Jesse went to join him.

17

At last Colonel Jesse Norwood's troops reached the foot of the hill leading to Sam Whitman's ranch house. They paused for a moment, gazing up at the shabby structure.

From where they stood, the place appeared to be undamaged. Jesse felt hopeful for a moment. Perhaps Dutch Kreuger had been wrong. Maybe he and Sam had gotten drunk together and it had all been a hallucination. It sounded like something the two of them might dream up. Jesse could not suppress a small grin.

His grin faded as he guided his horse upward, hearing the creaking of his saddle and the clip-clop of the animal's hooves. There was no other sound.

On closer view he could see where a portion of the roof had burned through. What looked like charred fingers reached around the window ledges and the door frame. He smelled a heavy scent of smoke and an underlying darker scent. The smell of death.

It was true, then.

Jesse dismounted and entered the house, turning his back to his men to hide his wet eyes. He thought back to the day he had left this place in anger, more than a year ago. That was the last time he had seen the man who now lay, mangled and bloated, beneath the table.

Sam had been drunk and abusive that last time, and now Jesse wished their parting had been different. He even wished that Sam could have died in the war instead.

He knelt beside the body and said a silent prayer. After a while he stood, his face set with determination.

"Clint. Tom. You're the burial detail. The rest of us will find the ones who . . . did this. Daniel, scout out the trail they took and—"

But Daniel was studying a paper he had found beneath Sam's body. A letter, torn in two stained with Sam's blood. He handed it to Jesse and saw the man jerk as though he had been struck.

This letter was in Jenny's hand.

Jenny's writing! What the hell was Sam Whitman doing with it?

Jesse tried to read it, his fingers trembling.

"Dear Mama . . ."

She went on to say that she had arrived there safe and well. Jesse was away at present, but a girl had been engaged as chaperone. . . .

The letter was obviously intended to allay Inga St. Germain's fears.

How long had Jenny been here? And what had she endured from a drunken Sam Whitman?

"I only wait for Jesse's return."

It was not true. If Jesse knew Sam, he had probably been drunk, and less than gentlemanly. He could envision what had probably taken place; the delicate girl fighting off a brutal man. Jenny had had to resort to fabrication to cover her shame.

But that wasn't important right now. The crucial thing was that she had been in this house, and now she was gone. Had the Indians taken her with them, or—

He swallowed hard and issued new orders.

The burial detail would continue as arranged. The remainder of the troops would scour the immediate surroundings for signs of an injured woman. . . .

Or a dead one.

He and Daniel would ride out on the Indians' trail. They would make good time if they were not encumbered. The rest could follow when they had completed their mission.

Jesse mounted his horse and whirled, galloping down the stony hill that led up to the house. Studying the spoor, he found that the Indians had a head start of several weeks. There was little chance of catching up to them soon enough to save Jenny.

Daniel followed, glancing at his colonel with concern. He could have sworn that the big man was crying.

"Jesse?" he asked hesitantly.

Jesse didn't answer.

Daniel did not interfere with his solitude. He rode along in silence, keeping on the trail, his mind working furiously.

Who was this woman Jesse had told the troop to search for? Surely it was not the girl Daniel had seen in Sam's house on that day they delivered the warning. She had been an Indian, without a doubt, with her ink-black hair and high cheekbones. Her tribe was unknown to Daniel, but her origin was unmistakable.

Daniel thought back, recalling what Sam had

said that night. He had claimed that she was unbalanced. "Tetched in the head," he said. And that "Jen-nee" belonged to him.

In spite of what Whitman had said, Daniel couldn't quite believe him. The girl didn't look crazy. And why had she made so many references to Jesse? He was, after all, a married man.

Something did not ring true. The woman's appearance at the door might have been a cry for help. Daniel could not let the matter rest until he proved it to himself.

He had ridden back to the house after the captain and his men had bivouacked, to stand outside her window. He wondered whether to wake her.

And then the door to the outer room opened to admit Sam Whitman. The drunken man was a grotesque shape against the light in the room behind him. He sidled toward the bed like a great hunched spider.

And the woman moaned and put up her arms to pull him to her.

Daniel had closed his eyes and backed away from the window, not wanting to see any more.

No, this girl could have no relationship to Jesse. It was better just to ride along, keep his mouth shut, and see what developed.

They rode in silence for several days, stopping only to rest the horses. Finally they reached a spot where the trail was confusing.

They had been following the tracks of a number of Indians Daniel had identified as Navajo. Many of them were mounted and they drove a number of cattle, possibly stolen from Sam.

Here the trail forked; new prints were superimposed upon the older ones of cattle being driven in a forced march. Daniel studied the ground and noted that all the people were mounted and the horses shod, in the white man's way.

Jesse and Daniel deliberated for a moment. It seemed the herd had been taken from the Indians. But by whom? Whoever these white men were, Jenny would most likely be with them. Jesse was unable to quench a small glow of hope.

He would follow the new tracks. Daniel could take the older route, which led toward the hot springs.

As Daniel neared the spot where the Indians had wintered for years, he smelled the odor that had clung to Sam Whitman's ranch house. It was a scent of fires that had burned down to cold ashes, along with a devastating, choking aura of decay.

He touched his spurs to his horse and rode into a clearing.

For an instant he paused, confused. The clearing was dotted with colorful bits and pieces of clothing, fluttering in the breeze. It looked like a garden of bright flowers.

Instead it was a garden of the dead.

Daniel Strongbow had lived with his people until he was ten years old. Then his parents were both killed, and Daniel was taken in by a family of settlers. They were devoutly religious people and had sent him to school. Gradually he forgot the old ways. But now he remembered.

His dark eyes watered and stung. He did not deny his tears as a white man might, but welcomed them. They helped wash away the pain.

Daniel rode into the middle of the grisly circle and dismounted. He began to search among the dead for faces he knew, as he had done as a child—and with the same dread he had felt as he looked for his mother and father. But they had been recognizable.

Animals had already been at these bodies. He paused by the side of a girl whose face had been destroyed, the ivory bone laid bare. She wore the remnants of a red dress that might have belonged to a white woman. But her hair was ebon-black, and the remaining shreds of skin clinging to her skull were very dark.

Daniel studied the fragile, broken body as long as he dared. He swallowed and moved on.

At last he found a man he had seen before, and it was a clue. This man was a miner from Silver City, a place that had borne the brunt of more than one Indian attack.

It must have been a case of revenge. The miners had come upon the Indians encamped here and had taken justice into their own hands. It was not a new story to the Indian scout. Daniel rose, the fringes of his leggings flapping in a rising wind.

Afte a moment the young Indian mounted and rode to the edge of the clearing. Sighing, he raised his pistol and fired a shot to summon Jesse, who could not have gone far.

18

Not too far from the charnel house the Indian encampment had become, Jesse Norwood found a camp with a dead fire. The miners from Silver City had paused here, to gather up the strays from the stampeding herd they had taken from their victims. There was plenty of sign: horses, cattle, and the heavy boots of white men. But there were no high-arched, slender footprints small enough to belong to a child.

There was no sign of Jenny.

He would return and search in the other direction. Evidently she was with the Indians. And she must still be alive! He could not imagine Jenny dead. Leading his horse, Jesse started back in the direction from which he had come, then stopped, stock-still.

He had to find her. But what in the name of God would he do with her when he did? He was a married man! If only she hadn't come out here.

But she had. And she had brought back all the memories he had thought were gone for good: the sweetness of her in his arms; her small, soft voice; her healing hands. Jesse had adjusted to the realities of this harsh land. He was happy with Elena.

His eyes wet with tears, he set his lips firmly for a moment. Then he mounted and rode back in the direction Daniel had taken. A small wind had suddenly sprung up, and he drew his cloak around him. Dust struck in a swirling cloud that took his breath away, blinding him for a moment.

The clear silence that followed was broken by a sound; a single shot from Daniel Strongbow's gun.

Jesse spurred his tired horse to its peak performance. Yet as he crashed through brush and up and down rocky hillsides, he felt as if he were moving in slow motion. His mind was filled with pictures—pictures of Jenny dead, perhaps tortured. Of Jenny alive and well, running to meet him—or shrinking from him in revulsion.

Surely Sam would have told her that Jesse had not been faithful to the girl he had left behind in Tennessee.

Again his gray eyes blurred, and he shook his head angrily. When they cleared, he saw Daniel waiting in the near twilight against a backdrop of trees.

Only Daniel, gesturing that there was no need to hurry.

He slowed his horse's pace, but when he reached the Indian scout, Daniel looked at the animal, then at him, in silent reproof. Jesse reddened. His mount was lathered, its mouth covered with bloody foam. Never before had he treated a horse in this way.

"Well, dammit, what did you find?" he said, exploding.

"They are all dead," Daniel said quietly. "There was no need to waste the strength of your horse." He turned away, taking a path between the trees. Jesse followed, his heart thumping with trepidation.

He saw the same sight that had met Daniel's eyes; a meadow blooming with the dead. The wind had come and gone, disturbing the bodies, fluttering their garments, and releasing the sweet, rich smell of death. The air was filled with its cloying, choking scent.

Ironically the field was full of butterflies.

Like a sleepwalker, Jesse moved among the dead. Most of the remains were so trampled that they were unrecognizable. But here and there he saw the body of a child. One small girl, whose lower torso was gone, hugged a corn doll close, as though to protect it.

He knew none of these people. Perhaps they were members of a small band who had hidden in the wilds, never coming in to the reservation. This was probably the chief. And here . . .

What lay at his very feet struck him like a blow to the chest. There was not enough left of the face or figure to identify. But the gown was Jenny's.

His brain was lanced through with sudden pain. He did not recognize the low howl of anguish that came from his own lips as he fell to his knees beside the girl who had been his love.

Jenny—Jenny—

Daniel moved toward him quickly, reaching out a hand to touch his shoulder. But Jesse shrugged it off. Lifting the girl's fragile remains in his arms, he struggled to his feet, his face a mask of shock and horror. Stumbling, he veered toward his horse, still carrying his precious burden. The animal laid its ears back but stood as Jesse mounted. He rode off into the trees.

Daniel did not follow.

Now he knew that this first hunch had been correct. There had been something between Jesse and this woman. But she was not deserving of Jesse's love, Daniel knew, and a fierce anger rose in him.

If Jesse chose to talk to him, he would listen but say nothing. The girl was dead and gone, and Jesse could keep his memories, go home to his wife, and eventually forget. It was none of his affair.

When night fell, Daniel built a small fire at the far edge of the clearing, away from the direction of the wind. Perhaps the ghosts of the slain would walk. No matter; he was afraid of nothing.

Squatting beside the blaze, his dark eyes yearned as he looked into the flames. There was no good or bad where love was concerneed. There had been such a girl for him.

Alice was his almost-sister, in the family that had taken him in after his parents were killed. He had loved her, and she had allowed a few stolen kisses, an unknown delight to the young Navajo. It was a forbidden love, but in his youth he had dared to hope.

Then he had found her tiptoeing into the house at dawn. Yes, she said defiantly, she had spent the night in the arms of an older man. But he was to keep quiet about it. When he tried to remonstrate with her, she sneered. "What do you know about it? You're only an Indian!"

He left the house that morning and never returned. If he had, he knew he would have to seek out the white man . . .

And kill him.

The sun was coming up when Jesse rode back into the field. His face was gray, his eyes red and swollen. Daniel's eyes took in the condition of the spade thrust in among the gear his horse carried. Its blade was covered with dark, moist earth.

It was over.

Jesse went down to the small, flowing river with its hot springs and bathed, scrubbing the odor of death from his big body. Drying himself, he changed to the auxiliary uniform he carried. Normally he changed just before reaching home, to avoid offending Elena's delicate sensibilities.

Now the action signified more than that. When he burned the death-tainted clothing, it would be the true end of an era in his life.

Last night he had gone into the woods, carrying the body of the girl he once loved.

And still loved, he admitted to himself.

In the deep, green-scented night he buried her. And there, beside her grave, he relived those days he had forgotten. Jenny's face was still before him, her great eyes looking at him gravely. He hid his face in his hands to shut her out.

"Oh, God," he moaned.

Daniel put a plate before him, and he pushed it away. "A cup of coffee, then?" Daniel asked.

Jesse accepted it and sat staring into its murky depths until his men arrived, their noise incongruous in this place of death. Then Jesse became Colonel Norwood once more. He issued his orders curtly, dispassionately.

"You will rest here a short while, to bury the

dead." He choked a little and regained his voice. "Then you will head for Silver City. There you may find some answers for this—this senseless massacre. Corporal Brackett will be in charge. I leave all authority in his hands."

"I am going home. Daniel," he said, turning to the Indian guide. "And you are going with me."

As they rode toward Santa Fe both men were silent. Daniel was thinking of his almost-sister, the girl he had once loved, who had betrayed him. Jesse was thinking of the girl he had just laid to rest, who deserved a happier ending to her short life.

Now she lay, lost in a sylvan glade, hidden away from prying eyes. He had buried her deeply, beneath the sheltering arms of a tall cottonwood tree, so that her eternal slumber would be undisturbed.

19

The Weldon baby posed no problems for the people at Sweethome. Zada was glad to serve as wet nurse to the unwanted infant, and Dinah kept the little one in the kitchen with her. It was a place Theron, now seeming a bit improved, never entered. Inga realized, uncomfortably, that the child had no name. She had to remind herself that the baby had only been loaned to her for a little while.

Dinah solved that problem.

"I'se gonna call her Honeybee," she said firmly. And Honeybee she became.

Honeybee proved to be a joy and a delight. From the moment she entered the house it was as though a charm had been draped over it. The slight improvement in Theron's health gave Inga hope. She lost her worried expression and presented a smiling face to the world. Even Dinah was affected by the difference in their lives, belting out Negro hymns as she worked in the kitchen and did the laundry.

"Swing low, sweet chariot," she would sing. "Comin' for to carry me home. . . ."

And Inga knew the black woman was thinking

of her father, Old Caleb, who had been home for a number of years and who, according to Dinah, was "sittin' at the right hand of God."

Could Inga's own faith carry her through with such enthusiasm if she lost someone near and dear to her? Theron, for instance . . .

She didn't know.

But she wouldn't think about that now. So much time had passed. Theron was better, and there was new life in the house, in the form of Honeybee. Each day the little girl grew sweeter, more lovable. She was beginning to talk, and her first word was *Minna*, her version of Mama Inga.

Still no one came from Eden even to ask after the child. It was beyond Inga's understanding. Dinah was puzzled too. She had reared her own grandson, Boy, and together they had walked to Sweethome from Memphis, after the war. Even now they had a closeness Inga envied.

"You just keep that baby, Miz Inga!" Dinah grumbled. "Don' you go givin' it back. Some folks ain't fit parents, no way, no how!"

Inga knew that Honeybee wasn't hers to keep and that one day Honeybee's father would return for her.

The summer passed, and suddenly it was fall. She was highly nervous as Thanksgiving approached. Surely Martha would want her baby on this holiday. Inga was so certain that she packed all Honeybee's things, dampening some of them with a few unbidden tears.

But still there was no word from Eden Plantation.

Theron was able to come downstairs to the festive dinner Dinah had prepared. To Inga's dismay he entered the kitchen, an unprecedented act since his illness. "Smells good in here," he said. Then he noticed the crib near the fire.

"And who is this?"

Inga froze, but Dinah threateningly waved a ladle. "That there's Zada's latest. Now, y'all git out of my kitchen befo' I throw you out!"

The figure beneath the blanket stirred, and Inga caught her breath at the sight of gray eyes opening. But Theron apparently didn't notice. Slipping his arm around Inga's waist, he led her back into the main house where he kissed her gently.

"We have so much to be thankful for," he said.

"Oh, yes," she whispered in answer. "Yes, we do!"

They had an enjoyable meal together, thinking back to other such occasions, then walked outside for a while in the crisp, cool air.

"Look at the fall colors," Theron marveled. "I never thought I'd see them again. I wonder if I'll see the spring. . . ."

It was the first allusion he had made to his terminal illness. And suddenly Inga could see his deadly pallor, the transparency of his fingers.

"Of course you will," she said. But she was suddenly cold all over and shivering.

"I think we'd better go in."

Theron, as usual, tired quickly. Inga put him to bed, kissing his hollow cheek, promising to return. Then she went downstairs, ostensibly to help Dinah clear up the kitchen. But that was only an excuse, since the work had long been done. Inga longed to see the baby.

She picked Honeybee up and cuddled her, making small, loving sounds. Then there was a rap at the door, and she turned, startled to see the figure of a man outside the screen.

She recognized Matt Weldon, and her heart sank.

Inga opened the door, holding the baby a little too tightly, releasing her hold as the child began to whimper. Inga opened her own mouth to speak, but nothing came out. Finally Weldon, turning his hat in his hands, asked, "May I come in?"

Inga nodded and stepped back as he entered, looking at him defensively. He reddened and swallowed.

"I expected Martha to want to bring the baby home today. But—she just isn't ready. I hate to impose...."

Inga found her voice. "She's no trouble at all, really."

"Then you wouldn't mind keeping her? Hopefully by Christmas..."

"Not at all," Inga said, on the verge of laughter and tears. "Not at all."

When Weldon had gone, Inga stared at Dinah and started to cry with happy relief. The old woman wrapped fat black arms around her and the baby. "We got us somethin' to be thankful for," Dinah said prayerfully. "We surely do."

Inga wanted to tell her that they would have Honeybee only until Christmas, but she knew even that wasn't definite. She would have to deal with this situation as she did Theron's illnesss: one day at a time.

Theron was still awake when she finally climbed the stairs. He reached up his remaining arm and pulled her down to him, burying his face in her hair.

"I love you, sweetheart! I love you so much!" And then he said, in a broken voice, "I haven't been much of a husband to you."

"You're all the husband I want," Inga whispered. "You don't have to do anything more. Just hold me, Theron! Just hold me!"

He did. She nestled against him, soft and warm, and they played their game of Let's Remember. They talked of the little summerhouse he had built in the glade beyond the fields, a bower for their wedding night.

"We didn't go there all this summer," he said huskily. "That is one thing I missed."

"We'll go next spring," she promised, holding her breath for fear that he would refute her statement. He didn't, but he sighed.

"That baby in the kitchen. You said it was Zada's child. But, Inga, it looked white to me. Has my sight failed too?"

"No," she told him in a muffled voice. "You must have misunderstood. The baby isn't Zada's. Its mother is sick. Dinah—Dinah is taking care of it until she's better."

Don't ask the baby's name, she prayed. Please don't.

Theron did not. His mind was already on another track. "Inga, we should have had a baby of our own. It would have given you something you need."

There was a note of resignation in his voice, a sort of giving up that terrified her.

"All I need is you," she said stoutly.

"And I am here."

She turned to him, holding him, trying to fill him with some of her strength, and finally he slept. She lay awake for a long time, then fell asleep, to dream of a scented bower in a flower-filled glade; of a man who loved her. She dreamed of waking in the morning to find the netting that enclosed a small white summer-house covered with dew; a million diamonds, sparkling in the sun.

20

That night, after a joyous day of Thanksgiving, was the last lucid period of Theron's life.
When Inga woke to a bright, cold morning, he
was cowering away from her, a bright spot of
red in each cheek, his eyes haunted.

From that morning on, Theron's condition was
difficult to predict. Some days he was easy to
handle, as sweet and childish as a little boy.
And at other times, when he believed someone
was about to take his arm off, it took four muscular field hands to restrain him.

It was almost more than Inga could bear.

Dinah approached her again about sending
for Kirsten or Jenny. Once again Inga refused.
Her daughters had their own lives to live. Theron was her responsibility. And he would hate
to have them see him this way. Sometimes she
felt as though little Honeybee were all that helped
maintain her sanity.

As Christmas approached, she thought feverishly of excuses to keep the child a little longer,
if Weldon should come for her. The weather was
dreadful: an ice storm followed by snow. Honeybee had a slight cold. If she was taken out, it

might deepen into pneumonia. Or whoever carried
her might fall. She had grown used to the people in this house. In a strange place, with strangers, she would be afraid.

No, Inga thought, there was no use grasping
at straws. After all, the Weldons were the baby's
parents. There was nothing she could say or do.

On Christmas Day Inga presented the child
with several little dresses and a rag doll she had
stitched while sitting at Theron's bedside. But
Dinah had outdone her. Her gift was a brightly
colored gourd made into a rattle, and the baby
cooed and batted at it with her rosy little hands.

Inga wondered what Martha would think of
the rattle; if she would even let the child keep it.
In spite of her mother's prejudice, Honeybee
was a true child of the South: nursed at Zada's
black breast, cared for by a black mammy, and
loved by everyone.

How could they take her away?

With Theron so ill, Inga hadn't been able to
get to Memphis to purchase gifts for the workers on the plantation. "Don' you mind," Dinah
said, "Nobody 'spectin' nothing."

Though the old woman had been behaving
mysteriously, Inga was still not prepared for what
happened. This year the gift giving was reversed.
Now the people of the big house were the
recipients.

One by one the Negro workers made their
way through the snow, carrying presents for
Inga, Theron, and the baby. There were pillow-
cases, bleached white and embroidered with
threads handspun and dyed. Dinah presented a
ham, cured in her own special way. There were
quilted pads for taking hot kettles from the stove;

homemade soaps, refined and scented with attar pressed from summer's flowers. . . .

And everyone had something for Honeybee. The crowning gift was a high chair made by John, the black overseer, who was also an excellent furniture maker.

Inga blinked back tears. "I don't know how to thank you."

"We need to thank you, missus," John said gently. "You give us a roof over our haids and work to do."

It was a heartwarming day but still a tense one. Inga waited for Matthew Weldon to come. It wasn't until the next morning that he appeared at the kitchen door, his shoulders covered with snow. He begged for a little more time. Martha wasn't well. Time, thought Inga, time and hope were all she had.

When he had gone, Dinah delivered her latest items of gossip. "Folks is still riled up over the way that man treated Massa Theron, buying his propitty up for taxes."

"I know, Dinah. But he did nothing wrong."

"That ain't all. You know that no-good Skaggs girl, runs after anybody that wears pants?"

"I know of her," Inga admitted.

"Well, she's all swole up like a punkin. Says it's Massa Weldon that done it."

"That isn't true! Weldon wouldn't touch her! Don't even repeat such a thing."

"Didn't say he did! But that's what she says. And that's what everybody's gonna think. They's gonna run 'im off, for sure."

At first Inga was concerned because Dinah hadn't told her in time to warn her neighbor. Then, as the days passed uneventfully and nothing happened, she put it out of her mind.

The approach of the new year brought another ice storm. On New Year's Eve, Inga stood at the window of Theron's room, idly tracing a design on the misted glass as she wondered where these last years had gone. At the stroke of midnight, 1871 would begin. What would next year bring?

She turned to look at her husband, deep in drug-induced sleep. How thin he had grown; how pale and haggard. She fought against a desire to wake him, to tell him she loved him.

Then suddenly Dinah burst into the room, her eyes wide in her dark face. Inga turned to her, shocked at the old woman's terror.

"I had tuh tell you," Dinah said in a low wail, too loud for a sickroom. "I had tuh tell yuh!"

"Tell me what?"

Dinah was babbling with fear as she caught hold of Inga, looking at her frantically. "Don' want no killin' on my conscience! No, suh-ree-bob! Been a God-fearin' woman all my life! Ain' gonna change none now!"

"For heaven's sake, Dinah, calm down! I don't have the slightest idea what you're saying!"

"The Klan! They's gonna get Massa Weldon tonight. John done heard it from one of Mistah Jenkins' hands. He come to me—"

Inga's mouth was white. "When, Dinah? Does John know?"

"When it gits good an' dark, I 'spec."

Dear God!

Inga was paralyzed with shock, but it was only an instant before her mind began to work. "Tell John to hitch the horse to the buggy, and then ..." This was the hardest thing she had ever had to say in her life, but after all, Honeybee was not her child. She belonged to her mother and father. Inga swallowed hard. "Then get the baby's things ready. They'll want to take her with them when they leave."

"No, Miz Inga! No!" Dinah was crying now, along with Inga. But Inga was adamant.

"We have to hurry." The window she had been staring out of was a black square, and outside, the wind lashed the house with frozen rain.

Within a few moments the buggy was waiting at the side of the house. Inga got in and reached down, taking the small, sweet bundle from Dinah's reluctant hands. She left the old woman, her apron over her face to hide her grief, and drove to Eden Plantation.

The house was dark, and she uttered a brief, irrational prayer that the Weldons were gone; perhaps they were celebrating the new year in Memphis. But the door opened to reveal the hastily clad figure of Johnson.

"It's the Klan," she told him. "They're coming tonight."

His face blanched. "I'd better call the master."

In a minute Matthew Weldon descended the stairs, his face lined with worry. Behind him trailed his wife, Martha, and Inga felt a sudden chill as she realized that Weldon hadn't told her the truth.

The woman was mad, her eyes wild, her hair unkempt, babbling something that sounded like "That awful woman!"

"Hush," Weldon said tiredly. Then, "Mrs. St. Germain, what is this?"

Inga explained. "They've been planning this for some time," she said. "I heard rumors of it

as early as last spring. It would be best to go
away, at least for a while. I have a buggy outside, and I've brought the baby to you."

Martha spoke for the first time. "It's just an
excuse, Matthew! She doesn't want the baby
anymore. She's trying to dump it on us!"

Weldon turned on her. "I told you to be still!"
Then, to Inga, "I'm sorry."

Inga averted her eyes from Martha's angry
face. "You'd better hurry," she said quietly.

"I'm going to stay and try to reason with
them. After all, they're human beings. If you
wouldn't mind taking the baby home with you—
and perhaps Martha?"

"I won't go," Martha stormed. "You just want
to get rid of me!" Johnson had been peering
through a front window. "It's too late," he said
hoarsely. "They're here, sir."

He pulled aside the drapery, and they could
see it: a blazing object, in the shape of a cross,
burning against the icy night. In the drive the
carriage from Sweethome had been set afire,
the horse cut loose from its traces. Sheeted figured moved cautiously toward the house.

Martha began to scream, and Inga stood transfixed, the baby in her arms.

Johnson had been right. She hadn't come in
time. There was no escape.

"I'm going out to meet them," Weldon said
quietly. He moved toward the door.

21

Theron awoke with the strange but distinct sensation that Inga was in trouble. She needed him. He took hold of a bedpost with a trembling hand and pulled himself up to a sitting position. He sat like that for a long minute, then drew a deep breath and hauled himself to his feet. His head swam, and for a moment he forgot where he was.

"Massa Theron!"

It was Dinah. He turned to the startled black woman with some of his old power of command.

"Get me my trousers and my boots!"

She obeyed, helping him dress.

"Now," he said, "where is Inga?"

His tone told her that he would brook no lies. Faltering, she told him of the Klan's planned attack on Eden; that Inga had gone to warn them.

"Oh, my God," he whispered.

Ordering Dinah to stay behind, he went downstairs and picked up the shotgun John had sawed off, so that it fit into the curve of his one arm. Then he was out the door before his weakness could catch up with him. Luckily the icy wind was at his back, though it made it difficult to maintain his balance as it swept him toward Eden.

When he reached the middle of the bridge, he paused, wondering what he was doing there. Then his mind dredged up a memory that was several years old.

That damned Yankee had Kirsten in his bed, and he was going to kill him. But he had lost his gun somewhere. No matter, he would do it with his bare hands. Hand, he thought, looking down at the empty sleeve of the nightshirt he wore over his trousers. He noticed that somehow he had lost his arm, too.

But he would manage.

The wind cut through his thin clothing; the freezing rain seemed to come from all directions as it lashed his face like a million tiny knives, but he went doggedly on. Now he had forgotten about Kirsten, and it was Jenny he worried about. Then he forgot everything but a mysterious something that drove him toward Eden.

When he passed the fringe of trees, he was soaked through with perspiration. He paused to admire the pretty flowers blooming on the lawn. Odd. Somehow he had gotten the impression that it was winter. After a while he blinked his eyes, and the lovely blossoms turned into fire.

It was a burning buggy, a fiery cross.

A horde of people robed in white.

A church wedding? he wondered. Then his mouth went suddenly dry.

Angels?

No, goddamn it! It was the Klan!

He saw Weldon go down as Inga appeared on the porch. Then someone fired a shot, and he knew why he had come. He broke into a shambling run.

the ... then someone tried a ...
knew why he had come. He broke into ...
blare the ...

—— 22 ——

Inga watched as Matthew Weldon swung open the great, arched door of Eden and stepped outside, raising a hand in a gesture of peace.

"Gentlemen," his voice rang out, "let's discuss this amicably, if you please."

There was a low growling sound from the mob. "Get the damn Yankee! String him up. Killin's too good fer him. 'Member Pittsburg Landin'? The Peach Orchard? They kilt Gen'l Johnson—ol' Albert Sidney Johnson—an' I was there! Hang the bastard!"

Weldon reddened. "Damn it, listen to me!"

From out of nowhere came a blob of fresh horse dung. It struck Weldon full in the face. He gave an angry roar as he went down the steps, two at a time.

"What the hell is this? Listen, you goddamn cowards! Step forward and name yourselves if you've got a gripe! Stop hiding behind those damn sheets."

He managed to yank off one hood, revealing an angry red face. The Klansman tried desperately to hide his face as Weldon reached for another's mask. The second fellow tried to back away, pointing a gun at Weldon with shaking fingers.

"Shoot the bastard!" someone boomed.

The man hesitated, and Weldon doggedly went after him.

Then the whole tableau was shattered by a scream—a woman's scream. Martha thought her husband was leaving her to the mercy of these terrible, sheeted creatures. Barefoot and clad in her nightdress, she ran from the house, screeching at the top of her lungs.

"You're not deserting me, Matthew Weldon! I'm going with you!"

She clawed at him hysterically, and Weldon turned. The wavering gun in the hands of his enemy exploded. The bullet tore through Weldon's shirtfront and into the body of his wife.

Inga put the baby in a deep chair and ran outside just in time to see Weldon tear into his enemy with an inhuman cry. Within minutes he was dragged down, arms twisted behind his back. His shirt was torn from his body, the icy ground stained red with blood from a split lip.

They're going to kill him, Inga thought. Dear God, they're going to kill him!

"Well, looky here," a man's voice said. He slipped an arm around her waist. "Looks like that Yankee wife of St. Germain's. Hear he's sick. Mebbe she's lookin' for a little fun—"

"No," she said. "No!" She gestured toward Martha. "Help her!"

"When we're through with her husband," the hood-muffled voice said silkily. "Mebbe we'll give her some of the same medicine. But not you. You're gonna get special treatment." His voice changed as he barked out, harshly, "Git a rope!"

Another hooded figure ran for his horse and brought back a roll of hemp cord. Weldon was dragged toward the trees at the edge of the clearing. Inga struggled vainly against the arms that held her, while her captor continued to shout orders.

"You, brother, you see to settin' the house afire. And my good brother, over there under the tree, if you will ..." The speaker paused and stared openmouthed, as he was suddenly interrupted.

"*Let her go! Weldon too! Now, by God!*"

The voice that rang out with such command came from an eerie figure that burst through the trees. Gaunt and emaciated, it looked like one of the walking dead as it made its way through the sheeted mob; they parted as it passed. His one hand held a sawed-off shotgun that fitted just under his arm, enabling him to fire at will.

And there were some there who remembered this man's deadly aim.

Inga gave a startled cry.

"Theron!"

He paused uncertainly. Then he saw that she was unhurt, and his expression was heart-rending. He moved to her side, and the man who held her backed away, the eyeholes of his hood reflecting fear.

"Sweetheart," Theron said shakily, "are you all right?"

"Yes, but—" Inga rubbed her bruised arm and looked down at her feet where Martha lay, a crimson blossom of blood welling from her heart. And then she buried her face against her husband's shoulder.

Released by a startled Klansman, Matthew Weldon crawled to his wife's side and frantically tried to revive her. Their blood mingled as he tried to breathe for her, forgetting everything around him.

The mob members were beginning to mutter among themselves, getting up their nerve again now that they had a good look at Theron; his once powerful body was clearly ravaged by illness.

"Be damned if it ain't St. Germain," said one man.

"Ain't seen him in a coon's age," said another.

"Looks like hell, don't he?"

"Heard he'd turned into a nigger lover. Mebbe he's a Yankee lover too," one Klansman said, sneering.

Theron spoke, his voice dark with rage.

"Get out of here! Go home!"

The Klansmen looked at each other and shuffled nervously. They had come here, united in their strength. Now they were not sure that they had done the right thing. After all, St. Germain was one of their own.

As they faltered, he continued.

"The war's over, goddamn it! We got whipped, fair and square! We're not rebels anymore. Weldon isn't a Yankee! We're all Americans."

"Now you listen, St. Germain," a voice called out. "I know you been sick and all, mebbe got religion, but goddamn it, this man don't belong here!"

"Then where does he belong? You men are

like little boys, playing games! And because of your games you've killed somebody!

"A woman—"

A sudden hush went over the group, followed by a guilty murmuring. "Didn't go to do it. Damn female got in the way."

"Does that make any of you more of a man? Are you proud of yourselves? Jenkins? Potter? Skaggs? Hargrove?" Theron taunted.

He went around the circle, deliberately giving the intruders names, despite their disguises. Finally one of the men said sheepishly, "Didn't go to cause no trouble. Just wanted to put the fear of God in him."

Theron's voice was ugly with its note of revulsion.

"You've done enough! *Go home!*" Turning to the fellow who dared lay hands on his wife, he said, "*Get! Or I'll blow the hell out of you!*"

The man cleared his throat, then stared at the body of Martha, who looked oddly small, almost like a child in her virginal gown. "Mebbe we ought to he'p you get the ... the lady into the house."

"You've done enough!" Theron repeated.

The members of the Klan began to slink away, one by one. When the last had disappeared, Theron seemed to wilt before Inga's very eyes, changing back again from the man he used to be to his state of invalidism.

But Inga was proud of him.

Taking his arm, she gently lowered Theron to a blue bench, out of the way of the wind, and went to check on Weldon's wife.

Her first thought had been a true one. The woman was dead.

Weldon had carried her into the house with Johnson's help. Now he knelt beside her, trying to warm her cold hands as he looked up at Inga and shook his head. Martha was dead.

Matthew blamed himself for marrying Martha, bringing her here to a place where she didn't fit in at all; for making her pregnant with a child she didn't want; for letting her think he was leaving her—all because of his damned hot-headed pride.

Inga could read the guilt on his face, but she had no answers for his problem. Guilt did not leave immediately; it had to wear away.

The important thing now was to get Theron home.

"I'll send John over to get the baby," Inga told Matthew.

She would keep it until Matthew got himself pulled together. Then, she knew, she would probably have to give the child up forever.

After a few words with Johnson, who loaned her a heavy cloak for Theron, Inga began the trek home with her husband. Their heads were bent against the wind. When they reached the center of the bridge, Theron was forced to rest. Putting her arms around his shivering body, Inga said softly, "I was so proud of you! And I was so surprised to see you there. I thought you hated Weldon."

"I remembered something," Theron told her. "I remembered the time he saved your life."

It was true. Weldon had come to rescue them all when Sweethome was invaded by the ragged leftovers of the Confederate Army. But Inga would have thought Theron had surely forgotten.

"I pay my debts," he said through chattering teeth.

"Yes," she said. "Yes, you do." Then, "Do you think you can go on a little farther?"

Of course he could. But first he took a long, long look at his surroundings; the frozen water that was the river, the trees and grass around it now turned into shards of shining crystal. It was as if he would never see it again.

Wait until spring, Inga prayed silently, when the river sings and the flowers bloom. Please, God!

They moved on, but Theron had to rest again almost immediately. They stopped near the tulip tree, now sculptured in ice. He pointed out the grave where Inga once buried a body she had thought was his; hoped was his, since she and the girls had laid finder's claim to Sweethome.

Theron had returned to discover his name burned into a marker that stood over the mound of an unknown soldier.

"Remember?" he asked Inga now.

"I remember."

"Inga, don't ever forget—anything."

They continued on. When he wavered, she guided him gently toward the house. Then the door opened. Dinah was waiting for them, her grandson, Boy, at her side. Frightened by the happenings at Eden and concerned for the safety of her master, she had called him in from the quarters.

"Praise the Lawd," she whispered. "Oh, sweet Jesus! Give me a hand, Boy!"

With the lad's help they managed to get Theron upstairs and into bed.

His chills subsided gradually, and he smiled up at them with eyes that were clear and sane.

"I think I will sleep for a little while."

Inga tucked the sheets under his chin, touching her lips to his.

"Sleep well," she whispered.

His eyes closed, their lids blue and transparent. The hand she held grew heavy. She could see no visible signs of his breathing. She was suddenly struck with a terrible premonition.

"Theron! Oh, God . . . Theron-n-n!"

There was no answer, and the big clock downstairs boomed out twelve deep-throated, macabre notes as Inga went to her knees beside her husband's body. It was the beginning of the new year. The old one was dead and gone.

23

Jenny rose to take her turn at tending the small fire that burned through the night in the Place of the Old Ones. A week earlier, sitting here in this same spot, she had realized that it might be Christmas Eve.

And she had thought nostalgically of the holiday at Sweethome. Her mother and Dinah would be busy in a kitchen filled with heavenly scents of Southern cooking, preparing the food for the morrow.

Jenny's mouth watered at the thought of the goodies they would provide: ham, candied yams, succotash, buttered squash, two or three different kinds of pie. Lordy, what she wouldn't give to sink her teeth into one of Dinah's buttermilk pies right now! But at least Christmas was over. If only she could dismiss it from her mind.

A stealthy movement from the curtain of falling snow outside the half-walled dwelling caught her eye.

Damn! There it was again!

A pair of round yellow orbs stared at her out of the frozen night. She had been woolgathering and had let the fire burn too low.

She took a burning twig from the sinking flames and tossed it, straight and true. She heard it strike home, and there was a faint smell of singed fur.

The creature stayed at its post for a moment, holding her gaze with its own. Then, with a low snarl, it disappeared into the darkness.

Sighing, she set about building up the fire again. The animal seemed to be growing more persistent as time went by. And with good reason. Their store of firewood was now precariously low. And if they ran out, they might freeze to death. Or be at the mercy of the beast that watched by day and night.

Maybe it was hungry too.

She had been terrified when she first heard the cougar's womanlike scream from the ridge above. But now Jenny had grown accustomed to it. She was able to return to her thoughts once she had a blaze going.

Thinking about Sweethome and Christmas had created an ache inside her. And tonight, which if she had counted the days correctly, was the last hour of the old year and the beginning of the new.

This, too, had its traditions. At home Mama and Theron would be sitting up late. Dinah would be bustling around the kitchen fixing hot gingerbread and eggnog. Then Theron, when the clock struck twelve, would go outside and fire off his gun. It would be answered by a spate of fireworks from the quarters.

Jenny thought of Theron and of how he had been right about Jesse. She had been wrong. She wished she had a chance to tell him so; to say that she was sorry for leaving as she did.

She had slipped away when he was sick in bed with a touch of lung fever, Mama said. And her mother had thought it was best that way, since the Washburns were leaving immediately. There was no point in upsetting Theron when he was ill.

Still, it didn't seem right. Theron had been a good father to her since he married Inga—the only true father Jenny had ever known.

She tried to hold Theron, Inga, and Sweethome in her thoughts. But right now she could think of nothing but New Year's and hot gingerbread.

She heard a sound and whirled to face it. It was only Ugly Woman, come to take her turn at the fire.

As if she had gussed that Jenny might be hungry, the Indian girl reached into a little pouch she carried at her waist and withdrew a piece of jerky, handing it to her friend.

Jenny's mouth watered, but she pushed it away. "I do not need it," she said.

"You do," Ugly Woman persisted. "You have eaten very little since the snow. You must eat to be strong."

"And so must you."

"This is not mine. It belongs to Tsi'dii, the old grandmother. She is not well and cannot eat. She asks that I give it to you, since you shared your portion with the children."

Finally Jenny gave in. She put the food to her lips, taking tiny bites and chewing a long time to make it last. She had never known a morsel of anything to taste so delicious.

"What is wrong with Tsi'dii?"

Ugly Woman shrugged. "She is old and does

not feel she is worthy of the food. I do not think she will eat again."

Jenny had swallowed the last bite of the jerky. But in the morning she would see that Tsi'dii got some food.

If only she had a gun! There were animals here. Although she had never killed anything before, she knew she could do it now, for the sake of these people, whom she loved.

They all had become her family, just as Tsis'na had. Ugly Woman with her lovely face and crippled foot; Tsi'dii; Bit'so and her small sister, So'tso; the toddler, Ey'yah, who clung to her skirts as she planted the seeds she found, tilling the earth with the sharpened fork of a sapling.

They made a good harvest, but it had not been enough.

They had expected D'zili and the warriors to return for them. They did not. Their only visitor was a small black bear that raided their scanty larder. Old Tsi'dii screamed at the top of her lungs, wielding a dead tree limb she had snatched, and sent him kiting. But not before the damage was done.

If the snow would only stop falling, Ugly Woman could set her snares for small animals again. Tsi'dii might be able to find edible bark and roots. And they could gather wood once more for their fires.

But right now the children went to bed with empty bellies.

"I saw the cougar again tonight," Jenny told Ugly Woman. Then she was almost sorry she had mentioned it. Tsi'dii claimed the animal was a ghost; the evil spirit of an Old One, haunting the dwelling. Tsi'dii was certain that its presence presaged her death.

Ugly Woman paled a little, but her only answer was a fatalistic yes, as she built up the fire.

Jenny said good night to Ugly Woman and went to her bed of dried leaves. She imagined she could smell hot gingerbread; taste the smoothness of eggnog on her tongue.

Surely it must be midnight by now.

She rose from her bed and visited those of the sleeping children, kissing each on the forehead. Old Tsi'dii was also lying wide-awake. Neither woman spoke, but Jenny touched her cheek with a loving hand.

And finally she went to Ugly Woman, who sat quietly by the fire. "I just wanted to wish you a happy new year," Jenny said.

Ugly Woman looked at her in confusion, not understanding. Jenny didn't explain but returned to her bed of leaves.

She was cold. And she was hungry. The warriors had not returned for them, and she had lost Jesse, and T'sis'na, her friend.

But the new year had to be better. It had to be!

24

Jenny woke the next morning to a crystalline world. The sun glittered harshly off a crust of ice covering the snow-white landscape; a sun without warmth.

Jenny tested the icy film over the snow. It held her weight. It was possible that they could gather wood for fuel. And if the cold held, Ugly Woman could set her snares.

She formed a work party. It consisted of herself, Ugly Woman, and small Bit'so. Tsi'dii, still unwell, would be left to look after little lame So'tso and Ee'yah, the toddler.

The ice was pretty slippery. Just to be on the safe side she would negotiate the steep hill leading down from the cliff dwelling first.

She lowered herself carefully, seeking hand- and footholds along the way. Once she nearly fell but caught herself. For a long time she hung, heart beating too fast, before she was able to continue on her way.

At last she reached the bottom. Bit'so followed her, scrambling down like a little monkey. Jenny hugged her close and looked up.

Now it was Ugly Woman's turn.

Jenny caught her breath. She had become so accustomed to Ugly Woman that she had forgotten about her infirmity. But she managed the descent without incident.

They moved through the narrow defile below the caves, semiprotected from the ringing cold as they chopped dead twigs and branches free from the ice that cut their hands like broken glass. While the two women accomplished this task little Bit'so dragged the firewood to the foot of the hill for them.

At last they were too chilled to work any longer. Freeing one last piece of wood, Ugly Woman unearthed a burrow where a hare huddled, petrified with fear. Sensing that it had been discovered, it leapt away. It was quick, but not quick enough. Ugly Woman brought down the branch she held, striking it dead.

They gathered around the little body, seeing not a small, dead animal but life—life for all of them.

They would go back to the cliff dwelling and make it into a stew; a tantalizing prospect for people who had been too long without fresh meat. Then, after they had eaten, Jenny would go with Ugly Woman to set snares.

They returned, calling to Tsi'dii. With Ugly Woman carrying the hare, they began to climb.

Halfway up, at the very spot where Jenny had slipped, Ugly Woman's crippled foot gave way. She fell all the way to the bottom, where she landed, buried deep in snow.

The snow had cushioned her fall, but she lay in a four-foot drift, one leg doubled beneath her, her dark hair spread around her.

Jenny and Bit'so knelt, looking down at her. "Are you hurt?" Jenny whispered.

Though the girl was bleeding from a thousand cuts caused by the ice, she tried to smile.

She was quite well.

Except for her leg; it was broken.

With the aid of one of the limbs they had gathered for firewood, they managed to get her out. It took a long time, and her lips were white in her dark face. Then came the arduous task of getting her back to the dwelling. Jenny supported her frail body on one side, Bit'so on the other, each of them moving carefully.

The afternoon was growing dark before they reached the top where they lowered the pain-racked girl to her bed of leaves. Tsi'dii clucked over her injury and helped Jenny set the leg, splinting it as they had done with So'tso's injury.

"We're almost done," Jenny said finally. She looked at the sky. It was twilight.

"Bit'so, go down—very carefully—and bring back the rabbit. We'll cook it for supper."

The little one obeyed, scrambling to the bottom of the hill. But the animal was nowhere to be seen. Bit'so remembered seeing its body hit the icy terrain when Ugly Woman fell. A stain on the snow marked the spot where it had struck.

But it was gone.

Slowly she returned to tell the others of the hare's disappearance. Perhaps a hawk had taken it.

"No," Tsi'dii said, quavering, "not a hawk. It was the one Who Walks by Night. The ghost in a cat's body."

The cougar?

Jenny tried to reason with Tsi'dii but to no avail. She knew it was her time to die, and the mountain lion was death's messenger. Finally

Jenny gave up. She had other things to think about.

With Ugly Woman unable to walk, who would set the snares? Perhaps she could teach Jenny how. But there was no time to learn from any mistakes she might make. Tsi'dii had deteriorated greatly, more from fear than anything else. So'tso was of little use, Ee'yah only a baby.

Jenny hugged Bit'so to her. They were now the sole providers for them all. She prayed to God that nothing would happen to either of them.

There was enough food, used sparingly, to keep six people fed for perhaps three more days.

After that there would be nothing. When the children slept, Jenny dragged the firewood they had gathered from the foot of the hill to a position between the walls.

Jenny would watch the fire through the night. Ugly Woman was sedated against her pain with the last of the medicinal herbs they had gathered in the spring. She was unable to help. Tsi'dii was too old, the children too young. And Jenny had not counted on her own weakness and weariness.

She fell asleep, waking in the morning to a dead fire with cold ash that retained only a spark to renew its blaze. It was snowing again, a different kind of snow this time: soft white flakes like feathers falling in a curtain across a gray sky.

After she had rebuilt the fire Jenny stood and stretched her limbs. They had stiffened from the cold and yesterday's grueling work. Then she went to check on the others.

The children slept peacefully. Ugly Woman was awake and weeping.

"You're hurting!" Jenny said accusingly. "Why didn't you call me?"

"I only hurt in my heart," Ugly Woman said. "Tsi'dii has gone. . . ."

Jenny stared at her for a moment, then ran to the old woman's bed. It was empty. She returned to question the Indian girl.

The grandmother had left before dawn, she said. She had gone for the long walk. It was inevitable, since the cougar would come for her, anyway. Now her small bit of food could be divided among the young ones.

"Why didn't you stop her?"

Ugly Woman shrugged. "It was her decision."

Jenny stared at her in angry exasperation. She would never understand these people! Then she whirled, going to Bit'so's bed. She shook the little girl awake. "Get up! I need you! We have to find Tsi'dii."

Every nerve jangling, Jenny moved food and water close to Ugly Woman's side. If she and Bit'so did not return, the supplies would only have to feed three. There would be enough food for six days. Bit'so pulled the firewood closer to Ugly Woman's side.

"Do not let the fire go out," Jenny said, admonishing the Indian girl. "So'tso will help you, will you not, So'tso?"

The little girl nodded gravely. Wrapping their blankets around their shoulders, Jenny and small Bit'so made their way down the hillside, following footsteps that were rapidly filling up with snow.

25

The heavy snowfall was brief; soon a lemony sun ventured out. Suddenly a great, white world opened before Jenny and Bit'so as the sun gilded the hills and made everything unbearably bright. It was also unbearably cold—as if the falling blanket of soft flakes had been there to keep them warm.

Jenny felt small and lost under the blinding sky that seemed to dwarf her. She took a firm grip on Bit'so's hand and went on.

Tsi'dii's tracks had disappeared in the snow. The trail they had been following led straight ahead, until it disappeared. While there was a chance they would continue on.

Bit'so came to an abrupt halt. "See?" the child said. "There is Tsi'dii in the snow. She looks like she is sleeping."

Jenny's untrained eye saw nothing but a vast, empty expanse of white. Bit'so broke away from her and ran on ahead, stopping beside a bundle of snow-covered twigs to wait for Jenny.

"Where," Jenny called as she caught up to the little girl, "where is she . . . ?"

Bit'so only pointed to the object at her feet.

Tears started in Jenny's eyes. "No!" she whispered.

Tsi'dii's face was chalk-white; as white as the hair that fell in thin, frozen strands from her scalp. She had left her blanket behind for the use of the children, and her faded Indian garb had frozen against her sticklike arms and legs. Her mouth was open, toothless and blue; her eyes were glazed with a film of ice.

Jenny dropped to her knees beside the old woman's body.

And then she saw them: the tracks.

The tracks of the big cat who haunted the cliff dwelling at night; who walked the ridge above that dwelling, uttering a woman's scream.

The cougar Tsi'dii had said was a ghost of the Old Ones. And she had said it would come for her. She had known that she would never leave that place alive!

There was no mark on the frail, frozen body. The thing had not touched her.

It had left only a circle of footprints, with no beginning and no ending, that surrounded Tsi'dii like a statement that she was the big cat's own.

Should she try to bury the old woman's body? Jenny knew such a course was futile. For one thing, she would have to dig through the snow until she reached the earth.

And it would be frozen.

She would make a snowbank to conceal the body from preying animals, mark the spot with a bright strip from her skirt, and then return to finish the job with the thaw.

She felt a little sick but set to work. And soon, with Bit'so's help, the job was done. Jenny tore a strip from her hem and tied it to the top of a small pine tree. Then she dashed her tears away and set her lips firmly.

The sun had come out for only a short time. The sky to the north had grown as black as ink. Jenny decided it was best to head back to the place they now called home, and to the others, before it began to snow again.

Again she took Bit'so's hand. They plodded along, half frozen, their hearts filled with sadness. And suddenly Bit'so raised her face, gazing about inquiringly. She pointed and said, "Look!"

In the distance Jenny saw two riders, and her heart lifted. They had seen no human beings since the warriors left them; she was certain they had come back at last. Leaving Bit'so standing alone, she ran toward them, waving to attract their notice. "D'zili! Here we are!"

"No! Jen-nee! No!"

Jenny heard Bit'so calling behind her. She paused, turning.

"They are enemies," the child shouted. "Run, Jen-nee!"

Then the little girl began to run; not toward the cliff dwelling but in the opposite direction.

"Wait," Jenny called.

She looked over her shoulder at the horses sliding as they plowed through the snow. Now she could see the riders clearly: two soldiers, rough-looking men.

"That's for me!" one of them shouted gleefully.

Jenny drew a quick breath, then she, too, began to run. She was not quick enough. They were upon her. The man in the lead slipped from his saddle and wrestled her to the ground. His ice-encrusted whiskers scratched her face as she tried to scramble away.

Let Bit'so get away, she prayed as she struggled.

Her prayer was not answered. Her captor's companion had ridden after the little girl. He scooped her up across his saddle and returned with her.

"Got us two live ones, by God!" the man who held her exulted. "Both these critters is female! Ain't had me a woman in a coon's age! What say we take the li'l 'un first, then bash her head in. We may want to keep this'n alive and kickin' for a while."

Jenny stared at him, uncomprehending. Then she realized that they were going to . . . to use . . . poor little Bit'so! And then they would kill her. After that it would be Jenny's turn.

And these were white men—people of her own kind.

The second man ripped away Bit'so's clothing, then tossed the small brown body into the snow. She lay still, looking up at him as she awaited her fate.

"No!"

Jenny jerked free of her captor and stepped forward. "You will not touch her," she said, her voice filled with hatred.

"Well, looky here! It can talk!" he said, surprised. "And it's white man's talk! Who the hell you been sleepin' with, girlie?"

The insinuation gave her an idea. If she could keep Bit'so safe until they reached Santa Fe, perhaps Jesse . . .

"Jesse Norwood," she said tartly. "Colonel Jesse Norwood. I am his wife. This is his daughter."

The man looked stunned, and then he grinned, clearly enjoying himself. "That's a damn lie," he said. "I've met the cunl's wife. She's a Mex. Purty little thing."

"I know of her," Jenny said tautly. "But I am his first wife. His Indian wife. If you wish. I will accompany you to Santa Fe in order to prove it. But if you injure his daughter, Jesse will kill you, and that's a promise!"

"You're lying." A note of uncertainty had entered the speaker's voice, and Jenny seized on it with hope. She reached into the bosom of her clothing and withdrew a worn bit of paper. It was one of Jesse's first communications, and she had been unable to throw it away. There was little left of the words that had once graced it, except for the signature: Love, Jesse.

The two men stepped to one side to discuss the situation. They didn't know anything about Norwood's past.

"But one thing's for damn sure, everybody knowed he was a Injun lover," the first man, whose name was Judkins, said. "The little gal's story just might be true as hell! The way I see it, we've only got two choices. Either we take the girls to Santa Fe and find out for sure"—he paused, licking his lips nervously—"or we have 'em here an' get it over with an' just hope the cun'l never finds out what happened."

"I dunno," the other soldier, a man known as Dermot, said cautiously. "I seen Jesse whup a man oncet. And all he done was kick a drunk Injun. 'Sides"—he grinned, hugely—"betcha that little pepperbelly he's married to don't know nothin' about this gal. Mebbe we oughta see to it she l'arns. Whaddaya say?"

Judkins snickered. "Last I heard, Norwood was out of town. We might just take these Injuns to the Norwood home and innerduce the little ladies."

He beckoned to Jenny, mounting his horse and taking her up in front of him. Dermot handed Bit'so her torn clothing, and she put it on, wrapping her blanket around her to conceal their condition.

As they rode toward Santa Fe, stopping only to eat and rest the horses, Jenny kept her face turned from the rank smell of the man's clothing. She tried to control her chattering teeth so that her captor would not know she was so cold. And so afraid.

She closed her eyes to the white expanse of snow as the horses struggled through it, the vapor from their nostrils rising like plumes to the sky. Her mind was filled with worry for those they had left behind them.

Somehow Jenny had to manage to find supplies and get back to the cliff dwelling as soon as possible, before the remainder of the people who had become her family starved to death. Their welfare, and her own, depended on Jesse; a man she had once thought she knew as well as she knew herself. Would Jesse still care enough for her to come to her rescue? And what would she do if he didn't?

Jenny thought of the cougar's footprints encircling the frozen body of Tsi'dii and felt a strange chill of foreboding.

Somehow she had to save them all, no matter what. Judkins' breath was hot on the back of her neck. He touched her as familiarly as he dared, and she knew that if she could, she would kill him.

26

Elena Ruiz Norwood was already dressed in
her finest gown, her dark eyes sparkling with
anticipation. Daniel Strongbow had ridden on
ahead of Jesse and his troops, to say her husband would be arriving soon. She had sent Daniel to the kitchen to be fed and hastily donned
her pretty dress. And now, all she could do was
wait.

She sighed, realizing that each time Jesse left
on a mission, he left her hoping for a miracle;
hoping that something would happen to put their
marriage back together. She had thought it
through again and again, searching for what
might have been the problem that led to the
destruction of the marriage. Now she thought
she had come up with a solution.

True, he had come to her bed at her request.
And did she not have a surprise for him to prove
it? But he had behaved so strangely since he
returned from his last mission, almost as if he
hated her. He had received word that his one-
time friend, Sam, was dead at the hands of
Indians.

He went to the scene, and when he came back,

he was so cold and moody that it frightened her. To lift his spirits she had prepared a fiesta, as a surprise, inviting all her family. Jesse had only seemed to endure it until, thinking to entertain the group, she had mentioned the odd-looking Indian girl who had come asking for Jesse when he was away on an earlier journey.

"It was beyond the imagination," she said prettily. "The woman asked for him by his given name! And the way she was dressed! In a faded red dress that was much too small."

"Did you give her a scolding?" her uncle asked, amused. "I can imagine you did!"

Elena tapped him on the arm with her folded fan in mock chastisement.

"Indeed I did not! I am married to the so-kind Colonel Norwood, remember? I suggested that she go to the back door for food, which is always available to members of her race."

She turned to smile at Jesse, then froze in alarm. His face had gone purple, his eyes bulging as though he were choking to death.

"Jesse! What is the matter?"

He gave a strangled cry that was almost incoherent. It could have been "Murderer!"

Or, "You murdered her!"

He had left the gathering then, locking himself in his study. Elena was left to try to explain his absence.

She had said he was ill. But what could be the excuse for his strange behavior since that day?

He had been polite—coldly, formally polite. And he had moved to his study, permanently. Away from her.

It had something to do with that girl. Elena knew it. She had learned of the massacre at the hot spring and thought perhaps the girl was dead. But still, it baffled her.

All she could do was wait it out: wait for Jesse to become his old self again. Wait for her miracle.

When Elena heard the sound of booted feet at the door, she ran, smiling, to answer it. The smile faded when she saw two soldiers standing there. She felt a rush of fear.

"The cun'l here?" one man asked.

She shook her head, her eyes wide. Then the men facing her moved to one side.

There, on the doorstep, stood the girl who had caused all her misery. The Indian girl, a little copper-faced child at her side. Elena recognized her. There was no mistake. She could never forget that face! Her fingers curled into claws as she confronted her enemy.

"Missus Norwood, meet Missus Norwood," one of the soldiers said, snickering. "And this here, this's Jesse's kid."

For Elena it was the ultimate in horror; far worse than she could have expected. She might have endured the thought of a mistress. But a wife! She had heard of white men taking Indian wives and then marrying later. But not Jesse!

"I do not believe it!" she said.

The soldier shrugged. "She got a paper to prove it."

He produced the letter and handed it to the woman. Elena's face went as white as milk.

"Come in," she said in a dead voice. Drawing Jenny into the house, she slammed the door, shutting out the others.

"What do you want?" Elena said. "What do you want from me!"

"To see Jesse," Jenny said hoarsely. "I—"

She was going to explain her story, telling the

woman that she didn't intend to make trouble, that she only needed food and supplies and to go free. But Elena silenced her with a raised hand.

"You should not have come here. I can have you killed! You and your daughter too."

Jenny lifted her chin. "I think not. I do not believe *he* will let you."

She looked past Elena at Daniel Strongbow, who had emerged from the kitchen at the sound of raised voices. His face went blank with shock at sight of her.

Elena glared at Daniel with smoldering eyes. "You know this woman?"

"I have seen her, yes."

He did not say that the last time he had laid eyes on her, she had been dead—dead and carried to her grave in Jesse Norwood's arms.

He didn't need to. Elena seemed to shrink away from him, as if Daniel had given credence to her worst suspicions. The important thing now was to get rid of the girl somehow.

"What will you take to leave us alone?" Elena asked, her eyes frantic.

And Jenny answered.

During the freezing ride she had mentally gone over the supplies they would need to get through the winter. She went through it now, as if she were reading it off a list. She wanted to be returned to the spot where they were captured. She also needed six packhorses, laden with food. A number of traps, garden seed, and a plow. A rifle with ammunition. Five woolen blankets. Needles, thread, five bolts of material . . .

All the horses, save one, would be returned, and Jenny would not come to Santa Fe again.

"I will have the soldiers fill your order," Elena said icily. "And they will return you to where they found you. Please leave immediately. If you're still here when Jesse arrives . . ."

Jenny shook her head; she was certain that if soldiers took them back, she and Bit'so would be violated, killed. "I want one more thing," she said deliberately. "I want him"—she pointed a finger at the startled scout—"to escort us. The others can tell him where they found us. I do not wish to see them again."

Elena turned to the Indian guide. His name on her lips was almost a supplication. "Daniel?"

He bowed his head in submission when Elena spoke. He was not quite sure what was going on, but it was clear that this woman was black-mailing the colonel's wife in some fashion. He intended to help get her out of the way as soon as possible.

He left Jenny and Bit'so in the lobby of the Exchange Hotel while, at the commissary, he filled the list of supplies she had requested. As they rode out of town, he could see the troops led by Jesse Norwood coming from the other direction.

It all had been done in the nick of time. Jenny didn't know how close she had come to seeing the man who had once been her love.

Daniel knew nothing about her feelings. Though he was courteous to the girl, it was obvious that he had nothing but contempt for Jenny. She bore his attitude in silence. After all, he was nothing but a means to an end; a guide to get them to where they were going.

And they were going home.

It had been a sickly woman. Apparently she thought Indian Jesse and his wife much [Redacted]

27

Jenny had reached the point of exhaustion. During the ride into Santa Fe she had kept her eyes open day and night, not daring to trust the men who had captured her and little Bit'so. Now, sensing they were safe in Daniel Strongbow's hands—no matter how he felt toward her personally—and with the knowledge that they were carrying food to those they had left behind, Jenny rode along in a half sleep.

Bit'so was weary, too, but more resilient. After a night on a moving horse, leaning against Daniel Strongbow's shoulder, she was completely rested.

As for the Indian scout, he was accustomed to riding for hours on end. He would not need sleep until he returned to Santa Fe.

Instead the two of them talked—the grown man and Bit'so—speaking in their guttural Indian tongues. Bit'so trusted Daniel completely, after all, was he not one of them?

Daniel learned the true story of Sam Whitman's death and the massacre at the springs. It had been Tsis'na who died there, whom Jesse had mourned—and buried. It would have been better if it had been this woman. Apparently she had brought both Jesse and his wife much unhappiness.

Uneasily he began to change his mind after listening to the small girl's conversation. It was strewn with Jenny-this and Jenny-that. He learned of the cliff dwelling; of the others there; of how Jenny had saved their lives. Bit'so told him of the cougar; of Tsi'dii's walk; of the soldiers who caught them and would have killed them, had it not been for Jenny's lie.

"And what was this lie?" he asked, obviously startled.

Bit'so clamped her mouth shut and would say no more. Daniel Strongbow was one of her people, but he had taken up the white man's ways. Perhaps it was better to be quiet.

Daniel, knowing he would hear no more, rode along in silence. It would seem that this woman, Jen-nee, was of stronger character than he had believed. But he could not, would not, forgive her for the unhappiness she had caused his colonel.

And he knew he would never forget that she had lived with Sam Whitman. He tried to banish it from his mind. Little Bit'so had just fallen asleep in his arms. He moved her gently to a more comfortable position.

They continued on, stopping only to rest the horses and eat a little. Jenny could not swallow, thinking of those left behind in the dwelling. Their food would have run out. They would be hungry. On the third morning a thaw had set in. Every tree, every branch, dripped with water. The riders were soaked through. Jenny caught a cold, and she was miserable.

Then she shouted out with joy. She knew this place. The strip of bright cloth she had tied to a tree dangled, wet and sodden, from a point much higher than she remembered. The melting drifts had made a difference.

But Tsi'dii's body was gone. The cougar had come. Jenny raised her eyes to the horizon. It was easier to think that Tsi'dii had risen and gone to her eternal home.

"We will stop here," Jenny said to Daniel. "If you will help us unload the supplies . . ."

He was tempted to argue with her. The child had told him where they were staying. It wasn't any trouble to carry the things a little farther.

But her face was set, closed against him. He cast a glance at Bit'so. The child's eyes looked panicked and guilty, silently begging him to be still about what she had told him. Damn it, if this was what the woman wished, he would do as she said!

He pulled the packs from the horses, placing them in the melting snow. Then, leaving behind the one animal the woman had requested, he left them there.

Jenny watched him go, trying to convince herself that she was glad to be rid of him. As soon as he was out of sight, she hurriedly led the one loaded animal toward the dwelling, Bit'so following. When they neared the structure that was concealed in the side of the cliff, her heart began to pound.

What if something had happened and they were dead?

Taking some food from one of the packs, she scrambled upward, catching her breath at the scent of smoke. They lived.

All of them were gaunt and weak with hunger, but they had endured. Jenny held the children to her, hugging them. Ugly Woman smiled broadly in welcome.

They did not ask about Tsi'dii. Jenny did not tell them but set Bit'so to building up the fire to make a stew. She still had things to do before nightfall. And a way to go.

She took the horse and returned to the packs that were stacked in the snow. There were numerous small footprints around them, as little animals had sniffed at what they contained. But nothing larger had come to rob her.

Jenny strained to lift the heavy packs, dropping them repeatedly before she managed to get them on the horse's back. For a moment she regretted not asking Daniel Strongbow to help her.

But then he would have known where they lived. And she wanted no one to know.

She made trip after trip, each time fearing that she wouldn't be able to lift another load. But by nightfall she had it all safely stashed away.

Sitting by the fire with a gourd of savory stew in her hands, Jenny felt comfortable in the warmth of the dwelling. She stretched her aching muscles and smiled. She was home and all was well. They would survive until the spring.

Then a small sound, like a footfall, alerted her. She sat up, instantly awake.

It was only the cougar, she thought. And it had done its worst. She wasn't afraid anymore.

Her eyes went to the gun that lay beside her, and she relaxed.

She would not have felt safe if she had realized that it was not a cougar but a man. Daniel Strongbow had gone a little distance, tethered the horses he led, and returned. He had stationed himself behind a pine tree and watched them throughout the day. A large animal had nosed about the packs in Jenny's absence, he ran it off. He had been concerned when he saw her try to lift the heavy objects, when it was so unnecessary. Then he remembered the set look on her face, the guilty one on Bit'so's, and he sighed.

Some people made things harder on themselves than they had to be.

He watched her carry her last load and still could not bring himself to leave. He laughed to himself as he followed the trail the horse had made on its trips to the dwelling. He knew where it was; he had always known. But even if he hadn't, the girl had made it a very easy thing to find.

He crept up to the half wall in the darkness. Melting in spots, the snow made it difficult to see outward. He might have been a shadow.

Then he saw Jenny, her dark features limned in gold as the fire blazed up. She had stripped off her wet dress and was clad only in a flimsy undergarment. She stretched luxuriously, and he caught his breath at the beauty of her slender body.

He must go, he told himself. He had only stayed to make certain that little Bit'so was safe, that the food had arrived for the sake of the others. He held no liking for a bad woman who would give herself freely to a drunken man, who would try to break up his colonel's home.

Silently he made his way down the cliff to the spot where the horses waited.

The long ride home was unutterably lonely, and Daniel did not know why.

28

In Santa Fe, Elena had waited for Jesse in vain. He stopped by the post, prior to going home, and discovered there was a problem in Taos to the north. He sent word to his wife but didn't even go to his house to change clothes.

When she heard he was on his way back from Taos, Elena was suddenly unsure of her emotions. She was afraid to face him alone. The thought of *that* woman, daring to come to Elena's very home, made her blood boil.

She decided to have an impromptu party to celebrate Jesse's homecoming. She waited for him, her nerves taut and brittle, wondering if this time he would come back.

And he did.

Her eyes lit up as Jesse, weary and still wearing his soiled uniform, walked in to find all his aristocratic in-laws waiting. Elena had outdone herself. The table was beautifully appointed, and she had carefully chosen all of Jesse's favorite foods for the cook to prepare.

"Very nice," he said lamely, making his bows to her relatives. "However, I need a few moments to bathe and change. If you'll excuse me."

"I'll go with you," Elena cajoled, clinging to his arm.

He felt the sudden revulsion that came over him at her touch lately. "*You*," he said, almost brutally, "will remain with your guests."

He went to the study that had become his bedroom, hating himself for his coldness. It was not Elena's fault that Jenny had come to the New Mexico Territory—nor that Jenny was dead. Yet Elena viewed the girl he had so loved as someone to laugh at: wearing a dress that was too short, too tight, because it had a meaning in their relationship.

And Elena had sent Jenny to the kitchen like a beggar!

Sweet Jenny, who had tried to follow him to the ends of the earth, and who had found a terrible death along the way.

He could never forgive himself—or Elena.

He changed quickly and went back downstairs. He was so damned tired. His eyes were heavy and he could hardly stay awake; it was all he could do to endure the superficial conversation. Finally he stood up.

"I must leave very early in the morning to hold court in Silver City," Jesse addressed the group as a whole. "A soldier has been accused of murdering a miner there. If you'll excuse me . . ."

Elena's nerves exploded. Silver City! That was near the spot where Dermot and Judkins had picked up that Indian girl and her brat! Elena had gotten rid of the soldiers, using her connection to have them transferred to Fort Stanton in Jesse's absence. But she had forgotten about Daniel. Daniel had arrived back at the post just this morning and reported to her on his success-

ful mission. She had assumed that because he
was Indian, he would keep his mouth shut about
a white woman's affairs!

Daniel must have told Jesse how she had gotten rid of that girl.

Elena was suddenly on her feet, tipping her
wine glass onto the damask cloth; her cheeks
were splashed with scarlet.

"He's taking you to her, isn't he?" she raged,
her black eyes flashing ebon fire. "If you go, do
not bother to come back!"

Jesse rose and reached out to her, shocked
from his fatigue. "Elena! What the devil?"

She scrambled free of his grip, spitting like a
wildcat. "Do not touch me! You—you squaw
man!"

"Elena—"

"Leave me alone!"

The wineglass sailed past his ear to crash
against the wall. Elena bolted for the stairs,
sobbing wildly. The guests flinched as they heard
a door slam; the click of a bolt shoved into
place.

Jesse turned to face the gathering, livid with
embarrassment.

His in-laws were courteous people, extremely
mannerly and understanding. Their little Elena
was known to have a fiery disposition, and they
made allowances for her. They left quickly, voic-
ing polite farewells as they avoided Jesse's eyes.

Jesse looked at the table. Their plates were
still full. Grimly he went upstairs to his wife. He
had to find out what was wrong; to try to make
some sense out of her accusations.

Elena would not open the door. Still weeping,
she flung all kinds of recriminations at him. The

name of Daniel, along with "that woman and that child" appeared quite frequently through her hysteria.

"I don't understand—"

"Just get out of my house!"

He obeyed. But he was angry, determined to get to the bottom of this. His first step would be a talk with Daniel. He was eager to speak with him, anyway. He had searched for him before leaving for Taos, but all he could discover was that he had been to the commissary, had bought a lot of presents for an Indian woman, then ridden off with her and a child. He knew the young Navajo wasn't a married man and that he had no living relatives. Somehow Jesse hadn't expected this sort of behavior from Daniel.

Then he paused, puzzled. Daniel's journey was what Elena had been referring to in her diatribe. But what could it possibly have to do with him?

He would damn sure find out!

Daniel, when he found him, was reluctant to answer Jesse's questions. Finally he admitted to knowledge of the incident.

"A woman came to blackmail the *señora*," Daniel said. "I do not know why."

"You had better know," Jesse snapped. "My marriage is at stake! Have you ever seen this woman before?"

"I have."

"Then dammit, man, tell me where—"

"She was with Sam Whitman."

"Then it was Tsis'na?"

Daniel didn't say anything. He didn't need to. Though his face remained expressionless, Jesse read the answer in his eyes. He reached out to him with shaking hands, taking hold of his shoulders in an iron grip.

"My God! It was Jenny, wasn't it! Jenny—alive." Jesse was weeping; great, hoarse sobs that tore at his throat. "Where is she? Take me to her!"

"It is a long way—"

"Dammit, do you think I care how far it is? Jenny!"

"You are tired. Go home to your wife. Consider this matter. Then, if you still wish to, we will leave in the morning."

He had forgotten all about Elena. And Daniel was wise. Before he went to find Jenny, he must discover what had gone on between the two women. Jenny couldn't blackmail anybody. Whatever had happened, it was probably Elena's doing.

"I will meet you at dawn," Jesse told the scout.

He turned and headed for home, his gray eyes steely and his jaw set as he prepared for a confrontation.

And there was none.

Elena was nowhere to be found. Her bed was disturbed where she had lain, crying her heart out. Some of her personal things were gone, as if she had packed hastily.

He knew where she must have gone. One of her uncles owned a *rancho*, some miles to the north of Santa Fe. She had gone there once before when she was pouting. He had gone after her. And she would expect him to do so again, riding all night after he had just gotten home.

He would be damned if he would go.

He went to his lonely bed to lie sleepless, the

memory of Jenny filling his mind: her sweet honesty, her coltish grace, her impish ways. Her lovely face smiled down at him from behind his lids.

How had he ever have forgotten Jenny, even for a little while?

29

Jesse and Daniel left at dawn the next morning. Daniel took his clue from Jesse, who was tight-lipped and silent as he rode. Finally Jesse asked a question.

"This woman. You're certain her name was Jenny?"

"She said it was."

"And you were there when she talked to ... my wife?"

Daniel's long body twisted uneasily in the saddle. He was damned if he answered and damned if he didn't. "It was between the two of them. I do not think—"

"I did not ask you to think," Jesse said harshly. "I ordered you to give me a simple answer! It would be better if you started at the beginning. When did you first see this girl? How did you get involved in this? And, for Christ's sake, what caused Elena to act like such a shrew?"

Daniel sighed and finally gave Jesse an accurate description of the events.

He had first seen the girl at the Whitman shack when they had gone there to warn Sam against illegal trading with the Indians. She had mentioned Jesse's name and seemed to be asking for help, but Sam had skillfully covered the situation, saying that the girl was not mentally sound. They had left her in his hands.

"Oh, no," Jesse groaned.

Daniel wanted to tell him that he had been concerned about the young woman; that he had gone back and looked through the window into Jenny's darkened bedroom; that he had seen Jenny and Sam in a compromising position. He had seen Sam's shadow looming over the girl, her hands reaching up to draw him down to her.

But he didn't, and he did not know why. Perhaps it was because he was embarrassed that he had worried about the girl's safety and had returned to find her in Whitman's arms. It was something he did not like to think about.

Instead he skipped to Bit'so's story, telling of the situation at the cliff dwelling where the group of Indian women and children had been left behind. Their food was running, out and the grandmother, Tsi'dii, had walked to find death in the snow. Bit'so and Jenny had gone to search for her when they were found by two soldiers who intended to rape and kill them.

Jesse's face went white. "They did not—?"

"They did not." Daniel's face contorted painfully. "They said the lady told them she was your wife—your *Indian wife*—and that the little girl was your child."

Jesse was astounded.

"Well, I'll be damned," he said.

"She also told that story to Señora Norwood," Daniel added quietly. "She was very definite in what she wanted. Her price for leaving your home and not returning included one horse, a great number of supplies, and my aid in delivering those supplies."

Jesse couldn't help feeling a touch of pride in Jenny. It took a great deal of courage to stand up to a woman like Elena. But he was torn in two.

Elena was his wife.

Though she was very different from Jenny, she was beautiful, exciting, and had brought him a way of life he never could have achieved alone. But he owed Jenny something too.

And Jenny had loved him—in spite of his poverty.

He remembered their last day together in his shack on Belle Terrain. How he had held her tightly, feeling the heat of her against him as he put his hands to her slim hips to pull her close.

Then, with a massive effort, he had pushed Jenny away. Her face—dazed with love, mouth swollen with passion—changed in front of him, its softness disappearing as it grew small and cold.

"You don't want me!"

He had cried out in denial telling her he was going west to make something of himself. He wasn't coming back until he could look St. Germain in the eye and tell him that now Jesse Norwood was somebody in his own right.

"Then I'll have something to ask you."

For a brief space, Jenny's night-black eyes had searched his gray ones, seeking out the love that was there, giving him a silent answer to his unspoken question—and then she was gone.

He had come west and had met Elena.

Marriage to Elena provided an opportunity to be someone of importance, while helping the plight of the Indian at the same time. He had thought he would never see Jenny again; there was too much time and distance between them.

If Jenny had died, eventually he might have gotten over his anger at Elena for turning her away. But Jenny lived—and she had tried to keep her commitment to him. He had not. Jesse was in the unhappy position of being unfaithful to two women. And he had to admit to himself that he loved and wanted them both.

The one night of rest before they started out proved to be a godsend to both Jesse and Daniel. They managed to ride all day and most of the night, spending a few hours in the eerie, burned-out shell of Sam's old cabin, in order to rest their horses. They spent another few hours at the site of the hot springs massacre.

But Jesse could not sleep. He insisted on driving on. And he told Daniel the truth about his relationship to Jenny.

Bit'so was not his daughter; Jenny evidently had made up that expedient story. But she was his first love, and only a small part Indian. Jenny's appearance was merely the reflection of an illicit liaison her grandmother had engaged in.

When Jesse met her, he was nothing but poor white trash, returned from the war. Jenny lived in the big house that he had never entered. He loved her. But he wasn't good enough for her.

Daniel wanted to tell Jesse that the girl's character wasn't all it should be. But Daniel was feeling a little guilty, himself.

When he learned that Jenny wasn't Indian, Daniel began to fear for the girl's safety. He should have known; he shouldn't have left them here in this desolate wilderness with no men to look after them.

True, the little Jen-nee was a liar, but she had saved small Bit'so and therefore deserved a little more care than he had given her.

Both men rode in silence, the same soft, dark eyes haunting both their minds.

On the morning of the fourth day they reached a high plateau. With the quixotic nature of the New Mexico Territory's weather, the snow had mostly melted away. It left small shreds that looked like dirty feathers strewn by some huge, molting bird. The sun-warmed earth had taken on a tinge of green that presaged spring.

Suddenly Jesse caught his breath. Above him, tied to a tree, was a bit of once bright cloth. It was a little sun-faded now, but it was snapping in the crisp breeze. He knew instinctively that Jenny's hand had put it there. As it melted, the snow had left it hanging high.

It was a sign of hope. An omen!

He turned to Daniel, a question in his eyes.

In answer Daniel kicked his horse into action with moccasined feet. Jesse followed him into a defile that led between two steep inclines. Finally Daniel stopped, pointing to a spot above.

"Up there."

It was a cliff dwelling, the Place of the Old Ones. Jesse knew of its existence, but he had never been there before.

It was enough that Jenny was there. *His* Jenny!

With a triumphant whoop he spurred his horse toward the incline that led to it. The animal went to its haunches as it attempted to assay the climb.

"Colonel, wait!"

It was clear that Jesse did not intend to announce his presence beforehand. Daniel shook his head and followed his friend.

Nodding over the night's fire, Jenny was startled awake. She leapt to her feet at the sounds below, automatically reaching for the gun she kept loaded against intruders in the night.

As she peered over the half wall, seeing soldiers' uniforms, her first thought was that her captors had found her. She gasped and aimed the rifle at the man who was leading, pointing it with trembling hands. Her finger was on the trigger in readiness to fire.

Then she recognized him—Jesse!

But it was too late. Her trigger finger had already received instructions from her brain. With a violent effort she managed to jerk the weapon.

She had missed him!

But she watched, frozen with horror, as the man who had guided Jesse to her clutched at his bleeding shoulder and went down.

30

Bit'so was awake and on her way down the side of the cliff before Jenny could move. The little girl knelt beside Daniel, keening a mourning chant for the dead.

Jenny ignored Jesse's outstretched hand as he attempted to halt her, and she fell to her knees beside the young Indian's body. She sobbed with relief to find he still breathed. He had taken her bullet through his shoulder and had gotten a nasty head wound as he fell from his horse.

Once Jenny would have given her life to see Jesse Norwood. Now, all that had passed between them was forgotten. She looked up at him with agony in her face. "Help me," she whispered.

Jesse bent to lift his friend. Together he and Jenny managed to get Daniel up the steep hillside. Bit'so ran on ahead with instructions to stoke up the fire and heat a pot of water to boiling. First they must make a tea of the herbs that brought sleep. Luckily the small girl and Tsi'dii had collected spider webs last summer; these would help to stop the bleeding.

"I'll get the bullet out," Jesse said, drawing a knife from his pocket.

"No," Jenny said. "Wait!"

This was something she had to do herself. She could not let a white man touch Daniel, not even Jesse!

Stunned by her own thoughts, she knelt beside Daniel, gently pulling the bloody shirt away from his bronzed body. Then she placed her ear to his chest as she listened to his heart. She put her arm beneath his head and lifted it, forcing some of the tea Bit'so brought through his clenched lips. He relaxed gradually, his head growing heavy against her breast. She reached for the knife.

She held it for a moment, shivering a little. Then, when Jesse moved to help her, she pushed him away gently. Drawing on an inner strength, she touched the knife to the wound, moving surely and deftly.

Daniel moaned in his sleep, his face taking on a greenish pallor. His upper lip beaded with perspiration as she probed carefully for the bullet, feeling the touch of metal on metal. She brought it from the wound and into the light, just as she had seen Tsi'dii do on that day so long ago, when the warrior had been wounded at the hot springs.

And it was done.

When both head and shoulder wounds were bandaged, the cloth startlingly white against Daniel's brown skin, Jenny rose to her feet. She dared to breathe normally at last. She swayed a little, and Jesse reached out to her.

But she stepped away.

Their eyes met. They both knew that except for what had happened to the man who lay between them, they would have rushed into each other's arms. Now they had time to think, to remember the years that had passed and that Jesse was now married to someone else.

Jesse was the first to lower his eyes.

"Jenny, I've got to talk to you."

Jenny looked down at the injured man. His eyes were still closed, but the dark face was contorted in pain as his fingers plucked nervously at the blanket. Daniel was another victim of Jesse's unfaithfulness, Jenny thought irrationally. She raised her face to his.

"Not here, Jesse," she said in a tight voice. "Come with me."

She led him to the half-walled circular storeroom where a small fire burned to control the dampness. She faced him, trembling as he took her small work-callused hands in his own. The touch of him brought back bittersweet memories.

"I had to find you," he said hoarsely. "I thought you were dead."

"I might have been," she said, wanting to punish him, for some reason she didn't understand.

"I thought I'd found you before," he went on desperately. "It—it was your dress. I thought I'd buried you."

"It was Tsis'na," Jenny said, the memory of her death still a horror in her mind. Jesse misunderstood the expression in her haunted eyes, thinking that the sadness there was on his account.

"Jenny," he whispered. "Forgive me!"

"There is nothing to forgive."

"Yes, there is, dammit!" He raised his voice. It was shaking with emotion. "Look at me! I love you, Jenny! There, I've said it!"

"And it doesn't make any difference, Jesse. Not now."

"*No difference?*"

He reached for her, pulling her into his arms, covering the sweet, remembered face with kisses.

They were not returned. And she did not resist him but stood stiff and silent as he held her. Finally, embarrassed, he backed away.

"You've changed," he said hoarsely.

"Yes," she said, "I have!"

She was thinking of how she had given up everything to come to a man who had not kept his promises; of the way she had been mistreated by Sam Whitman. She had seen her friends murdered by a group of white men, suffered indignities at the hands of Jesse's own soldiers. She had been cold and hungry and afraid, yet all these things had only made her stronger.

Strong enough so that she did not need Jesse anymore. She did not need anyone!

The thought came as a surprise to her. Jesse saw the starry look that came into her dark eyes and thought it was there for him. He ached with wanting her, and words came to his lips, unbidden.

"I love you, Jenny," he whispered. "Believe me, I've always loved you. But you were so young when I left you, and it was so far that I—I didn't think we'd ever get together. I can explain about Elena! Listen . . ."

He launched into the story of his arrival in New Mexico, of Sam's unlawful activities, and of how he had met his wife. Elena was from an influential Spanish family. Her father had taken an interest in Jesse, getting him a commission from Washington. In his position with the military Jesse was able to help the Indians and see that they were treated fairly.

"Now I know I made a mistake," he told her. "But, Jenny, it's not too late. I can talk to Elena, tell her I don't love her. I'm certain I can make her understand. We can go away together, just the two of us, maybe to California. Please . . ."

But Jenny imagined she heard a softness in his voice when he mentioned Elena; a reluctance when he made the proposition she had dreamed of.

Jesse was not lying. He did love her. Jenny could see it in his gray, honest eyes.

But he also loved his wife and didn't even know it.

"You are tired," she said gently. "You must rest. Then we will talk."

Two days later Jenny stood by the wall, fashioned by a people dead for several thousand years, and told Jesse good-bye. He reached once more to take her in his arms, but this time she backed away and shook her head.

Jesse had changed, and so had she. He did not love her as a man should love a woman. And she no longer loved him, she told herself. She no longer loved the gray-eyed boy who had left a drawing of a heart, a message of love, on the kitchen table at Belle Terrain. What they had shared together was first love. Like a bubble filled with rainbows, it was too beautiful to endure, too fragile to survive.

"Go home to Elena." Jenny said now. "She is your wife."

"But, Jenny—"

She cut him short. "Go home."

He stared at her. This was not his Jenny;

laughing, pixyish little Jenny. In the several days he had spent here he realized he didn't know her. This girl wore lines of pain around her mouth, while Jenny once had been all smiles. She had been with the Indians so long, she even sounded like them at times.

He studied her face. For a moment he looked so much like his old self that her good intentions wavered. *Don't touch me*, she prayed silently. *Don't touch me!*

Instead he grinned crookedly and touched his fingers to his forehead in a mock salute. Then he turned and climbed down the steep incline that led to the valley below. There he mounted his horse, and Jenny watched until he was out of sight. She thought how like a little boy he was. A little boy who wanted everything in the world and who would never be quite satisfied with what he had.

She went back to Daniel. It was time to change his dressing. Now he was conscious, and his dark eyes watched her every move.

"Jesse is gone?"

"Yes."

Daniel lay quietly. Then he said, "I am supposed to convince you to come to Santa Fe with me when I am well."

Jenny carried a clay pot of water to his side and knelt to wash his wound. "I will not leave my people," she said decisively.

Her words jolted him. He had not believed that she was capable of such loyalty.

"I am to bring them also," he told her. He explained that Jesse wanted to send Jenny back to Tennessee, to her mother. He would find a position at the Exchange Hotel for Ugly Woman and put the children in an Indian school.

Jenny was through with the bandaging. She rose and emptied the contents of the clay pot over the wall, drying her hands on her skirt.

"No," she said. "We will not go with you. D'zili and his warriors will return for us. I have seen what happens to *tame* Indians, and we do not want that kind of life. Now, if you will excuse me . . ."

A deeper color tinged the darkness of Daniel's features as he watched her go. Was this woman, whom he had seen engaging in immoral activities, daring to hint that he, Daniel, was less than a man? That perhaps he was a traitor to his race?

Damn her!

Jenny did not mean her remarks in the way that Daniel heard them. She was remembering the streets of Santa Fe; the drunken Indians sleeping in doorways; the children with their soft, doelike eyes, lost between two cultures. That would not happen to those who had been left in her care.

A little part of her would always remember Jesse, though she had closed a door in her mind against him. She would live without him because she must. It hadn't taken him long to forget her, and it wouldn't take her long to forget him, either.

She hated himself for having such thoughts and would certainly have denied them, but she hoped that Daniel Strongbow wouldn't be in too great a hurry to get well.

31

Jesse rode some distance from the dwelling and paused. Maybe he should have forced Jenny to come with him instead of giving the chore to Daniel. He couldn't stand the thought of leaving her behind. He still loved her. She would be all alone with small children, an injured Indian woman, and a wounded man to care for.

Jenny was capable, though. He had to admit that. And someone had to look after Daniel until his injury healed. Daniel shouldn't travel for at least a week, and Jesse couldn't remain here that long.

Why couldn't he?

He made himself face the truth. He was going home to end his marriage. "Go home to Elena," Jenny had said. "She is the one you love."

He had to admit that she had seen into his mind to some extent. He had a certain fondness for Elena, and the way of life she'd brought him. Elena was beautiful, glamorous, exciting. But she wasn't Jenny. He wondered now how he ever could have forgotten his little sweetheart from Sweethome. He rode on with his head bowed, Jenny's face fixed in his mind. But he knew he wasn't free to think of her.

He would have to tell Elena it was over. But she was a devout Catholic in spite of her teasing, flirtatious ways. If he left her, she would be tied to a husbandless marriage for the rest of her days. Elena would never give him a divorce.

And how did he know that Jenny would have him?

It didn't matter. No matter what Jenny thought, he had to be free. He wasn't being fair to anyone. It was as if he had been asleep and dreaming. Now the dream was over. He could not, in all honor remain with Elena.

Look who's talking about honor, he told himself. A poor white trash country boy, charmed out of his britches by the daughter of a Spanish *grandee*. Or was it the importance that came along with marrying her?

Moodily, Jesse made his way home.

Elena's mother saw Jesse in the doorway and rushed to envelop him in her arms, bursting into a shrill spate of Spanish he could not understand.

"Slowly," he said in her own language. "Slowly, *por favor*."

Finally he managed to piece together what she was saying.

Her daughter, his wife, was very ill. Elena was close to death.

And Elena had kept a very important secret from her husband. Elena was pregnant.

Jesse felt a massive wrenching of his heart at her words.

"I didn't know," he whispered. "I didn't know!"

"A man has eyes," Señora Ruiz said enigmatically.

Jesse thought of all the time he had spent

away from home. Whenever he saw Elena, in
their few brief moments together, she had been
dressed in voluminous gowns with flowing shawls.
Why hadn't she told him? Was it because she
realized it was something he wouldn't want to
hear?

Choking on a sob, he pushed past Señora Ruiz
and ran up the stairs, suddenly conscious of
how his home had changed. Once it had been a
place that was scented with Elena's dancing
presence. Now it smelled of illness and medication.

He entered Elena's room to find her handmaiden, Juana, bending over her bed. He waved
Juana away and took her place, looking down at
the white face on the pillow. The dark eyes were
sunken beneath their shadowed lids; Elena's
vivid, sensual mouth was pale and silent.

He lifted the slight body in his arms and held
her against him, trying to instill her with his
life, his warmth, his energy.

"I love you, Elena," he whispered. "I love
you! You have to get well."

Her eyes fluttered open, and for an instant he
thought he saw a brief recognition in their depths.

Then they closed again.

In the days that followed, Jesse did not leave
Elena's side. From his father-in-law he learned
that Elena had indeed gone to her uncle's *rancho*
north of Santa Fe. On the journey she had caught
a cold. Then, after a day or two, she became
obsessed with the notion that Jesse would soon
be back. She insisted on coming home, and the
cold had worsened, becoming a lung fever.

What had he done to her!

There came a night when the post surgeon

despaired of Elena's life. Jesse held her hands tightly, refusing to allow her to slip away.

And when morning came, he was told that the crisis had passed. With tender loving care Elena would be well.

Worn-out from the days and nights spent at Elena's side, Jesse finally slept. He dreamed of Jenny, a younger Jenny: a half-wild little creature who spied on him from the woods surrounding the tenant house where he had lived after the war. She had played at being an Indian, slipping from one tree shadow to another, concealed by a dappling of autumn leaves.

He had caught her and carried her, kicking and biting, to the shack he called home. She bandaged his bitten hand and cared for him later when his leg was injured, defying her parents.

And he fell in love.

He fell in love with Jenny's sweet, confident self; a pair of dark, dancing eyes; with a mop of dark hair; with her impetuous nature and gamin-like grin. He fell in love with a girl above his station, and he left her, vowing to return for her when she was grown-up, when he had made his mark in the world.

Jesse woke with a start to find that his dream had changed. Jenny's face was replaced by that of Elena, who lay worn and haggard in the next room.

The walls of the beautiful house seemed to close in on him, creating a prison from which he would never escape. Because for now Elena needed him.

He rose and went back to her room to find that she was awake, her eyes like dusky lanterns through rain-streaked windows.

"It *is* you, my Jesse."

"Yes, *querida*," he whispered softly. "It is."

He held her tightly, his face against her hair, until she slept again. And his life stretched out before his eyes, a long and lonely life without Jenny.

One month later Jesse's daughter was born. She was very tiny, with just a suggestion of nails on her miniature fingers and only a hint of the beauty to come, from her father's blondness and her mother's huge, dark eyes.

Elena held the infant in her arm, marveling at her little doll, then smiled and asked to be allowed to rest. Juana remained beside her. And Juana fell asleep. When the handmaiden woke, she woke screaming.

For her mistress lay as white and still as a figure carved from marble, the sheets around her soaked with her life's blood.

Elena was dead.

32

The day Theron St. Germain was buried was violent with wind and storm—a day as tempestuous as the master of Sweethome had been. Inga stood shivering by the graveside as John, the black overseer who was also a minister, performed the service in his soft, musical voice. It ended with, "We now commit ouah brothah to yo' han's."

Theron would have liked the service, Inga thought numbly. Just as he would have liked the spot she had chosen next to Caleb's grave. Theron's mind would never wander again. And he was hers no longer; he belonged to the earth of Sweethome now.

Dinah stood next to Inga. Dinah's grandson, Boy, was at her other side, his strong, young arm supporting her. Though Boy was only in his early teens, his presence was comforting. Dinah, Boy, and Caleb had been the first to return to Sweethome after the war.

They had become Inga's family. Her only family, she thought, now that Kirsten, Jenny, and Theron were gone.

Dinah was looking anxiously into her face.

Inga wanted to tell her not to worry, she was fine. But she couldn't summon the energy to speak.

"It's awright if yuh cry, honey," the old black woman whispered. "Nobody gonna think less of yuh."

Inga couldn't cry, though she wished she could. She felt numb all over, too tired after the long ordeal of Theron's illness. Too weary after the situation with the Klan that killed Martha Weldon and contributed to Theron's death.

"Here, honey." She was conscious of Dinah pressing a sticky, wet clod of earth into her fingers, propelling her forward to the yawning hole. She looked down on the casket John had built with loving hands. A frozen rain hissed against the lid as it closed on Theron forever. Inga was motionless trying to envision Theron's face, his eyes closed in eternal sleep.

Now Dinah was prying at her hand. What was expected of her?

Oh, yes.

She opened her fingers and let the dirt dribble from her palm, its dull thudding a counterpoint to the hiss of sleet.

And Dinah led her away.

When the warmth of the house seeped through her, putting an end to her shivering, Inga slept for twenty-four hours straight. The long days and nights of worry had taken a terrific toll; the episode at Eden had drained her of further strength. For a time she became as mindless as a newborn baby, while her body worked to repair the damage this last year had inflicted on her. If she dreamed at all, it was that Theron slept beside her.

And then she woke.

Before Theron was buried, she had not slept in this room. In fact, she couldn't remember sleeping at all. But she had insisted on resting here when she returned from the funeral. The bedding had been changed, but as Inga turned, she could see an indentation left by Theron's head on the pillow.

She reached to touch a ghostly hand. There was nothing there, and never would be from this time forward.

Now she could cry.

She cried for a long time, weeping for her dead husband, her lost children, even for Birgitta, the mother she would never see again. Yet combined with her sorrow was a sense of relief— relief that the girls had not had to see Theron deteriorate as he had this last year; relief that her prayers had been answered. He had been the old Theron for a short while, in command of himself when he passed from this world into the next.

Finally she rose and poured water from a pitcher into the washbasin, laving her eyes until they were no longer red and swollen. Then she went downstairs.

"Good morning, Dinah."

The old woman jumped as if she'd been shot. "Miz Inga! Praise the Lawd! You was sleepin' like the dead!" Her eyes rounded in horror at what she had said, and she finished lamely, "I figgered you wasn't gonna never wake up!"

As Dinah babbled on, trying to conceal her own feelings, Inga's eyes scanned the kitchen. It was bright and clean but strangely empty. Finally she asked the question that was troubling her.

"Where is Honeybee?"

Now it was Dinah's turn to burst into tears. She wiped her streaming eyes on a corner of her apron. "That man didn't bring her home, Miz Inga!"

Inga was dazed. She had always known this day would come, that Weldon would want to keep his own daughter. But it was a cruel blow coming at this time, when Inga had no one. But wasn't Matthew Weldon in a similar situation?

Finally she managed to say, "You're forgetting, Dinah. Honeybee is home. She doesn't belong to anybody but Weldon. We only kept her for a while."

Inga knew her words did not reassure Dinah. Nor did they make her feel any better. Her hands and her heart were empty, she knew that she needed to find something to do.

The weather was still inclement, so she could not visit Theron's grave. Dinah had vented her sorrow in cleaning and cooking. The kitchen was shining, and there was enough food prepared for an army. Soon the sun would warm the land and the planting would begin. Then she could walk through the fields and talk with the workers. But that was a someday thing. Now her tension would not let her rest.

She wandered down the passageway and through the breakfast and dining rooms to where the great, new living room replaced the burned out section of Sweethome, set ablaze during the war. The renewal of the mansion was the culmination of Theron's dream.

Right now this spacious chamber was cold

and unheated. Here Theron's body had lain in state. No one had bothered to light a fire since. Inga looked at the spot where the coffin had rested and shivered. This would always be a haunted room, it seemed to hold a lingering smell of death.

A loud banging at the front door paralyzed her. For an instant a foolish thought flickered through her mind. Theron had come home! Then, shaking off the notion, she hurried to open the door. Whoever it was, he was standing outside in the storm.

Matthew Weldon!

And in his arms a tearstained Honeybee!

The little girl wriggled and reached out for Inga with a cry of frightened desperation. Inga took her and held her close. Then she studied Weldon's face.

It was white, his normally neat hair tousled. As she watched, he ran his fingers through it nervously. "I heard what happened," he said. "I'm sorry. I hope what occurred at Eden didn't contribute to it."

"He would have died in any event," Inga said evenly. "And I'm sorry about your wife."

He shifted from one foot to another, then blurted, "There's no easy way to say this. I feel as though Martha's death is my fault. I should never have brought her here. She was right. Neither of us ever belonged in this place."

Inga opened her mouth to speak, and he silenced her with a raised hand. "What I'm trying to say is that I'm going away."

Inga clutched the little one more tightly, her heart beating in her throat until she thought she would suffocate. Weldon continued.

"This may be a presumptuous suggestion. I don't know. But I do know I trust you more than anyone else in this world. I can't feel anything for this child, who only reminds me of how I failed her mother. She doesn't know me. I don't know how to take care of her, and I don't have any female relatives to my name." He tried to smile.

For the first time she felt a ray of hope. *Dear God*, she prayed, *let him say what I think he's going to say*!

"So I thought," he plunged on, "that maybe you might want to keep the baby. It's obvious she loves you. Of course, I would pay you for her support. I owe you for a year, in any case."

He reached for his pocket, and she stopped him.

"Are you saying you want to *give* me the baby?" she asked in a choked voice.

He reddened. "I had hoped you would take her."

"Then it will have to be on my terms," she said decisively. "The baby will be mine. Should you remarry, she will still be mine. There will be no talk of remuneration." She began to cry. "I don't mean to sound hard, but she's been mine for a whole year. And every day I've expected to lose her. I couldn't stand for it to happen in the future, especially now that I've lost Theron."

Weldon put his arms around Inga and the baby, and the two of them wept together. And finally Weldon left them.

Inga carried the little one into the warm kitchen. It suddenly smelled of good things; of baking bread and spices and love. It was not nearly as empty as it had been earlier. "Dinah," she said, smiling through her tears. "Dinah, look who's here! It's Honeybee. Our little Honeybee's come home."

If she thought about Kirsten and Jenny, it was only for a moment. Her empty arms were filled again.

33

Kirsten wasn't thinking of her mother, or of anyone but herself. For once everything was going quite well. Lydia seemed to have disappeared from Slim's establishment, and Nick had let old Pete go reluctantly. They were the only drawbacks to the plans she had made.

In addition, she had managed to talk Nick out of redecorating the card rooms, extracting a promise from him to allow her to handle the funds. She managed to convince him that she was saving up for a special surprise.

She had invested the money she had stolen from Slim Morley right back into The French Rose. Soon she would be making a profit off Slim's own money.

It was a big joke on everyone. She was having more fun than she could have imagined, playing Nick and Slim against each other. Lately her life had become very exciting. She hugged herself with glee as she studied her face in the mirror. Her blue eyes were sparkling. There was color in her creamy cheeks. Her lips were a soft rose-pink. She looked like a Swedish princess, she decided. But there was something more: a polish, a glitter that took her out of the ordinary and made her even more beautiful.

Nick's dark face appeared behind her, one sardonic brow lifted. "Well, do you think you look passable?"

Eager for his compliments Kirsten flushed. "Don't you?"

Nick shook his head and took hold of her shoulders, turning her from side to side. "No," he said judiciously, "there's something missing."

Kirsten's eyes darkened, and she began to pout as he moved to face the mirror again. "I would say you need this," he said.

She caught her breath as he clasped a sapphire-and-diamond pendant at her throat. "It's beautiful," she breathed. Then she wondered how he had paid for it. It must have been terribly expensive! If he went to the bank for funds, the money would not have been there. Still, Nick didn't seem to suspect anything.

"W-where did you get this?" she faltered.

"I was hoping you wouldn't ask," he said ruefully. "A fellow lost his shirt at the tables last night. Wanted to know if he could bet the pendant. It looked like you. So"—he shrugged, grinning boyishly—"don't worry. I kept my promise, little Miss Miser. Every cent that comes in goes to the bank. Nothing comes out."

Kirsten put her arms around him. "I love you, Nick."

Nick wasn't too sure about that. He didn't think Kirsten was capable of loving anyone but herself. But he was grateful for all small favors. And now her fingers were unbuttoning his shirt, slipping inside to caress his bronzed chest. Finally, half out of his mind with teasing, he picked

Kirsten up and carried her to bed. Soon her golden hair was spread over a blue satin pillow, and she was clad only in the sapphire-and-diamond pendant, which rested between her creamy breasts.

She smiled as she lifted her arms to him, knowing that she had the ability to drive him mad. And if she had that effect on Nick, what would she do to Slim? Slim Morley, who could take his pick among many lovely quadroon courtesans? She tried to imagine Slim's face if he saw her like this. And soon it was no longer Nick who made love to her but Slim Morley, with his dark, reptilian eyes and slender mustache.

When Nick had finished with her, he smiled sweetly, then rolled over and went to sleep. Kirsten hated him for it. How dare he grow so accustomed to the act of love?

She tried to sleep but was unable to shut out the street noise outside, the thin ray of sunlight that peeped through a parting of the draperies. It was just a little after noon when she gave up, rose, and dressed. She would check on last night's receipts. If there was enough there, she might take another deposit to Slim Morley. Guiltily, she realized that she was looking forward to seeing him again.

There was not enough money to bother with. Kirsten looked down at her pendant, wondering what it would bring if it were converted into cash. Of course, she didn't dare to do that this soon. Nick would miss it and start asking questions. But she might as well check out its value.

Donning a sweeping hat with a heavy veil, she went out onto the street. Today the wind was off the water. Cold and humid, it cut through her

clothing, chilling her. Kirsten ignored the calls
of "Fresh fish, she t'am fresh, I gah-ron-tee,"
and the smiling black faces beneath bright ker-
chiefs hawking pralines, roasted nuts, and pas-
tries.

When she reached a small store where, it was
rumored, stolen goods were received to be re-
sold, she was greeted warmly by the proprietor.
He had dealt with her before and admired her
knowledge of fine things, as well as her ability
to haggle. He smiled as she entered.

"Ah, Miss Kirsten! You have been thinking
over what I say to you? You weesh to work for
me?"

She laughed at what had become a standing
joke between them. "No, but I've brought something better."

He gasped at sight of the pendant, then screwed
a jeweler's glass into his eye. "Priceless," he
muttered before he could stop himself. "Priceless!"

Kirsten took the pendant from his clutching
fingers. "I will sell it to you but not just yet. It is
a gift and would be missed. I only need to know
its worth."

He regained his composure and named a price.
Kirsten knew that she could double it and he
would pay gladly. She smiled mysteriously and
left the store. Let him worry for a while.

Out on the street again, it seemed even colder.
She shivered, perhaps she was coming down
with something. There was a tiny shop ahead, a
place where the thick, rich coffee the Louisianans
preferred was made and sold.

It would be warm, Kirsten thought, unable to

control the chattering of her teeth. She would go in and purchase a cup.

She entered, pausing in the coffee chop's miniature foyer to toss back her heavy veil. Then she froze as she heard her name mentioned on the other side of the partition.

"It's all that blonde's fault," came Lydia's sharp voice. "I tried to tell Slim, but he threw me out. She stole that money, I didn't! I'm gonna kill her if it's the last thing I ever do!"

"Mebbe" came Pete's blurred tones, rumbling a reply. "We oughta scare hell out of her first, whaddaya think?"

Lydia began to laugh—a high, shrill giggle that somehow sounded more venomous than the hatred she had expressed previously.

"Let's!" she said gleefully. "Let's get her on the run. She won't know when or how it'll happen! A bullet through the brain is too easy for that bitch!"

"Hell, yes," Pete said in a maudlin tone. Kirsten realized that he was drunk, despite Nick's work to straighten him out. "Nick was my friend," he said, slurring. "And that woman pizened him agin me. She's bad for him. Ba-a-ad! We gotta get rid of her. Lemme think on it a little more. Now here's sump'n we might do. . . ."

The voices lowered to ugly, suggestive whispers, and Kirsten stood, her mind whirling, her hands clutched tightly against her sides. Supposedly, Pete had left town, purchasing a little place far upriver with the pay he had saved. And though she had no idea what had happened to Lydia, Slim had indicated that the girl was far away. But she still had both of them to contend with, and she was afraid.

It dawned on her that while she stood, too terrified to move, the pair had left the table. She heard them paying for their coffee. They had to leave by this same door.

She tugged at the veil, lowering it to conceal her face, and hastily left the foyer. Once outside, she began to run. Her life was in danger! Where could she go for help?

Nick would never believe Pete would do this.

And Slim Morley had lied about Lydia. Evidently he still retained some affection for the girl. And Pete and Lydia were planning to kill her.

The hucksters and hawkers of New Orleans turned their heads to watch a beautiful woman as she fled down the street. Then they returned to business as usual.

PART II

34

February passed, and March. An early spring brought a strewing of butter-yellow flowers to the high mountain country, along with scattered coral blooms on tall stems. The New Mexico days were the color of the heavenly blue morning glories that opened their eyes at Sweethome in the day. The sky was close at night, black velvet, studded with a million stars.

Jenny was already preparing the earth to receive its seeds. And seeds she had aplenty, after her trip to Santa Fe and her confrontation with Jesse's Spanish wife. She hoped he had found some way to appease Elena's anger; to make things right between them.

In the meantime she worked doggedly while trying to forget what was taking place in the cliff dwelling. Daniel Strongbow tended to ignore her. Was he angry because she had shot him? It had been an accident. And it had been she who had removed the bullet from his wound; she who had cared for him in the beginning.

Now Ugly Woman was able to limp about, and she had completely taken over Daniel's care. The splints that supported her broken limb concealed her defective foot. Jenny hadn't really noticed before that the girl's face was so beautiful. There was something serene, madonnalike, about her.

For some reason Ugly Woman's attentions to Daniel upset Jenny. She recognized her feeling as jealousy because he seemed to prefer the Indian woman's ministrations to her own. It was only natural, she thought as she hitched the horse she had bargained for in Santa Fe, that Daniel would rather have the company of his own kind. But still, it bothered her.

Daniel's interest in Ugly Woman seemed to begin when she trimmed the hair around the head wound he received when he fell from his horse. The girl placed the long, dark clippings in a small bag to preserve them against the evil machinations of witchcraft.

Alienated from his people for so long, Daniel was enchanted by her tales of ghosts and witches that took him back to his childhood. His lean, coppery features were alive with interest, his dark eyes filled with memories, as Ugly Woman explained what she was doing.

If an enemy possessed nail parings, hair, or clothing containing sweat of the victim, Ugly Woman told him solemnly as she snipped away, the material can be buried in a grave and, through ceremony or prayer done backward, can cause great harm.

"I do not believe I have any enemies," Daniel said with a smile.

"Do not be too certain," Ugly Woman told him. "Maybe Jen-nee's hand was guided to do you injury, guided by witchcraft. Perhaps someone is jealous and wishes you evil. I will make you a charm of gall medicine, mingled with ground corn. It will protect you from spells, from corpse poison, and from other bad things.

"Unless, of course, it is a ghost who haunts you."

Ugly Woman grew silent, and Jenny understood how she must feel. The death of a relative was terrifying to the Navajo because it created a burst of uncontrollable power. They had all lost someone at the place of the hot springs. For Jenny it had been Tsis'na.

And there was the more recent death of the old grandmother, Tsi'dii.

The woman's frozen body had completely disappeared, creating a story that frightened children and adults alike. Ugly Woman continued to spin tales of Indian lore while Daniel listened, fascinated. The children, even little Ee'yah, were equally enthralled. Only Jenny felt awkward, an outsider.

As soon as the weather permitted, she escaped the confines of the dwelling, going to work in her garden with dogged determination. As Daniel's health improved, she often saw him standing in the distance. But this time his presence bothered her. How dare he behave as though she didn't exist!

"Notice me," she said under her breath, her fists clenched. "D-dammit, just see me! Speak to me, just once!"

Then he was out of sight, and Jenny was angry with herself for even caring.

It was the loneliness out here, she thought. There were so few people to know, to speak to. And there were such wide-open spaces in this high mountain country.

The small piece of earth she had cleared was now smooth and weed-free. But instead of being pleased, she was sorry. It only meant that she would have nothing to do for several days and thus would have no excuse to leave the dwelling.

As Jenny stood there, wondering whether to go back or not, she heard a man clear his throat to speak. Every nerve quivered as she turned to face Daniel Strongbow, who had come up behind her.

"I am sorry," he said. "I did not mean to frighten you."

"You didn't," she said, more crossly than she had intended, for indeed he had. He had literally scared the wits out of her!

He stood still for a moment, turning his hat in his hands. He had come to tell her that he was well enough to make it back to Santa Fe; that it was time to go; that he owed her a debt of gratitude.

He did not tell her that this had been a time of torture for him, seeing Jenny, wanting her; that he had recovered from his wound many days ago but that it had taken him a great deal of time and effort to come to this decision. He did not say that he had nearly steeled himself to settle for another man's leavings, trying to shut his mind to the memory of Jenny in Sam Whitman's arms.

Now, face-to-face with her, he knew he couldn't go through with it. He remembered that he had offered his heart to a white girl once, and she had laughed in his face. Daniel Strongbow was a proud man, and he would not make the same mistake again.

If Jenny had only reached out to him, expressed

concern about his going, he might have changed his mind. For an instant he thought he saw a shadow of disappointment in her eyes. Then he decided he must have been wrong.

He turned and walked away stiffly.

Jenny watched him go, wanting to call him back, to beg him to stay. She saw him reach his horse. He mounted the animal and rode away.

He did not look back.

Jenny drew a harsh breath that sounded almost like a sob, then threw herself into digging out a yucca root, so near the edge of her plowed field that it didn't interfere with her planting.

Finally she gave up and stepped back, wiping a dirt-smeared arm across her face. She couldn't erase the vision of a tall, copper-colored man with dark, impenetrable eyes, his black hair held in place with a beaded leather band.

What was it about Daniel that drew her so irresistibly? He had never touched her, had hardly spoken to her, yet here she was mooning over him like a lovesick girl. She supposed this feeling, too, could be laid at Jesse's door. In vowing never to think of Jesse again, she had transferred her affection to Daniel.

At least, she thought dully, he was gone now. And he would not be coming back.

A churring sound from a pile of brush she had raked from the garden area immobilized her. Damn, she thought. A rattlesnake! It sounded again, and she decided it must be some harmless creature. She approached the pile carefully and probed at it with her hoe, only to become stiff and still once more.

A skunk!

But such a tiny little thing, with its black

nose bisected by a white stripe, its white-plumed tail. Where was its mother? The other babies?

Either they had become the victims of predators or this poor infant had gotten lost from its siblings. It was very weak and, from all appearances, hadn't eaten in some time.

Jenny's heart melted.

Her mother had always said Jenny was closer to the animals than to humanity; that she could speak their language. And it was somewhat true. Now she knelt and held out a hand for the little one to sniff, so it would understand that she posed no danger. Then softly, sweetly, she began to talk to it, just as she had talked to the flickertails in Minnesota, tolling the prairie-doglike animals from their holes that honeycombed the meadows; just as she talked to birds and squirrels and frogs—and a deer who had been her friend for some time now.

"You'll be all right," Jenny whispered. "I'm going to take you home."

Holding the animal to her bosom, she hurried toward the cliff dwelling, thinking of how she would feed it. Perhaps a thin gruel at first, then bits of dried fruit and insects.

But when she reached the dwelling, the absence of Daniel struck her like a blow. She was going to miss him! Lordy, how she would miss him! Her voice was too tense, too shrill as she tried to cover her emotions.

"Bit'so, So'tos, look at what I have! See, Ee'yah, I've brought you a little friend."

Then she unaccountably burst into tears.

35

Bit'so named the little animal Kwass'ini, or "friend." And it truly became a friend. Kwass'ini loved to play hide-and-seek with Ee'yah, who toddled after it on his chunky, baby legs. Only when Ee'yah slept did Kwass'ini deign to curl up in Jenny's lap for a little while.

As Jenny sat fondling Kwass'ini, she watched Ugly Woman closely for any sign that the Indian woman was mourning Daniel Strongbow's absence. She was calm and taciturn as usual. If Jenny mentioned his name, she evinced little interest. Jenny longed for Tsis'na, her dead sister; for someone she could talk to.

Keeping her feelings toward Daniel to herself probably had contributed to their importance, she thought.

Spring wore on, and Jenny planted the seed in the tilled ground. Soon it sprouted and grew, showing above the earth in even, cultivated rows that stood out against the wild countryside around them. Jenny was nervous at first, for fear someone would come upon her garden and know there was a caretaker nearby. But as time wore on and there were no intruders, she began to feel safe.

Occasionally the others helped Jenny with her weeding. Later on, when it was under control, they went their own way. Bit'so and So'tso picked wild berries, trying to keep ahead of little Ee'yah, who ate them almost as fast as the little girls filled the baskets old Tsi'dii had woven through the winter. Ugly Woman spent her time finding edible plants and setting snares for wild animals, in order to conserve their precious ammunition. When she emptied her traps, the meat of rabbits, squirrels, and other small animals was cut in strips to be smoked and cured over an open fire.

Soon Jenny was working by herself, with only Kwass'ini to keep her company. The little animal usually retired to the brush pile where Jenny had found him, to curl up and sleep until she was ready to return to the dwelling. Then he would run along beside her. Jenny often wondered if he felt closer to the members of his missing family this way. Or if he enjoyed the solitude as she did—the pleasure of being left alone to dream.

Time seemed to pass so slowly here. It seemed like years since D'zili's warriors had left them, promising to return with help when they reached Cochise. At first the women and children had spoken of "*when* they come." Then it had been "*if* they come." Now they were rarely mentioned. They all seemed to know, even down to little Ee'yah, that it was possible that the warriors were all dead, either at the hands of the white man or from hunger or thirst. Now it was up to the people left behind in the cliff dwelling to survive on their own.

Jenny fell to her knees with a glad cry. One of a myriad of yellow blooms had culminated in a tiny finger-length squash. During the next week or so the vegetables would come on heavily, but this one would be her special treat. She broke it off the vine and nibbled at it, tasting the crispness of spring. Then, laughing, she shared the remainder with Kwass'ini, who had come from beneath the brush pile, his small, white-striped nose twitching with curiosity.

Finally Jenny lay back on the sun-warmed earth, the little animal cradled in her arms. The sky was a dazzling blue, the day so beautiful that she felt a kind of pain.

She felt so old and yet so young. And it was spring.

At last she slept—how long she had no idea. She woke as Kwass'ini made his churring sound, which meant danger. He leapt from her arms and fled to his brushy haven.

Jenny blinked. The sun had been directly overhead, and now it was slanting toward her. And there was a strange sound. At first she couldn't place it. Then a horse stamped and whinnied, and she knew it for what it was: the creaking of saddle leather.

Someone had found her garden! But was it friend or foe?

She raised her head cautiously, and her heart sank.

She recognized the man, though he had changed vastly. His hair was long and stringy now, and he was not in uniform but dressed in ragged civilian clothes. It was Judkins, one of the two soldiers who had found her and Bit'so in the snow. They would have killed them if she hadn't taken Jesse's name in vain and then blackmailed Jesse's Spanish wife.

Judkins rode his horse into the center of the garden and wheeled it around, facing the other way.

"Come out, damn ye! Show yerself! I know yer here!"

Jenny began to creep backward, hidden from his view by a patch of young corn that was barely knee-high. She wriggled into the pile of brush, praying he would not find her, that he would go away. Apparently he had no such intention. Judkins dismounted, crushing tender plants beneath his heavy boots. Despite her fear, Jenny felt a helpless anger that made her sick to her stomach. This was food he was destroying. Food her adopted family needed desperately.

"I figger yer sommers around here," he growled. "And I'm gonna fix ye good if it's the last thing I ever do! It was you what got us transferred to Fort Stanton, where my pardner got kilt! It was all yer fault, ye little Injun bitch!"

He had picked up Jenny's hoe, and as he spoke, he poked through the garden, leaving a swath of destruction behind him. Once in a while he paused to tip a bottle to his bearded lips.

"I'll find ye! Damn ye, I'll find ye!"

Jenny shivered. The man was drunk or crazy; maybe both. The sharp ends of a twig were cutting into her arm, and her cheek was presseed against a piece of thorny brush. She suppressed a whimper of pain, and Kwass'ini made his churring sound, assuming a position he had taken so many times at play. Then Judkins came directly toward her, his lips drawn back over yellowed teeth in an expression of hellish glee. He was so close, she could smell the sweat that stiffened his filthy shirt. Jenny shrank at his nearness.

"Hah! Gotcha! Knowed ye was there! Knowed it all the time!"

Judkins bent down and thrust out with the hoe, missing Jenny completely. She realized he hadn't seen her at all. He had only seen Kwass'ini move. She drew in a quick breath as she recognized the small skunk's crouch: balanced on his front feet, tail high and forward.

Kwass'ini! No!

The little animal exploded into instinctive action. The devastating discharge that was its only protection shot into the man's face, a choking, blinding cloud that permeated the entire area. Jenny was a little to one side and shielded somewhat by the brush. She leapt to her feet, gagging. And then she began to run.

"Eee-yow!" Judkins screamed in agony. He shook his head, but the stinging pain remained. His eyes burned and he could not see. But there was nothing wrong with his ears. He could hear the sound of running feet. That goddamn woman had caused him trouble again, and he was as mad as hell! By God, he would even the score!

He raised his rifle, steadied himself, and fired toward the sound just as Jenny tripped over little Kwass'ini. She fell, triggering another, weaker wave of scent from the small animal.

The bullet went over her head, and in the distance she heard the sound of another horseman pounding his way toward the scene of the shoot-

ing. Dermot, she thought. It must be Dermot.
But hadn't Judkins mentioned in his ravings
that Dermot was dead?

Jenny lay still, gasping for breath, clutching
blades of grass convulsively in both hands. She
was trapped between the two of them, Judkins
and the stranger. There was no point in running
anymore.

36

For Daniel Strongbow it had been a busy time of year, and an almost intolerable one. He had returned to Santa Fe to find Elena dead, and Jesse a shattered hulk of a man, left with a child who hovered between life and death.

Jesse asked for a leave of absence, and Daniel was placed under a new officer, Captain Gomez. The two shared a mutual dislike. Gomez was arrogant, overbearing, and prejudiced against Daniel's people. He had just dismissed him in the presence of the commander of Fort Stanton, where he and Daniel had been called in an emergency.

"You have an hour," he ordered. "Stay out of the bars, and don't mingle with any of your filthy people. Be back"—he consulted his watch—"at fourteen hundred hours, and dammit, don't be late."

Daniel left, his face still burning with dark fire.

Jessse had treated him like an equal, both in rank and race. He wondered how long it would be before he returned to active duty. Or if he ever would. Daniel remembered the last time he saw Jesse. He had come to the barracks just before lights out, asking about Jen-nee. Daniel had not brought her to Santa Fe as Jesse had requested.

Daniel saw the mental exhaustion in his friend's face and knew that somehow Jen-nee had caused the awful guilt in Jesse's. Evidently the man still loved her.

The woman was a witch! Daniel had seen her reach up to Sam Whitman with loving arms. And Bit'so said that D'zili, their tribe's new chieftain, wished to take Jen-nee as his wife. Even Daniel, himself, had almost succumbed to her charms!

Daniel tightened his lips. At least he would save his friend. The thing he told Jesse was not the truth, but neither was it a lie.

He had left the Place of the Old Ones, because D'zili and his men were returning for Jen-nee and the others. It was said that D'zili wished to make Jen-nee his wife.

Jesse flinched as if he had been struck. But he would get over it. It was the best way.

Now, if only Daniel could forget her!

He did owe Jen-nee some thanks. She had saved his life, even though—his lips twisted wryly—she had been the one who had shot him. With some vague idea of evening the score he stopped at a blanket spread on the ground, laden with Indian jewelry. He purchased a turquoise necklace for the girl. Then, embarrassed at his action, he bought one just like it for Ugly Woman, along with bracelets for Bit'so and her little sister, and a beaded headband for Ee'yah.

He put the gifts in his saddlebags. He would drop them by, if he was ever in that area. And, of course, if they were still there. Meanwhile he would try to forget that the girl existed. He had problems enough of his own.

Daniel prowled through the raw little settlement that had grown up around the fort. Suddenly he stopped, immobilized by shock. It was as if his thoughts had come alive.

Jen-nee!

Clad in bright Navajo garb, she walked ahead of him, her bare brown feet kicking up little puffs of dust as she went. Her black hair was swinging, and she had a provocative sway to her hips.

What the hell did she think she was doing? Daniel asked himself angrily. She looked like a chippie!

He swallowed hard and called her name. Jennee pretended to ignore him, the swish in her walk becoming even more exaggerated. Daniel swore under his breath as he hastened to catch her, then grabbed her arm.

Then his heart sank.

This was not Jen-nee, nor anyone he had ever known. The eyes in the delicate face that looked up to him were wise and knowing. They surveyed his long body with admiration, and her lips tilted up as she greeted him in a dialect he recognized.

He was too stunned to answer immediately. Fearing that Daniel didn't understand her, the girl made an obscene gesture with her hands. And he knew her for what she was: a woman who followed the camps, living off what she could get from the soldiers. If she were not diseased already, the girl soon would be. And she would live out her life with her beauty destroyed, until no one wanted her anymore.

Daniel shuddered away from her. He saw the

light go out of her eyes. It was replaced by a
dull indifference. She shrugged her shoulders
and turned to go. Impulsively he touched her
with a staying hand. Reaching into his pocket,
he took out the remainder of his pay and spilled
it into her palm. Her eyes widened, and her face
lit up. She made that gesture again, then pointed
to a narrow, dusty alley between two buildings.

Daniel Strongbow was a man with a man's
needs. Yet his first experience with a woman
had turned him against them. None of the women
he had known were worthy of the kind of love
he had to offer. Yet this one looked so much like
Jen-nee that it made his heart hurt. Quickly,
before he could succumb to her charms, Daniel
walked away.

Mounting his horse, he rode toward the post.

Captain Gomez was leaving the fort. His lips
were tight beneath the pencil-thin-mustache. It
seemed that two soldiers, once attached to the
troop he had taken over from Jesse, had been
transferred to Fort Stanton before Gomez took
command. He could not recall either man, but
their names, Judkins and Dermot, were familiar.

That was beside the point, however. The two
men had committed a crime. They had bullied
some Indians, and a man named Captain Riggs
had tried to remonstrate with them. They had
killed him in cold blood.

When they tried to get away, Dermot was shot
but Judkins escaped. The commander had the
nerve to suggest that Gomez go after him and
bring him in. Surely he knew Gomez had more
important things to do!

Daniel turned ashen. "Request permission to
go after him, sir."

"Permission denied. What the hell are you trying to do? Be a hero? Now, I'm going in here. You wait outside." He went into a bar, and Daniel watched him go, sick at heart.

He knew Judkins. He had borne the brunt of his bullying many times; borne it stoically, like an Indian who knew his place and wished to avoid trouble.

But it was different now. The man was a killer. And if Daniel's hunch was right, he would blame his predicament on Jen-nee.

Even now she might be dead.

Daniel wheeled his horse and was gone.

He slowed the animal once he was away. Perhaps he had jumped to conclusions and Judkins had left the country. Maybe he had gone down to Mexico. Daniel should probably seek out some clue to his whereabouts before he went off half cocked. One thing he knew was that Judkins was a womanizer and that there were few women here, other than officer's wives.

Yet there was one woman he could ask.

He reined his mount to a lazy, ambling walk, surveying both sides of the street. And then he saw her. She came out of the narrow alleyway between two buildings where she had invited him to go earlier. A seedy-looking soldier with a stubbly beard and a cast in one eye followed her, buttoning his trousers as he came.

Daniel felt suddenly ill.

The Indian girl waited until the soldier had gone, then ran toward Daniel, clutching at his stirrup, her eyes hopeful. He shook his head, and she moved a step backward, head down, as she listened to him.

"Yes," she said with a shiver. She had known

the man named Judkins. He was a bad man, very bad. He and his friend had killed a man.

No, she did not know where Judkins had gone.

Had he mentioned a woman who lived in the Gila wilderness?

Only when he was drunk. And then he always wanted to hurt her, Dolores, afterward.

The Indian girl turned her cheek to the light. Daniel could see that it was bruised and swollen. It had happened four days ago, the girl told him. Just before the murder of Captain Riggs.

Now Daniel knew, without a doubt, where Judkins was heading. He prayed to the gods of both the red man and the white that he was wrong in his thinking, or that Jen-nee had already left the Place of the Old Ones; that the Indian warriors had returned for her and for her companions. He kicked his horse into a trot and rode away, leaving Dolores behind him, standing in the dust.

Despite the urgency of the situation, Daniel tried to maintain a steady speed that did not push his horse beyond its limits, stopping often to let the animal rest. At several way stations he traded his mount for a fresh one. In Tularosa and in Silver City he asked after Judkins. No one had seen him.

Still Daniel forged ahead, climbing upward and onward into the mysterious Gila wilderness. He rode swiftly. He had a feeling that time was running out, that Jen-nee was actually in danger! He had no eyes for the beauty around him as he ducked low beneath reaching branches that tore his shirt from his lithe, muscular shoulders. More branches ripped his beaded headband away to allow his dark hair to float in the wind of his passing. Now he did not slacken his speed. If the horse died beneath him, so be it.

He rounded a boulder and reached the gentle swell of earth that led to a high plateau just in time to hear the crack of a gun and to see Jenny fall. A mournful, howling sound issued from Daniel's lips. Judkins, intent on his prey, ignored the sound.

In that moment Daniel Strongbow, who had been adopted by a white family as a small boy, became all Indian.

For the first time in his life he fired on a white man. His bullet struck Judkins in the back, dead center. And Judkins went down. Daniel rode to where Jenny lay, flung himself from his horse, and knelt at her side.

37

Jenny hugged the ground, frantic with fear. She knew that Judkins's bullet would have struck her if she hadn't fallen. A second rifle was fired almost simultaneously, from farther away, by the unknown rider. It, too, had missed. But with her ear to the ground Jenny could hear the horse and rider pounding toward her.

Perhaps if she lay very still and pretended she was dead, they would both go away. It was her only chance.

If only she could breathe! Kwass'ini's scent was very strong. Jenny tried to swallow the gagging coughs that shook her slender body and succeeded for only a brief moment.

The rider dismounted. Through a blur of terror Jenny could see the legs of his fringed trousers and a pair of soft leather moccasins; could feel a hand on her shoulder, turning her. She closed her eyes and braced herself for what was to come.

Then she heard her name!

"Jen-nee. Are you all right?"

Only one person ever said it that way. Daniel! She sat up and looked into Daniel's concerned face. She blinked, her eyes still streaming with tears. Impulsively she threw her arms around Daniel, drawing a deep breath that ended on a sob of relief. Then she burst into a paroxysm of coughing.

Daniel drew back hastily. He had been so relieved to find Jenny still alive that he had paid no attention to the odor of skunk surrounding her. He brought out a bandanna to cover his mouth and nose. The gesture reminded her of her predicament, and she was embarrassed at having given in to impulse. What was worse, the dark eyes above the bandanna held an unmistakable twinkle.

This man was laughing at her!

Jenny glared at him and got to her feet. She began to run, stumbling across the plowed ground, not caring what direction she took. She only wanted to get away. And Daniel was following. She could hear his breathing, close behind her. Then he caught up with her, knocking her to the ground and straddling her. She felt her bones melt at his touch.

Lordy, what was he doing?

She tried to struggle free, and to her horror Daniel took fistsful of dirt from the garden and rubbed them into her face, her hair.

"Water only makes it worse," he explained. "Now take off your clothes!" His voice took on a husky timbre that shook her to her toes. He reached for the buttons on her gown, and she slapped his face..

"I will not," she gasped.

"Take them off!" He growled, attempting to hold her and to hold his breath at the same time. "Damn it, woman, do as I say! I have no wish to look at you! We've got to get rid of that smell!"

Jenny reddened and stopped struggling. "If you will let me go," she said haughtily, "I will undress behind the brush pile!" He complied, and she stripped down, cowering in the brush as she threw her clothes to Daniel.

Then, at his direction, she scrubbed her nude body with dirt. She was like an old hen taking a dust bath, she thought scornfully. And she wasn't even certain this was necessary. This man had always treated her as less than woman, from the first time she saw him at Sam Whitman's place. In fact, he had treated her like a—a common prostitute. If this was all some stupid joke to humiliate her, she would kill him!

While she accomplished the task Daniel kept his back turned, rubbing more gritty soil into her clothing. When he handed her dress back, it was filthy, and so was she. She donned it and marched toward the cliff dwelling, looking like a mobile statue made of dirt. Two small streaks of mud crossing her cheeks betrayed tears of embarrassment.

She ignored the anxious little Kwass'ini trotting along at her heels. He may have saved her life, but he had ruined it too.

When she reached the cliff dwelling, Jenny was greeted with screams of dismay, followed by giggles and teasing from the two little girls who smelled the skunk's spray. When she told of her narrow escape from Judkins, the teasing turned to shock. And when the others learned that Daniel had come back, there were murmurs of pleasure. Jenny's trials were all but forgotten in the excited preparations for his arrival.

Ugly Woman put the coffee on to boil, and Bit'so, giggling again, whispered to Jenny that perhaps she should sit a little farther from the cook fire, especially since they were expecting a guest.

Jenny did better than that. She retired to her own area. The knowledge that Daniel wouldn't smell much better than she did sustained her.

It was quite some time before Daniel arrived. He had buried Judkins, then caught the man's horse, now munching away at Jenny's green corn. He removed the animal's saddle and slapped it on the hindquarters, hoping that it would return to wherever it came from. Then Daniel took great pains to cleanse himself. Kwass'ini had not struck him firsthand as he had the others, but his clothing suffered from his efforts to hold the struggling Jenny.

He draped the Kwass'ini-scented clothes over the pile of brush and donned the fresh uniform he carried in his saddlebags, noting the gifts he had bought for Jen-nee, Ugly Woman, and the children. He would leave them here and distribute them when the time was right.

If there was ever a right time, as far as the small Jen-nee was concerned.

At last, the necessary chores performed, and with no one to see, he could give in to very un-Indian-like laughter. It began as a small chuckle and gave rise to mirth that brought tears to his eyes.

The entire episode had been most amusing. The scrappy little girl had endured enough to give the ladies of Santa Fe the vapors. Yet Jenny had stood there, after narrowly escaping death, or worse, surrounded by a cloud of scent, glaring at him with those great dark eyes!

Daniel finally sobered. He glanced at the edge of the woods where he had buried Judkins.

There would be trouble over that.

But he would not think about it now.

He made his way toward the Place of the Old Ones, the cliff dwelling that had become Jennee's home.

Peeping over the half wall, Jenny saw him coming. Clearly Daniel had not taken his own advice regarding a dirt bath! Her heart pounded in her throat at how handsome he looked, but she refused to acknowledge the feeling consciously.

She ducked down and waited for the giggling and the teasing to begin, in the great central room. She heard nothing but the warmest of welcomes and a burst of laughter when one of the children mentioned her name. She was certain they were laughing at her predicament.

Most frustrating of all, Daniel didn't seem concerned enough about Jenny's well-being to ask where she was.

Somehow that made her even angrier.

When Ugly Woman called her to dinner, she didn't answer but pretended to be asleep. Later Bit'so was sent to her with a small clay pot of soup. She called Jenny's name softly. And when she received no answer, she placed the food near Jenny, to eat when she awoke. After the little girl had gone, Jenny sat up, folding her arms around her knees and resting her chin on them.

Nobody wanted her, she thought, her great eyes filling with tears that she blinked away angrily. Not Jesse, not Daniel, not anyone. Nobody cared—except Kwass'ini. And he probably thought she smelled like his mother!

After they had retired, Jenny rose. She made her way carefully down the side of the cliff and went to a sandy creek bed. There she stripped off all her clothes, scrubbing them—and herself—once more. At last she visited the spring and waded waist-deep in water, washing herself off with the leaves of the aloe vera and drying off with bunches of the fresh mint that grew by the spring.

She did not know that she was being watched. Daniel knew that he had buried her enemy, but it was possible that Judkins had friends somewhere in the area. He had followed Jenny to be sure that she was safe.

Now he stood transfixed by the loveliest sight he had ever seen. The girl's small, firm body was outlined in silver by the moonlight; her hair a tangle of mystery that, at one moment, hid her face; at the next, revealed it. All at once she was Every Woman. She was Eve in the garden. She was Changing Woman of Indian legend. She was Jen-nee.

And in her innocence at being unobserved at her bath, her movements free and unrestrained, she was the wanton little camp follower from Fort Stanton. Daniel backed into the shadows of the trees as she waded to shore, still unable to take his eyes off her. She sat on a stone at the edge of the spring, showing the beautiful curve of her waist and back as she picked up Kwass'ini and held him high, murmuring little love words in her gentle, slightly husky voice.

Daniel knew, more than anything, that he wanted this girl but that she was not for him.

The girl he would marry would be someone like Ugly Woman, who had never lain with a man. Besides, if Jen-nee discovered that he had invaded her privacy, she would hate him forever.

He took one last look and drew a shuddering breath. Then he backed away, soft-footed, without a single snapping twig or rustling leaf to mark his passing. He made his way back to the dwelling. He had only gone to watch over Jen-nee, to protect her. But he had discovered that the greatest danger to the girl was himself.

38

At Sweethome, far to the south, spring had turned into the lushness of summer. During these last months since Theron's death, Inga had felt the effects of age for the first time. Her step was not as light, her smile not as ready as it had been. And there were several silver threads among the golden ones she braided into a coronet each morning.

She supposed she had good reason for aging so rapidly. Theron's death had been the most difficult blow she had ever had to face. It was even harder when Eden, Weldon's plantation, was sold to one of the men who had been with the Klan the night Martha Weldon was killed—the night Theron died. Living with the knowledge that someone who contributed to Theron's death lived just across the way was a terrible drain on her strength.

It wasn't Weldon's fault. He had left the sale in the hands of his Memphis attorney, and he couldn't have known to whom it would go. But the new owner was a man by the name of Potter. He and his wife were filled with hatred for Northerners, as were the two grown sons who lived with them. Their hatred was especially directed toward their Yankee neighbor, who no longer had a husband to protect her.

She would not think about that today. Today the world was so beautiful, it touched her heart with sunlight and her feet with the dancing step they once had. And she steeled herself to face a thing she had long been avoiding.

In all this time she had not visited Theron's grave.

At first the weather was too inclement. Then she used the excuse of being occupied with the planting. Only to herself did she admit the truth. As long as she did not see the grave, with its bare mound of earth, she could make believe that Theron still lived.

Today she knew that she could put the visit off no longer.

Without saying anything to Dinah, Inga took little Honeybee with her, holding the toddler's hand. She suited her pace to Honeybee's as they left the tilled lands and walked through fields of sweet clover and alfalfa, where bees droned lazily in the sun. Halfway there, they stopped to rest.

Sitting in the soft grass, Inga picked a yellow flower, holding it beneath the baby's chin. It cast a golden glow on the little girl's tender skin.

"It says you like butter." She smiled, quoting an old wives' tale her own mother had handed down to her. The little one chuckled and gurgled, then tried to eat the flower before it was pulled away.

How long Inga sat there, feeling the soft touch of the warm sun, she had no idea. But for the

first time in months she felt truly at peace.
Finally she rose, and they walked the remaining
distance, to pause by Theron's grave.

It was not a bald patch of earth as she had
feared. There was no stone as yet. It had been
ordered to be sent out from Memphis. But the
grave, itself, was covered with a carpet of fine
new grass in contrast to that of Old Caleb, its
tall growth touched with waves of silvery shadow.
At the head of the grave, wild primroses blew in
the breeze, seemingly sprung from out of nowhere.

Inga sank down beside the mound that covered her husband's body. This was where he
would want to be, she thought.

As she sat there she remembered another graveyard, another time. Theron had taken her to
Shiloh to find some evidence of her lost brother.
They had found only a half-crazed man, a self-
appointed caretaker of his dead friends. He said
he didn't know Sven.

"But don' y'all worry, ma'am. Ah'm watchin'
ovah 'em. Watchin' ovah them all."

As he talked on about the wars, commenting
on his dead friends as if they still lived, the sun
broke through, turning the mists into rainbow
veils that shimmered and finally disappeared.
The light revealed that the devastated trees had
sprouted new leaves to cover their wounds, that
the grass grew over pocked and cratered earth.
A bird sang a single long, sweet trill. The battlefield of Shiloh was healing itself.

Inga jumped at the sound of bird song, so like
that other time when Theron had been beside her.

Perhaps he was still beside her, here in the
midst of this blue day; here with the perfume of
the flowers and the droning of the bees; with

the butterfly that balanced on small Honeybee's finger to palpitate, opening and closing its bright wings.

"No! Don't eat that!"

Inga caught the child's hand as the finger with the butterfly headed toward an open mouth. Inga laughed, the silvery trill that Theron used to love; that she had never expected to hear from herself again.

"I love you," she said, hugging Honeybee tightly to her. "Oh, I love you so much!"

And she knew her time of mourning was over. Theron wasn't hurting anymore. He wouldn't want her to be sad. The tears that seeped from beneath her lashes were tears of happiness.

"Minna?"

Honeybee was looking up at her with huge, questioning eyes. Inga held her close.

"It's all right, baby. Everything's all right."

And it was.

It was late afternoon when they started back to the mansion known as Sweethome. Inga's feet were light again as she pretended to race with the stumbling, giggling toddler. Honeybee tripped and fell. Inga picked her up and cuddled her hurt away, pretending that this was her own little girl. Hers and Theron's. This child who had taken away the hurt of losing not only her husband but Kirsten and Jenny as well.

A shadow touched her face at the thought of her daughters. Theron had found his peace in death, and Inga's grieving had come to an end. But what had happened to the girls—had they found the happiness they sought?

Inga hoped so.

Shaking her worries from her shoulders, Inga

sat Honeybee's feet on the ground. She took the child's chubby little hand in hers and hurried toward home, where Dinah would be waiting and grumbling because they were late for supper.

She had almost reached the house when she saw Dinah coming to meet them. She sighed. Leaving without telling the old woman where she was going had been most unkind, yet this excursion today was something Inga had to do for herself.

The plump housekeeper was huffing and puffing as she came toward them at a jiggling trot. "Miz Inga," she shouted when she was within hearing distance. "Miz Inga, you got compn'y."

When Inga reached her, Dinah was completely out of breath, the bosom of her print dress heaving beneath its white apron. "Oh, Lawd," she said with a moan. "I'se gittin' old! Too old to run no more!"

"Why didn't you send John or Boy?" Inga scolded affectionately.

Dinah wiped the perspiration from her gleaming face. " 'Cuz I figure this is too impawtant," she said with dignity. "This yere's a man."

Inga was shaken. Weldon, she thought. It was Weldon, the child's father. He had come back, after all, breaking his promise to her.

"He's a man, an' he aks for Miz Inga *Johansson*. I never said nothin'. Jes' come to git you." Dinah stopped to stare at her mistress.

"Miz Inga, what's wrong?"

Inga's blood had run cold. She was freezing, despite the heat of the day. Everyone here in the Southland knew her as Inga St. Germain.

She had not been called Johansson since she'd left St. Paul, Minnesota, when she had killed the man who'd given her that name in marriage. Olaf Johansson had been the father of her children, and she had murdered him. Now, at last, the crime must have caught up with her.

"Miz Inga!"

Inga came back to the present; she stared at Dinah through blurred eyes. Then she snatched up Honeybee and put her in the old woman's arms. "Take her out to the kitchen, down to the quarters to Zada—anywhere! But keep her out of sight. If—if anything happens, take care of her. Promise me!"

"But Miz Inga!"

"Promise me!" It was a cry of anguish torn from Inga's heart. Dinah looked at her fearfully and bobbed her head.

"Yes, ma'am."

Inga went toward the great living room where the stranger would be waiting. The double doors leading into it were closed, and Boy was standing there, his skinny rump protruding as he pressed his ear to one of the panels. When he saw Inga, he backed away, grinning nervously.

"Granny say this here a stranger-man. I'se s'posed to keep a watch out on 'im, ontil y'all come."

"Thank you, Boy. You may go now."

If she was right about the identity of her visitor, this wasn't something she wanted anyone else to overhear.

Inga paused to brace herself, trying to get her emotions under control. She had a pretty good idea who the man waiting for her would be.

He would be the man she had called Father, come to save her immortal soul!

Pastor Gustav Lindstrom was a fanatical man.

He believed in only the black and white of things—the right and the wrong—and saw himself as an instrument of the Lord's vengeance. He had accused her, his own daughter, of adultery. Standing in the pulpit like an angry, graybearded god chastizing a sinner, he had pointed the finger of condemnation at Inga.

No decent woman belonging to his small, obscure cult had dared speak to Inga following his indictment. No decent man would look her way.

What had made her think she could get away with murder? Gustav Lindstrom would follow her to the ends of the earth. Inga sensed that her day of reckoning had come, at last.

Trembling, Inga drew a shuddering breath. Then she squared her shoulders, stepped forward, and opened the living-room doors.

39

Inga stepped inside the living room, and the man who had been standing at a window admiring the view turned to face her. She was unable to speak for a moment. She had been so certain that the visitor would be Pastor Lindstrom. This fellow was little more than a boy.

Her gaze swept over him, taking in his height, his wide shoulders, the raw, unfinished look that showed him to be in his late teens. He wore a lumpy, ill-fitting suit. His tow-colored hair, cut in bowl-fashion, proclaimed him to be from home.

Then he seemed suddenly, startlingly familiar. Could this be Sven? No, if Sven had survived the war, he would be much older. Yet there was an amazing resemblance.

She hesitated, and the boy stepped toward her, smiling.

"Inga?"

At the sound of her name on his lips, at the odd Norwegian inflection in his voice, her memory came rushing back.

This was Paul! Paul, the younger brother she hadn't seen in so long.

But he had grown up now, he was so different.

Inga reached out her arms to him and found herself crying again, sobbing out her relief against his broad chest while he muttered gentle words of comfort, his face scarlet with adolescent embarrassment. Finally she managed to compose herself.

"Mama? Birgitta? Is she well ... ?" Inga's voice faltered, trailing off as she saw his change of expression.

"Mama's dead, Inga."

Oh, dear God! His words left a vast emptiness inside her. But what had she expected? That Birgitta would live forever? Her breath caught on a sob.

"I expect she's happier now," Paul said awkwardly. As though he knew what Inga was thinking, he said huskily, "Mama made me come. It was the last thing she said before she died. Papa was praying and he didn't hear. She said I was more like you than the others. She told me to take her egg money—"

He choked up and couldn't continue, but Inga knew the rest of the story. When she had struck her husband down, Inga had gone to Birgitta. Birgitta had given her an old coat into which she had sewn what little money she was able to hide away from her husband. It had been enough to take passage on a ship going downriver, to take her and her children far away.

Now her mother had sent her a final gift. Her brother.

"Did you know about Olaf?" Inga asked. He nodded. And now Inga was crying once more. Again Paul put his arms around his sister to comfort her. But when she felt his body stiffen,

Inga pulled free of him and turned to follow his gaze.

Dinah was standing in the doorway, black arms crossed over her starched apron, her rolling pin in her hand. She fixed the newcomer with an implacable glare.

"This fella botherin' you, Miz Inga?"

"Yes!" Inga laughed through her tears. "Oh, Dinah, I mean, no! Look at him! Just look at him! Isn't he beautiful? This is my little brother, Paul!"

Dinah's grimace disappeared as she studied the tall, gangly boy. "He do look like you," she said at last. "But he needs to be fed up some. I speck he's hongry. I'll fix somp'n in the dinin' room."

"No, Dinah," Inga told her. "The kitchen. He'll like it better in there."

"I'll dish it up," Dinah said. "Then I go out an' get that little package back from Zada." She winked at Inga, and Inga almost laughed. For a moment she had completely forgotten little Honeybee. Paul knew nothing about her. He would be so surprised!

Sitting down to a meal of ham, black-eyed peas, and corn bread, Paul and his sister argued over who should begin the recital of the happenings in their lives.

"You first," Paul said. He looked at his surroundings. "Only wealthy people could live like this. I'm sure your story is more interesting."

"No," Inga said, "you." Her mouth quivered. "I want to know how Mama died."

It was a simple story. Birgitta just grew more tired every day, until one day she didn't get up when Gustav Lindstrom ordered her to. She hadn't been well for several years. But Paul supposed that Kirsten had told her.

Kirsten? Kirsten had gone to see her mother and had said nothing? Inga was bewildered. Then Paul spilled out the whole story of how Kirsten had come, planning to stay with them. And one day his father discovered that she was pregnant. Birgitta had hidden her, then helped her to escape on Paul's horse, wearing Paul's clothes.

"Papa nearly beat me to death," Paul said ruefully. "You remember how it was."

Inga reached across the table to touch her brother's hand. "I'm sorry, Paul."

But the dates in Paul's story didn't coincide at all with those Kirsten had given her. So the tiny body lying in the graveyard on the hill could never have been Nick's daughter. Inga remembered the day she and Theron had caught Kirsten in Matthew Weldon's bed.

It was probably his child, sister to little Honeybee.

Inga's tears were close to the surface again; she swallowed them hastily.

"Paul, there's something I want to tell you—"

"An' here she is!" Grinning from ear to ear, Dinah arrived through the back door, carrying Honeybee. She set the child on her feet. "Don' need tellin'. Jes' showin'!"

Paul looked as though he had just been struck. "Who," he asked, "who—?"

"My little daughter." Inga smiled, reaching out to the giggling toddler.

"But you—you didn't—you can't!" Paul's face was almost apoplectic.

Inga looked at him uneasily. "Perhaps I should have said *adopted* daughter, though I fail to see that it makes any difference." Paul's face cleared, and she continued. "She's been such a joy to me since my husband died."

"Husband?" he croaked.

Then Inga understood. Paul hadn't known she was married. Of course, he was upset! "My husband was Theron St. Germain," she said softly. "He was the owner of Sweethome. And he was injured in the war. He finally died of his injuries. I loved him. I loved him very much."

"I don't understand," Paul said helplessly. "I can see Olaf writing you off as dead and marrying again, but you . . ."

He paused, and Inga leaned forward, her face ashen. "What are you talking about, Paul! My God, what are you saying! Are you trying to tell me that Olaf is still alive?"

"I thought you knew."

His words crashed through her head, bouncing off the walls of the kitchen, echoing in her brain. Suddenly she could hear Olaf's drunken ravings as he dragged Jenny toward the door; she could hear him say that he was giving her to a man who wanted a woman and didn't give a damn if she was a bastard.

Inga struck him down. And now she could smell the scent of blood and whiskey. She could see what she had left on the floor of the house when she and the girls had fled. She could see the long body of a big man with a mop of coarse yellow hair; one side of it a mass of blood and gore that matched the stains on the poker she had struck him with.

He couldn't have lived! He couldn't! Yet he had. Inga knew she would never close her lids again without seeing that enormous shambling form, coming at her with blank, unseeing eyes.

Theron was dead! Dead! And he had never really been her husband.

And Olaf still lived.

It was too much to absorb. The room began to spin around her, and Inga toppled to the floor in a dead faint. Dinah hurried to her side, dropping to her fat knees and frowning up at Paul.

"What did you do to mah baby?" she asked. "What did you do to mah chile!"

Paul had no answer. He could do nothing but spread his hands helplessly. And Honeybee began to cry.

40

In New Orleans, Kirsten couldn't care less about what was happening at Sweethome. Time had passed since she overheard Pete and Lydia's vengeful conversation, and nothing had happened. She decided it was just talk and tried not to think about it, though she now carried a loaded pistol wherever she went. It was protection enough.

Meanwhile Kirsten's life was full and brimming with excitement. Her investment in The French Rose had doubled, just as Slim Morley said it would. And instead of returning half of it to Nick's bank, as she had originally intended, Kirsten had taken another gamble and reinvested the whole thing.

"On one condition," Slim said imperatively. "Kirsten, come here."

She approached him, trembling a little. She ought to be getting home. Everyone said there was a storm on the way. But she knew what Morley wanted. She had learned to recognize it in his eyes.

Morley's lovemaking had been every bit as exciting as she had thought it would be. It wasn't as spontaneous as making love with Weldon had been, nor as sincere and sweet as it was with Nick. But Morley was more adept. He knew the art of taking a girl to the edge of madness and desire and bringing her back slowly, carefully, to reality.

The stories that were spread about Slim, his illegal activities, and the very danger of him all added spice to their illicit relationship. And, of course, there were the dresses she now modeled for Slim.

Slim took pride in presenting the most attractive girls in New Orleans at The French Rose. To that end he employed several French seamstresses to make their gowns. Kirsten had discovered that although she hated the tedium of stitchery, she had a talent for designing costumes that were both provocative and revealing. Slim had insisted that she have the first of each made up for herself. Now she modeled them while Slim watched lazily from the crimson velvet bed they had shared a short time before.

Today there were two. The first was an amber satin that hovered at the edge of modesty. It was cut a little too low, revealing the tops of her lovely breasts, clinging in front to mold every curve of a body without undergarments. It was a dress made to wear for the street, calculated to raise a man's passions, yet sedate enough for polite company—if one didn't look too closely.

Morley laughed and clapped his hands. "It is a liar of a dress," he said teasingly. "Like the woman who wears it! All praline-sweet on the outside, deliciously evil beneath!"

Kirsten looked at him saucily. "This gown lies?" she asked. "Then you would prefer honesty?"

At his grinning nod she stepped behind a screen. Within a few short minutes she was back again, her arms held up as if to receive applause.

Instead she met dead silence. Slim Morley stared at her, openmouthed.

Kirsten wore a dress with a jet-black bodice. It was a startling contrast to the scarlet walls of the bedroom and to the whiteness of Kirsten's skin. It fit her tightly, revealing her long, pale legs, cut deeply to bare her thighs, with row after row of ruffles at the hips. Behind her fanned layers of stiffened, spangled net, rising like a peacock's tail to frame her face and body. She wore her hair down, and on her head was a jeweled coronet.

Morley's eyes narrowed for a long moment. Then he said, "Come here, baby!"

With sure, deft fingers he found the snaps and fasteners, as she remonstrated with him to be careful. "I made this dress for Elyse—"

"No one will ever wear it but you," he whispered. "And then only for me. You're not going back to Tremont, Kirsten! You are staying with a man who has sense enough to appreciate you! I can give you everything you want. And I will, I promise you."

Kirsten merely kissed him and put him off. Her affair with Slim was a new, exciting experience. But she was reluctant to leave Nick, for some obscure reason that she didn't understand herself. She let Morley make love to her again, smiling at his insatiability. Finally, exhausted from their passion, she fell asleep.

Morley watched her for a while, then grinned.

This had been a pleasant interlude, but he had work to do. It was time to open The French Rose for business. But first he would take her clothing, just as insurance that she would still be here when he came back. As an afterthought, he also took the amber gown, leaving the wicked little peacock outfit behind. He chuckled to himself. She wouldn't dare wear that outfit out on the street, yet she couldn't say he had left her with nothing.

Kirsten awoke to a dark room. For a moment she didn't know where she was. "Nick?" she whispered. When there was no answer, she swung her legs over the side of the bed, feeling the texture of the spread against the back of her bare legs.

Damn!

She knew where she was now. Morley had left her here deliberately, hoping she would do what she had just done—sleep until Nick was up and worrying about her. This had happened once before, and she had managed to cover with an acceptable story. But that didn't mean Nick would believe her this time.

She lit the bedside lamp and looked for the clothing she had worn earlier. All she could find was the little black creation she had just worn for Slim. She damned him for putting her into this predicament, slamming her fist into the crimson bedspread. He had no right! And Nick had no right to expect her to be home when he woke up, either!

But, she finally supposed, forlornly, that she had no business spending the afternoon in another man's bed. If she could convince Nick that she was innocent of any wrongdoing, she would work toward replacing all his money, and she would never, ever see Slim Morley again.

First, however, she had to find a way to get home, then concoct a story for Nick. She would think about it on the way.

She put on the peacock costume and doubled the crimson bedspread, wrapping it around herself like a cloak. Then she snatched up her handbag and started downstairs. At the landing a door opened on a set of stairs that led to a side entrance. If she could just make it to those!

Before she reached the landing, a man and a girl passed her. Kirsten leaned over the railing and turned her face into the shadows until she heard them reach the top floor and close a door behind them. Then she ran on down, negotiated the side stairs without incident, and was out into the night.

It had been very hot and humid all day. Now the expected storm was just a low grumble in the distance. An occasional gust of wind broke off twigs and sent them skittering into Kirsten's path as she ran for the Card Parlor, head down, seeing no one.

Rounding the corner, she crashed into a feminine form, losing her grip on the spread. It fell away in the wind, revealing her scanty costume. Kirsten stared at the girl who faced her. She was green-eyed, her orange-red hair blowing in the wind like a flame. And her features were set in a mask of hatred.

Lydia!

Kirsten turned from the girl to see a familiar figure in the distance. He was approaching from the other direction, his clothes whipping about his scrawny body.

It was old Pete, who once worked for Nick.

And she was going to be caught between them—the two people who had talked of killing her. She turned toward Lydia again, trying to plead with her; she would tell her that the affair between herself and Slim Morley was over. But Lydia didn't give her the chance.

Since leaving Morley's protection Lydia had fallen on hard times. The regulars who patronized The French Rose knew her as Morley's property and were afraid to have anything to do with her. She had managed to pick up an occasional stranger, or a sailor from a ship in port, but of late the pickings had been thin. She had been evicted from the shabby room where she had been staying, and she'd had nothing to eat all day.

And here was this woman, *Nick Tremont's* woman, who had taken Slim Morley away from her. The sight of Kirsten, her lower limbs bare, standing before her in that ridiculous, provocative costume, drove her mad.

With a cry of rage Lydia reached into the top of her stocking, taking out a small dagger. She came at Kirsten, her teeth bared, the dagger drawn back in a stabbing position. She slashed forward with the glittering blade.

But Kirsten moved even faster.

The pistol she had purchased for just such an eventuality was in her hand.

She fired.

And just then the wind rose to the pitch of a woman's scream. Kirsten clapped her hands over her ears to shut out the sound as she gazed numbly at the sight that lay on the ground before her: the body of Lydia, who, in her own way, had truly loved Slim Morley and had now died for him. The bullet had entered her heart, and the breast of her gown was crimson, the same red as the decor of The French Rose.

Kirsten cowered against the wall of the building behind her, the back of her hand to her lips, to cover a whimpering cry. For a moment everything stood still. She was sure Pete had seen her. But he had not seen Lydia at her feet.

Kirsten dropped the pistol at Lydia's side, snatched up the bedspread, and ran in the other direction. The tempest began to scream again, rising to a crescendo.

All Kirsten knew was that she had just killed a woman. And now she was running for her life.

41

Kirsten ran until she could run no longer. The wind was at her back, and every step was taking her farther away from Nick's Card Parlor. The street was cleared of people and filled with flying debris. Many of the streetlights along Royal Street were broken, and the swinging lanterns that graced some buildings had been blown out by their proprietors, in fear of fire.

Finally, with a stitch in her side that took her breath away, Kirsten dropped to the ground in a narrow, cobbled alleyway. Evidently one of the buildings bordering on the alley was a saloon. The alley stank of ale and urine, and the cobbles gleamed with broken glass.

Above Kirsten's head, a shutter banged ceaselessly; the shrieking of the gale was horrendous. A bit of broken tile left the roof above and narrowly missed her as it was blown to the ground. She folded her arms above her head to shield it.

And then, over the scent of the alley that surrounded her, rose another, stronger smell.

Smoke!

A vendor of roasted corn had left his cart with its vat of smoking coals in order to get out of the weather. The vendor's cart had tipped, and the coals were blown against one of the structures that abutted the alley. Once a fine old French home, it was now a saloon with an addition created of creosote-treated timbers from a wrecked ship. The wooden section was burning like tinder.

The customers who had taken shelter from the wind poured from the saloon, all of them coughing and shouting drunkenly as bells clanged out an alarm. Kirsten drew back, dazed by the sudden uproar.

"A damned nigger done it," one man bellowed as he saw the tipped cart. "A damned nigger set this place afire! Gawdammit, let's find the bastard an' hang 'im!"

Kirsten cowered in the alley, afraid of the fire, afraid to leave. Nick always insisted she be off the streets before darkness fell. It was Reconstruction, and violence in the streets was not uncommon. Just the other night there had been a riot involving Metropolitan Police and Klansmen, and an innocent bystander had been killed. These men were too drunk to notice if she was black or white, or that she was a woman.

She finally chose her moment and ran, choking, against the wind. She was running toward the Card Parlor and Nick, who would protect her. Her eyes were streaming until she could hardly see.

Then she realized she had not been quick enough. Two men had caught sight of her, and they were pounding after her. The smoke had diminished her breathing power, and she already felt the stitch again. But she didn't dare pause. They were too close for her to take evasive action.

They were going to catch her! She gave a little sobbing cry as the man in the lead reached out and caught hold of the scarlet bedspread she had wrapped around her. It fell away from her running figure, stopping her followers in their tracks for a moment.

"Hell," the man said. "You see that, Ramon? By God, that's for me!"

Her pursuer lenghtened his stride once more, ducking to avoid flying slates that left a roof like huge blackbirds. Then an empty wine barrel spiraled before the wind, catching him dead center. It knocked the breath out of him with a *whoosh*, and he fell to the ground. He sat up, shaking his head blearily. His fatter friend, who was following him, tripped and went down on top of him.

As if it were a signal for the storm to begin in earnest, the night sky was suddenly silver with sheeting rain. Kirsten could see the two men no longer, nor could they see her. She heard their footsteps splashing after her for a while. Then they paused in confusion.

They had no idea where she was, and this was a regular frog-strangler. The rain had surely put out the fire in Henry's saloon. They would go back and have a drink. And by damn, they certainly had a story to tell! How they had chased a golden-haired mermaid down the street and she had knocked the pair of them down with one sweep of her powerful tail. Then the rain came, and she swam away. They couldn't follow her. They had to come back to the saloon because neither of them could swim.

Kirsten would gladly have traded places with a mermaid at the moment. A mermaid wouldn't have minded being soaked to the skin, cold and wet, tramping ankle-deep through water that rapidly filled the streets and ran into low doorways. And a mermaid wouldn't have to explain to anybody where she had been. Right now all she knew was that she was miserable and afraid, and that she wanted Nick.

She edged along to the side of the street, feeling her way most of the time. She recognized a low, ironwork grille set in a doorway; a narrow space between two buildings; and then the rain slowed for a moment and she saw the Card Parlor. Every room was ablaze with light, and she drew a shuddering breath as she started toward the entrance, fighting against a wind that slammed into her, almost knocking her down. The rain that struck her full in the face, almost drowning her.

Finally she made it through the door, leaning against it in complete exhaustion. Her spirits rose when she saw that the card room was empty. Evidently, when Nick found that she was missing, he hadn't opened up for business. He was probably out looking for her. And that would give her time.

She looked down at herself. The costume that had been so lovely was now a bedraggled mess; the peacock tail she had devised was dragging against the back of her legs, which were now covered with mud. Her ruffles drooped, and her hair hung in darkened streaks against her shoulders.

She could never let Nick see her like this!

Aching in every muscle, she limped toward the stairs and hauled herself up, holding on to the railing. The banister suddenly felt wet and sticky to the touch. She looked down, and to her horror it was red with blood.

It was her own, welling from a deep cut in her palm. She hadn't realized that Lydia had gotten close with that knife. She felt nauseated, and her head began to spin.

Finally, steeling herself, Kirsten moved up the staircase, listening all the while. The house was as quiet as a grave. She shuddered a little at the analogy. It made her think of Lydia and what she, Kirsten, had just done. She had to put it out of her mind. The woman was dead. It had been a case of self-defense. And nobody had seen it happen!

Reaching the top of the stairs and her room, Kirsten rested a moment. It was obvious that Nick wasn't there. She was weak with loss of blood, but she had made it back. She would concoct a story while she changed.

First she took off her wet clothing, rolling it into an unrecognizable ball. Then she swathed her bleeding hand in bandages. Her injury would be easy to explain, since she had been out in this weather.

Selecting her most demure down, of pale yellow lawn with a white lace collar, she hastily donned it. Then she dried her hair with a fluffy towel, braiding it into a halo, as her mother often did. So far she was unable to fabricate a reason for her absence. But it would come.

Now all that remained was to get rid of the damning evidence.

Picking up the soggy costume, she used it to wipe the blood from the stair railing on her way to the lower floor. There was a storage pantry and a small kitchen for staff use in a room behind the bar, as well as a large trash container that Nick paid an old Negro to empty. The man was due to come tomorrow morning. She grinned a little. If he pawed through the trash this time, he would surely have a surprise.

Kirsten went through the storage pantry that served the bar. She entered the kitchen and headed directly for the trash container, opening it and pushing the ruined costume down among the garbage and the empty bottles from the liquor that had been served. There! It was gone. No one would ever see it.

And she had her excuse! She had come downstairs this afternoon before Nick woke and had cut her hand on a broken bottle. She had rushed out to a doctor, who had treated her and made her lie down. Then the storm had come.

She would talk to Dr. Simms in the morning. He was none too reputable and had an eye for a pretty face. She was certain she could get him to cover for her, just in case Nick asked any questions.

"Hello, girlie."

Pete's raspy voice came from behind her. She whirled to see him sitting, like a cadaver, in a kitchen chair. His hands were beneath the table's edge. Kirsten was sure he was concealing a gun.

Her eyes went quickly to the bottle before him. It was almost empty. Pete was drinking again, and he looked dangerous. Her heart stopped as she realized what he might have seen.

"What—what are you doing here," she stammered. "And where is Nick?"

He grinned, showing the rotted stumps of his

teeth. "I come here direckly after findin' you kilt Lydia. Told Nick what you done, and this time he hadda believe me."

"But I didn't—"

Pete ignored her interruption and continued his dissertation with relish.

"Nick went over to The French Rose huntin' for you. By now he's found the body, talked to Morley, an' the po-lice will be lookin' for you."

The police! She had to get out of here.

Kirsten half turned and Pete was suddenly on his feet.

"No sense in runnin', girlie," he rasped, "cause I'm gonna kill you, and nobody's gonna fault me for it."

In his hand was the same gun she had used to shoot Lydia, its barrel pointing straight between her eyes.

42

Kirsten turned white, but she stood her ground, trying to bluff the man. "I don't know what you're talking about!"

His eyes went to the bandage on her hand. The blood had seeped through the white wrappings. Kirsten put her hand behind her back.

"Looks like you tangled with a knife," Pete said insolently. "Mebbe a knife like the one layin' next to Lydia, there in the street."

"I was making a sandwich," she babbled. "I—I cut myself."

"Shee-yut." Pete sneered. "An' I s'pose you was wearin' this when you made your sammitch!" He strolled over, the pistol still pointed at her, and rummaged in the trash container, pulling out the soaked, flimsy bit of material that was streaked with blood. "Don't try to lie to me, girlie. You're guilty as hell . . ."

He paused and turned, his jaw dropping. He forgot his weapon as he threw up his hand to ward off a blow.

Kirsten had picked up the poker from beside the stove and moved behind him. She swung, then heard his forearm snap. The sound was immediately followed by a dull clunk as Pete took the main force of the blow on his forehead.

His eyes bulged for a moment, then glazed over, and he went down.

Kirsten went to her knees beside him, searching for a pulse. A moment later she rose to her feet, staring at the body of the old man in horror.

She hadn't meant to kill him!

But she knew she could never prove it. Not even Nick would believe her now. And she knew, instinctively, that the cold-blooded Slim Morley would never come to her aid. It would be bad for his business, and besides, he was incapable of love. Kirsten had known all along that she was just another woman to him.

Why had she never admitted it to herself? If she had, then she wouldn't be in this dreadful mess.

But now she had to get away! What was it Pete said? He had told Nick what she'd done, and Nick had gone to The French Rose looking for her. Soon the police would come.

Maybe this weather would hold them back for a while. This was no time to act impulsively. She had to think this out carefully.

Kirsten forced herself to stand still. She looked at the old man's body reflectively. He was the only witness to Lydia's death, she thought. *Nick only had Pete's word for it*! And if Pete's body were out of the way, along with any other signs that she had returned to this house . . .

The wind shrilled away outside. The shutters banged, and the lamp flickered. She stared at the lamplight, mesmerized. Everyone knew it was dangerous to leave lamps lit in a storm like this.

And she knew immediately what she was going to do. Except that she had to have time!

Kirsten raced up the stairs and threw some clothing into a bag. She selected several of her favorite gowns, seized her warmest cloak, then emptied the contents of a kerosene lamp onto the blue satin bed. She swallowed a lump in her throat as she did so. Then she flew into Nick's study, dousing some papers and the couch where he slept occasionally.

Her next stop was the card room where Nick kept his gaming money in a locked drawer. She found the key where he usually hid it, and counted out the cash. Thank God there was enough.

Finally Kirsten went down to the storage pantry, timorously opening the door that led to the kitchen. Perhaps, by some strange magic, Pete would have come to life again.

He had not. He still lay sprawled where he fell, looking strangely shrunken and small; a figure made of sticks and wax.

He's not real, Kirsten told herself. It isn't a real man lying there. It's some kind of a scarecrow, like we had back at Sweethome.

Sweethome! Kirsten felt tears come to her eyes at the thought of the place—its slow, dreamy beauty; the goodness of the people who lived there. Suddenly Theron, Inga, and Jenny seemed more real than the spot where she now stood.

Why hadn't she stayed there?

Kirsten squeezed her eyes shut, but only for a moment. She went to the storage closet, found a can of kerosene, and poured it over the scarecrow, averting her eyes. Finally she picked up the lamp, went to the door, and, shuddering, tossed it straight into the spreading pool around Pete's body.

There was an explosion of flame.

Kirsten picked up her packed bag and cloak and fled the burning building. The wind, shrieking in her ears, was like the screaming of a lost soul. Her gown was soaked through instantly as she ran mindlessly, wanting only to escape the terrible sound. Then she slowed as she realized what it was.

And that she had no place to go.

Ducking into a doorway, Kirsten forced herself to look back at the inferno that had once been Nick's pride. She could see the fresh bursts of flame as the kerosene she had poured in each room caught and bloomed in savage bursts of red and yellow. The downstairs windows were squares of fire that bellied out into the wind; a wind that caught burning brands and carried them along the narrow street, setting other, new fires.

Soon a group of screaming, gesticulating people from neighboring buildings gathered in the street, their faces reddened by the flames. One brave soul ran inside, and Kirsten held her breath until he returned, slapping at his scorched trouser legs. She could hear his voice rising over all the rest.

"Kerosene! Somebody doused the goddamn place with kerosene! And there's a body in there!"

Then, as Kirsten watched, the roof of Nick's building fell in with a *whoosh* and a roar that brought a concentrated moan from the watchers below.

Kirsten wondered if Nick was among the crowd and what he could be thinking. The Card Parlor had been his dream. He had worked the riverboats for years, gambling, trying to earn enough money to purchase that building.

And he had said that Kirsten was what was needed to give the place class. He had been so proud of her.

Yet it would be impossible to return to Nick now. The man would tell his story, and Nick would know exactly what had happened.

Feeling a kind of sick relief, Kirsten realized that old Pete, with his evidence, was gone. But still, she could not be sure that she was safe. It would be better to go far, far away.

Kirsten knew the firemen would be sent for, and along with them would come the police.

She ran again, the wind buffeting her, her hair slipping from its braids. Her packed bag slammed against her legs. She had to find a quiet place to hide, to think. Oh, God, where was she?

Shutting her eyes tightly, she stopped and waited for a brief cessation of the storm. And then she saw it. She knew she had found her sanctuary.

Before her, out of the wind and the rain, loomed the Cathedral of St. Louis. It had stood on this site, Jackson Square in the Vieux Carré, since the beginning of New Orleans. Though not a religious man, Nick was absurdly proud of the old landmark and had often suggested that she visit it. But Kirsten dismissed it as being of little interest. It had been—until now.

The church's doors were always open. And now its dark interior, with only a single lamp flickering near the altar, beckoned to her.

Kirsten slid, shivering, into a seat, placing her

bag beneath it. She noted that there were others present, their heads bowed. Perhaps they were praying for the safety of their homes throughout the storm.

What would these pious souls think, she wondered, if they knew there was a murderess among them? A woman who had just killed two people and set fire to the house of the man she claimed to love?

Kirsten had never been especially moral, she had committed minor crimes of theft and blackmail. She had borne an illegitimate child and had lied to Nick, telling him that he fathered her baby, who had died at birth.

But she had never done anything like this. She had never caused anyone's death before!

Kirsten thought of the day her mother had taken her and Jenny, running from Minnesota after Inga thought she had killed Olaf. And she, Kirsten, had accused her of his murder.

Yet when Kirsten went to her grandparents' home in Minnesota, she had discovered that Olaf still lived. He had declared his family dead so that he could marry again.

How strange that Inga was innocent. It was Kirsten who was now a murderess.

She laughed, a hard, little, mirthless sound that made several of the St. Louis parishoners, less absorbed in their worship, look up briefly. It didn't matter. No one would recognize her there, at least not as wet as she was, and without the cosmetics she normally wore. Then, too, these were not the kind of people who would consider frequenting a gaming place, nor a house of prostitution like The French Rose.

Kirsten had decided where she was going and

what she was going to do. She intended to return to Sweethome. At least she could rest awhile while she decided what to do.

Her mind finally made up, Kirsten lowered her head demurely and sat silently, as if in prayer. Anyone who saw her, noting the sweet curve of her cheek, the lashes like golden silk that were lowered in sweet humility, might have thought her an angelic vision, a woman with her mind on things beautiful and holy.

Actually Kirsten was wondering how soon the storm would be over and how she would get from the church to the riverboat landing without being seen. And all the while she was thinking of multiple explanations to cover all eventualities.

43

Spring deepened into early summer in the New Mexico Territory. The high meadows were vistas of blossoms, visited by butterflies and birds. Jenny rose early in the morning and tended her garden all day, spurning Daniel's tentative offer of help. The offer was an impulsive gesture; Daniel had been trying to avoid Jenny since the night he watched her bathe at the spring. There was something about the girl, a beauty that made his throat catch. It was a struggle to remember that she was not for him, so it was better to stay away from her.

"I didn't think the men of your tribe did manual labor," Jenny said silkily.

Daniel wanted to grab her and shake her, tell her that he was no ordinary Indian. He had been raised like a white, though he was treated with a condescending kindness. His role in his adoptive household had been to remain silent, remember his origins, and work fourteen to eighteen hours a day.

Now, his offer spurned, he shrugged and said, "Have it your own way, Jen-nee," then turned his back to converse with Ugly Woman.

Perversely Jenny was exasperated by his attitude. He might at least have argued with her, and he did not offer his assistance again. It was better that way, she told herself haughtily. She much preferred to be alone.

Each day she went to the garden to hoe and weed, her face grim when she left the dwelling. But in the field it would soften into that of a hurt child as she thought of Daniel, of Jesse, of her life.

She had come to join Jesse, and he had found himself a new love. Daniel hardly knew she existed. Her real father had rejected her, long years ago. Even her mother, learning that she had found a way to get to New Mexico by joining the Washburn family, hadn't put up any argument. Maybe Inga, too, had always felt a little uneasy because Jenny was so Indian-looking. Or maybe it was just that she wanted to be alone with Theron. But the fact that Inga had accepted her departure so matter-of-factly was painful.

At least she was out of the way now; out of everyone's way.

Today the sun was hot. Jenny's garments were sticking to her body, her hair soaked with perspiration and coming loose from its braid. She pushed it back with a soiled, brown hand and stretched to ease the ache in her back as she thought longingly of the cliff dwelling with its cool shadows; the spring with its icy water.

She looked around at the garden she had created. The damage Judkins had done by riding his horse through the center of it had been cleared away and replanted. She wondered vaguely where Daniel had buried the man. Then, resolving not to think of the Indian scout again, she went back to her study of the garden. The undamaged plants were just at the verge of bearing fruit. From where she stood, Jenny could see a few green beans, still slender and young. Another squash. Lately, all her work here had paid off. There was not a weed in sight, the rows between the plants as clean as if they had been swept.

Then what was she doing out here in this heat? She felt a sudden surge of anger. Daniel had no right to displace her in her own home—that was the way she had begun to regard the cliff dwelling. She was going back, and if he didn't like her presence there, he could just— just go away! Come to think of it, why was he still staying around? Unless, of course, it was on Ugly Woman's account.

Jenny left the field and started home, her footsteps lagging now that she had come to a decision. She paused to watch a lizard scamper through the grass. Then she found a horned toad sunning itself. It blinked basilisk eyes as she picked it up and carried it back to her garden to join the others she had taken there as protection against insects. Finally she could think of no more excuses to linger and made her way back up the steep side of the cliff to her own half-walled room. Then, bracing herself to face Daniel, she stepped into the main room. Bit'so ran toward her, her small face shining with delight.

"Oh, Jen-nee! You're back early! Daniel has brought you a surprise!"

Daniel reddened. He had just given the others in the household their gifts, but he had had vague plans of taking Jenny's gift to her in the field; of seeing her eyes light up as he placed the bit of turquoise around her neck. Now his fantasies had been spoiled. It was just as well. He fumbled in his pocket, removed something, then moved toward Jenny and dropped the leather thong over her head. The chunk of turquoise, hanging between her breasts, was a light, cerulean blue, free of greenish casts. It was so beautiful, it took her breath away. Daniel stepped back quickly, his fingers burning from their slight graze against Jenny's warm flesh.

"It is a thank-you gift, for your care when I was hurt," Daniel said almost formally, averting his eyes from Jenny's startled brown ones.

Jenny was surprised. "But it was my fault. I shot you."

"But you worked to make me well." Daniel was embarrassed, and so was Jenny. She tried to smile, to show her pleasure at the unfamiliar stone.

"What is this?" she asked, touching it with a curious finger.

Ugly Woman, usually so quiet, answered for him. "Turquoise is the sacred stone of the Navajo, which we use in all our ceremonies. Have you never noticed the small blue bead I wear tied in my hair?" She turned to face Jenny. "Turquoise is a sign that the wearer is under divine protection. Now you will never be struck by lightning, nor bitten by a rattlesnake."

It was a thoughtful gift and an unexpected one, especially after the way she had ignored Daniel lately. Jenny's dark eyes filled with tears, and she stood on her tiptoes and impulsively kissed his dark cheek. He flinched, and she mentally damned herself for being so demonstrative. Her new little family had grown accustomed to her ways, but this man was practically a stranger.

He mumbled something about having bought the necklace a while ago. He had carried it in his saddlebags for a long time.

Jenny pressed her hands to her hot cheeks and backed away. "It—it's very nice," she said lamely.

"It is," Ugly Woman answered. "This turquoise is very old and will keep its blue color. It is not like the soft stones that drink in grease and moisture, which causes them to become green." Her lips curved softly in an affectionate smile as she spoke. "Your necklace will be a thing to take pride in forever, as will mine."

Jenny stared at the pendant that swung between Ugly Woman's breasts. It was, in every way, an exact replica of her own. The children crowded around her, clamoring to show their gifts: bracelets for the girls; a beaded headband for Ee'yah. Jenny tried to be properly appreciative of them all, until she managed to get away.

"I only returned for some more squash seed," she explained hastily.

Then, taking a small bag, she hurriedly left the dwelling. It was hotter than ever, one of those still, humid days before a summer storm. Jenny reached the haven of her garden and burst into tears.

She had made an absolute fool of herself, making much of a small gift, taking it as a compliment for herself. Yet Daniel had brought them all presents. It was his way of saying that he thought as much of each of them.

Yet he had given Ugly Woman her present first. And then the children. He might not have even intended the necklace for her; he had presented it rather reluctantly. Maybe he had purchased it for some other woman.

Jenny sat down at the edge of her garden in the heat of the blazing sun, folded her arms around her knees, and sobbed her heart out. The worst part of it all was that she didn't even know why.

44

By early evening, when Jenny still had not returned, Ugly Woman began to worry. The girl had not been her usual cheerful self of lately, she told Daniel. Ever since the episode of Judkins, Jenny had been silent, shutting herself away from the rest of them.

Jenny's share of the special treat Ugly Woman had prepared for the evening meal, Navajo fry bread, was ruined. It had been sitting on the low wall for over half an hour, waiting for Jenny's return. Now it was cold and sodden.

Daniel offered to go and find her.

It was a stupid thing to do, he thought morosely as he walked toward Jenny's garden. It was surely not a night for any man to be with a girl as pretty as Jenny. The moon was already in the sky—a full moon that turned the grass to silver and touched the whole world with a kind of haunting magic. He breathed in the scent of cedar and blooming sage, of the purple-berried juniper, and lifted his head to see the stars; too many of them to count. Most of the constellations were the subjects of Indian legends, which he believed, yet did not believe.

He wondered how Jen-nee saw them, then was angry at himself for even caring.

He saw the small figure hunched at the edge of her garden and picked up his pace, alarmed. Maybe something was wrong. Maybe she had been bitten by a snake or had become overheated.

"Jen-nee?"

She lifted her swollen eyes to his, and he saw that she had been crying.

"Jen-nee, what is it? What is wrong?"

"I don't know," she said forlornly, scrubbing at her eyes. "I can't seem to stop."

Daniel lifted her to her feet and put his arms around her, intending only to comfort her as he would a child. He held the small, tearstained face close to his heart, a heart that was pounding wildly out of control. He was panicked at the thought that something had hurt her, and he wanted to make it right.

"Don't," he said, the words bursting forth, not of his own volition. "Jen-nee, sweetheart, my little love—don't cry!"

Jenny stepped back, looking up at him with amazement that slowly turned to an expression of happiness; a look of innocence and trust that broke his heart.

Oh, hell, he thought savagely. *Now I've done it!* He couldn't call back the words he had just spoken, and he hadn't dreamed that his feelings for the girl would be reciprocated. He had to get out of this some way.

"Jen-nee," he said unsteadily. "I am sorry."

The light went out of her eyes, and she surveyed him for a moment, as impassive as any Indian. "Would you mind telling me why?"

"I—I only came to say good-bye," Daniel said,

stammering. "I am leaving tonight. I cannot go back to Santa Fe, not now. I suppose I will head for Mexico."

"Because of me?" Jenny asked, her great eyes fixed on his face, their depths reflecting the silver of the moon like the eyes of a cat.

"No—yes. Well, not exactly." He took her hands in his. "Jen-nee, you've got to understand. I am a deserter from the army. And I have killed a man. A white man. It does not matter that I tried to save you. I shot him in the back and there were no witnesses."

"I will tell them."

Daniel shook his head. "You did not see me shoot him. You are a woman of—of uncertain reputation, and they will not believe you. They will say I did it because of my Indian blood. The fact that Judkins is a murderer will not count. If he is found, I will go to trial and I will hang."

Jenny was disturbed by his description of her as a woman of uncertain reputation. She was about to question him, but his last statement, that he would go to trial and would hang, made her heart skip a beat. She shivered, her face white and frozen in the moonlight. "Then it *is* my fault! Daniel, take me with you!"

"No, Jen-nee! There are other things to think of." His copper complexion was suddenly burnished with red.

"Please understand, Jenny." Daniel's voice faltered. "I can only marry a woman who is ... pure—"

Jenny's mouth fell open as she stared at him. "What? You think you are too good for me?" Her anger rose. "What the—what the devil makes you think—"

"I saw you with Sam Whitman," he said gently. "That night, when you were at the cabin, after the soldiers were there. I came back and saw you through the window with Whitman—"

Jenny finally found her tongue. "You fool," she spluttered. "You pious, self-righteous idiot! You—you great stuffed owl! You window peeper! I wouldn't marry you if you were the last man on earth! As far as I'm concerned, you can go to Mexico! Or for that matter, you can go to hell!"

She began to run, sobbing with anger. And after a few moments hesitation, he followed her. She was running away from the direction of the cliff dwelling and into the woods beyond the garden. Her tiny, moonlit figure was almost out of sight. And Daniel suddenly knew that no matter what she had or hadn't done, he wanted this woman.

He had to find her and tell her so.

"Jen-nee, wait!"

Jenny heard him call, heard his feet pounding after her. She stumbled a little, then increased her speed, determined that he would not catch up to her. If she could only reach the shelter of the trees, she would hide. She could stay out here for several days, raiding the garden at night. Eventually he would have to leave this part of the country.

Probably, she thought angrily, he would be taking Ugly Woman with him. At least the Indian girl wouldn't be one to back-talk or sass him. They should be very happy together.

She had reached the shelter of the trees. She ran a few paces to the right and stopped, holding her breath, until she heard him pass, crashing through the trees like a great bear. She might think the whole thing was funny if she weren't so—so damned mad!

Daniel's footsteps faded out of earshot, and Jenny leaned against a tree, allowing herself the luxury of gasping for breath.

It was then that she noted the odd smell of the place, the sickly sweet odor of decay that brought the taste of nausea into her throat. Something was dead in the area. A deer, perhaps, or a bear, but something large. Jenny put her hand to her mouth, covering her nose, but still the scent was nearly overpowering.

Then she heard Daniel's footsteps as he returned, her name on his lips as he called her repeatedly. Jenny forgot the smell around her as she hastily moved to the other side of the tree, where she would be concealed.

And then she screamed.

For there, lounging against the tree's exposed roots, was the figure of a man, his jaw fallen open in a horridly jovial grin. His eyes were empty sockets that caught the moonlight and gave off a red glow. He looked as Judkins would have, had his face fallen in, but this man wasn't dead, for he was still moving!

With a sense of shock Jenny saw that what she took for movement was actually the activity of fat white grubs writhing in the stomach cavity; of red ants crawling in and out of the open mouth. And at that moment the delicate balance of the obscenity was disturbed, and it half rolled over to face her with its dreadful hollow eyes and awful grin.

Jenny shrank away and, for the first time in her life, began to scream uncontrollably.

45

Figuring that Jenny had somehow doubled back, Daniel was halfway to the garden when he heard her screams. He halted and listened, immediately thinking of snakes. But even a snake-bite wouldn't cause that mindless terror in Jenny's voice. He ran back toward the trees, following the terrible sound.

"Jen-nee," he called. "Jen-nee."

Jenny didn't answer. In her fear she was deaf, blind to everything but the horror before her. At last Daniel crashed through the trees, his eyes taking in the scene. First they went to Jenny, who stood immobile, her head thrown back as she uttered those awful cries.

Then he saw what lay at her feet.

For a moment even he was taken aback at the gruesome sight.

"*Chindi*," he whispered, remembering his Indian ancestry. The spirit of the dead!

Then he saw what it was and returned to his senses. On the ground before Jenny lay what was left of Judkins, his body disinterred by wild animals, half eaten away and crawling with vermin. It was a terrible sight for a woman to see; but other than suffering from shock, she seemed unhurt.

Daniel put his arms around Jenny and led her from the trees, holding her, murmuring soft words to calm her.

"It's all right," he whispered. "It's all right. Come, I'll take you home."

Jenny was glassy-eyed and numb when he returned her to the cliff dwelling. Daniel alerted Ugly Woman, asking her to sit with the girl until he came back. Then he took a shovel and walked toward the woods. This time he intended for Judkins to stay buried.

Grim-faced, Daniel dug a new grave, far deeper than the first. Then he shoveled the body into it and covered it over, noting as he did so that all traces of the bullet that caused the man's death were gone, eaten away by the wild things. At last he smoothed every sign of the burial away, finally setting a small fire atop the mound to destroy any scent of Judkins's body or his own.

Then he left the place and went to the spring where he had watched Jenny at her bath.

Stripping, he waded into the water. It cupped his lithe brown body like a woman's cool hands. He groaned and said Jen-nee's name.

After his bath Daniel left the water and squatted on a rock that still retained the warmth of the day. He was all Indian, now that he had divested himself of white man's clothing. He sat motionless, so still that the frogs took up their chirruping once more, and a green lizard ran along the rock beside him without fear.

This was what he had missed: this time of solitude in the wilderness. His life at the post had consisted of orders and confusion. He had been surrounded by men who thought less of him because of his race. Here in the wild country he felt he could be king of all he surveyed. He felt . . . healed.

After examining Judkins's body Daniel knew he could go back to the post without being tried for murder. But did he want to?

He only wanted to stay here in the wilderness, to be a man in his own right, to make peace with Jenny. He would return to his own.

Daniel raised his face to the moon above. It touched his profile with silver, like the face on a coin. And he sang a song he remembered from his childhood. It was one of the Blessingway rites, used for the installation of tribal officers, for the novice who is singing for the first time, for blessing a new house—

For the departing or returning soldier.

Daniel was returning to his own kind. For many years he had been away. He had lost the goodwill of the Holy People, and now it must be regained. From this time forth he would move from time to time and place to place, as his kinsmen did.

For he knew he had come home.

Leaving the water, Daniel rubbed his body with handfuls of mint that grew around the spring. Then, feeling clean and refreshed, he pulled on his trousers. He carried the uniform jacket over his arm as he returned to the cliff dwelling. Ugly Woman had promised to make him a shirt and fringed vest of the kind his people wore, in exchange for the gift he had brought her.

All the way back to the dwelling the night wind spoke to Daniel. It carried the balmy fragrance of flowers, the sounds of small things in the grass, ruffling through his dark hair with a woman's fingers, touching his lids with a woman's kiss.

It was very late. As he had hoped, Ugly Woman and the children were abed.

Jen-nee was awake.

She was as pale as death but calm now, as he seated himself beside her. He was silent for a long time before he began to speak.

"I am an Indian."

Something told Jenny not to reply but to wait.

"I have tried to fit myself into the white man's mold, but I have failed. I intend to go back to my people and live as they live. If I marry, my wife must join me in that life." Another silence followed, then, when he spoke, there was the sound of agony in his voice.

"I did not know who I was, nor what I was. I made a vow to marry a virgin, because of a god I did not know. And I made it because I was a coward. Jen-nee, do you hear me?"

"Yes," she said faintly.

"Will you forgive me? Go with me as my wife?"

"Yes." It was little more than a whisper.

With a glad cry he gathered her in his arms, holding her, kissing her soft mouth, setting his own afire. Kissing was a custom of the white man, but in that area Daniel would never become completely Indian, nor would he ever think of a woman as less than a miracle.

Daniel touched Jenny's soft cheek, her throat, her shoulders, with wondering fingers. Then, after a time, dizzy with her presence, he forced himself to lay her down. He knew by the way she trembled that she expected something more, but he shook his head.

He would be back. Right now he had many things to do.

When he had gone, Jenny lay in a love-drugged haze, going over everything they had said and done together. Suddenly, startled, she sat upright.

Daniel had not asked if she was, in fact, a virgin. For a moment she was angry again. He had no right to believe such a thing!

Then she giggled. He had seen her with Sam Whitman and thought she must have slept with him. Let him believe it! She wouldn't tell him otherwise until their wedding night! Then he'd feel like such a fool.

Wedding night? Jenny was suddenly disturbed and a little frightened. She knew nothing of the Navajo ways. How would the marriage take place? Would it be a legal ceremony, at least in Indian eyes? Or would it merely be a matter of going to Daniel's bed?

Jenny knew instinctively that it would be nothing like Inga's wedding.

It worried her, but at least, when she slept, it was not to dream of that horror among the trees but of a slender brown man, wide-shouldered and slim-hipped, with eyes that were dark and deep enough to drown in.

The next day Jenny did not see Daniel. When she mentioned his name, it provoked an outburst of giggling from Ugly Woman and the little girls. Apparently, wherever he had gone, he was coming back. It could not be soon enough, however, for Jenny was sick with missing him.

Just before dusk he appeared, tired-looking but smiling. All of them, he said, were to go

with him. There was something he wanted them
to see.

At the edge of the spring, blending into the
scenery, stood a new building: a hogan Daniel
had constructed with his own hands. It wasn't a
permanent structure, he said. But just for tonight, and as many nights thereafter as Jen-nee
wished. He had taken care to observe all the
rituals he could remember as he built it for his
bride. If he had forgotten anything, perhaps the
gods would still smile on him and on his new
wife.

At last Jenny had an inkling of what was going
to happen. She remembered the bower Theron
had built for Inga. Like Theron, Daniel had built
this structure out of love.

46

The hogan was pointed at the top, the doorway facing east, to receive the blessings of the gods. Daniel touched the post to the right of the doorway. It represented thinking and reasoning. The post to the south stood for planning or philosophy; the one to the west represented life; and the northern post stood for confidence. The entire hogan represented the Navajo's religion.

As he worked to build the hogan Daniel had tried to remember the proper formulas, the proper prayers. There was much he had forgotten, much he had never known. He only knew that it was important to find the right location, based on the wind trails, the Ant people's trails, the Lizard People's trails. Everything on earth must occupy certain spaces.

The hogan must look to the rising sun, and the sun must be given entry through its smoke hole at noon. There must be a fire obtained, for this is the heart and life of the hogan.

In the next few hours an ancient ceremony took place. Blessingway rites were performed, in song and prayer. Corn pollen was smeared on

the hogan's ridge pole to dedicate the comple-
tion of the hogan and the start of a new life.

Thus Jenny and Daniel were wed.

After the others had gone back to their dwelling
under the cliff, Daniel gently removed Jenny's
dress. The moonlight shone on her face, deline-
ating her rounded breasts and the curves of her
body. Then he dropped his own clothing to the
grass. Taking Jenny's hand, he led her into the
water, which pooled around their moon-gilded
bodies, black with concentric circles of silver.

It was like a baptism; a baptism that washed
away all traces of civilization, creating two new
pagan creatures with a love that transcended all
the slights, the hurts, the loneliness that either
had ever known, and made them one.

Only the frogs in the reeds around the spring,
and the night birds in the trees above, heard
Jenny's soft voice as she whispered, "My husband," in Daniel's native tongue. And he answered, "My wife."

Then his mouth closed over hers. The stars
above them shimmered as he carried her to land,
then went out in an explosion of silver shards as
they consummated their love.

Later, when Jenny slept, Daniel left the hogan, looking at the star-studded sky for answers.
Jen-nee had proved to be a virgin. She had never
lain with a man before. And once, dizzy with
lovemaking, he was certain that heard her whisper another man's name: Jesse.

Could it be that she still loved Jesse? Daniel
had not told her of Elena's death, just as he had
neglected to tell Jesse that Jen-nee was still here.
At the time he had thought it was for Jesse's
own good.

Had he made a mistake? Would the two people he loved be with each other now, if he had not interfered?

"Daniel?"

It was Jen-nee. She had awakened to find him gone. She joined him, and they stood together, the cool night wind laving their bodies, and pledged their love again. Suddenly he thought, with triumph, that Jen-nee was now his, and they were leaving their other lives behind them.

A night bird called, and he led her gently back to the house he had built with love.

47

At Sweethome, Inga had just stepped out of the house. Honeybee hadn't been feeling well of late; today the child had been cross and demanding. Now she was asleep, and Inga, on a whim, had walked out into the little glade beyond the fields. Here she had spent her honeymoon.

She hadn't been out here for more than a year, not since Theron became so desperately ill. She had forgotten how beautiful it was as she walked ankle-deep in grass and smelled the flowers that blossomed in the meadow.

The summerhouse Theron had built for the two of them was still there. But now the veiling that surrounded their marriage bed was rotting away; the knots of ribbon that fastened the wind bells to the roof had faded into small, colorless tangles.

Inga closed her eyes, summoning a vision of the summerhouse as it had once been, years ago. Theron had brought her here, and there had been a soft bed, a low table set with glasses, and a bottle of Dinah's wine. He had loosened her hair with his one remaining hand, letting it fall like golden rain. Then that hand had gone to the fastenings of her soft blue dress—her wedding dress. The confining garments fell away, and he carried her to a bed where satin sheets covered a mattress filled with sweet grass. And all night they made love, to the tinkling sound of little fairy bells.

Inga shook her head as thoughts of the present intruded on her lovely reverie.

Potter, across the road, had recently spread the word that Theron's Yankee wife had actually murdered him. Inga's brother, Paul, refused to believe the gossip, but still he ducked his head and blushed whenever Inga mentioned Theron's name.

He was embarrassed for her.

She had lived with a man she wasn't married to. It made her life with Theron seem like ... something dirty. Inga had even seen Paul look askance at little Honeybee, perhaps wondering whether Inga had lied—perhaps Honeybee was really the product of an infamous union.

She wondered what Paul would think if he knew of his own mother's affair; that Inga, herself, wasn't the child of Gustav Lindstrom but an unknown French-Indian boy who had worked as a hired hand on the Lindstrom farm. That in reality she was only a half sister to Paul.

Inga sighed then and began the long walk home. She saw someone coming in the distance and increased her pace. Finally she was close enough to recognize Paul's approaching figure. And he was running as though he were desperate. Even at this distance she could see that he was as white as death. Something must be wrong at home.

Inga, too, began to run.

When she reached Paul, he was gasping. "The baby! Sick! Choking! Dinah says hurry."

It was enough. Inga was already running again, leaving Paul behind.

There was a small group of Negroes on the back porch. The men had removed their wide-brimmed straw hats and held them at their sides. They said nothing, just stood there with grave, downcast eyes, as if praying.

Inga flew through their midst and into the kitchen door. Dinah and Zada were working over a small form stretched out on the kitchen table.

On the table were two pies, still bubbling from the oven, and a ham in the process of being sliced.

And little Honeybee.

"Dinah, what is it?"

Dinah didn't answer. Just then the child gave a crowing sound and stopped breathing. Dinah expertly turned her upside down and ran a black finger around the inside of the child's mouth, removing the white mucus that was choking her. Honeybee breathed again, then gave out a thin, wailing cry. Then Dinah said one word tersely.

" 'theria."

Diphtheria! The word that every mother cringed to hear. Dear God! Oh, dear God!

"Let me hold her!"

"Better you stan' back, Miz Inga. She cain't hardly git no air, nohow."

As if to prove Dinah's statement, little Honeybee made a chirruping sound, ending in that terrible, cawing gasp for breath that tore Inga's heart in two.

"Them men waitin' out there," Dinah said gruffly. "You take 'em out some cawfee."

Inga complied. The Negroes took their cups with downcast eyes and thanked her in the soft voices they reserved for funerals and deathbeds. Inga's anger flared. They had given up on Honeybee. They had no right to!

Then she remembered the Negro graveyard, the dozens of tiny wooden slabs with names burned into them, their death dates all the same year—the year of the diphtheria epidemic that Dinah had told her about. Inga realized that these men were remembering it too.

Now the dreaded killer had returned.

Inga left the quiet congregation on the porch and went back into the house. Soon she forgot the men outside; forgot Paul, who had finally arrived and was standing in the doorway, his forehead knotted with worry. His eyes were fixed on the little girl who struggled for breath.

"Can I help?" he asked uncertainly.

Inga looked up and saw the terror in his face. She knew that Paul thought Honeybee was going to die and was now regretting his earlier feelings toward the child he considered a bastard.

"No, Paul," Inga said quietly. "We're doing all we can. Go on to bed."

He didn't leave but stood watching, a scared little boy in the body of a man.

Night was coming on, and there was much to do. Kettles were set to boil, filled with aromatic herbs that permeated the kitchen with choking steam. In the oven a concoction of onions and honey was baking slowly down to a syrup. To this would be added a few drops of turpentine; it would be used as a cough medication.

Old Rufus, one of the workers from the quarters, had shamefacedly presented a jar of his own homemade whiskey. It was a godsend. Dinah rubbed it on Honeybee's small body and tipped an occasional spoonful to the child's pale lips.

Nothing seemed to help.

Inga's throat hurt as she realized that she was trying to breathe for the little girl. And she knew she had come face-to-face with her greatest fear. She would not be able to endure the loss of Theron and Honeybee too.

"It's allus wuss at night," Dinah said.

Inga reached out blindly for the old woman's hand. Her words were somehow comforting. If only they would keep the baby alive until morning . . .

When the big clock struck three, Inga felt her knees give way beneath her. She had never been so exhausted in her life. Dinah shot one look at her white face and said, "You go lay down, Miz Inga. Me an' Zada's doin' all we can."

"I think I just need some fresh air," Inga whispered.

She went to the door. The Negro men were still standing on the porch, as if to keep death from entering the house. Inga realized now how grateful she was for their presence.

Then, a few minutes later, Dinah, who had been a rock to cling to through all of Inga's sorrows, began to cry; great, round tears slid down her plump cheeks and plopped on her ample bosom.

She had done all she could. The little girl was dying. Black Clara, who cooked for the Potters, had once saved her own child with a mixture she had made. But Dinah didn't know what it was.

"I'se gonna go over there an' git some," Dinah said, scrubbing angrily at her tears. "Them folkses is born mean, but they cain't go agin helpin' a sick baby."

"No, Dinah."

Inga put a hand on the old woman's arm. Mr. Potter not only hated Yankees, he hated blacks. Dinah had told her how he mistreated those who worked for him. Once John, Sweethome's black overseer, had crossed the road to look for a stray cow. Potter had shot at him. He had missed, but he swore to kill anyone who trespassed on his property.

"I'll go," Inga said.

"No, I will!" Paul was still standing in the doorway, his fists clenched, his blond hair standing on end like a cock's comb. He had been there through the long night, taut with frustration, wishing that there was something he could do to help. And he had been told of the neighbor's hatred of Northerners.

"I wasn't in the war," he said stoutly. "And I'm a white man. He wouldn't dare touch me!"

Paul's not a man, Inga thought. *He's only a boy. But maybe he's right; we've got to try.*

Inga went to him and stood on tiptoe to kiss his cheek.

"Be careful," she said.

"I will."

Then Paul was gone, and Inga turned her attention once more to the little girl who lay so limply in Dinah's arms. She prayed that Paul would be able to obtain the medication and that he would return quickly.

She held out her arms for Honeybee. "Let me hold her," she pleaded. Dinah looked down at the child, her tears starting again.

"Mought as well," she said dismally. "Ain' gonna make no difference, nohow. Mought as well."

48

Morning came to Sweethome, and a finger of sun probed through the window, touching the little girl's damp curls with a dust of gold. Honeybee had made it through the night.

Paul still had not returned.

John selected several men from those gathered on the porch. Armed with one gun and hoes and shovels, they marched toward Eden. They knew that if one of them harmed a white in any way, it would mean certain death.

But Inga was their friend. She had given them jobs when there were none, saved them and their families from starvation. In addition, they all loved Honeybee. And Paul had worked beside them in the fields.

Their conversation was a low, growling sound as they approached the little bridge.

And there they found him.

Paul was still alive but so badly beaten that he resembled nothing human. Potter had a friend visiting; a man of similar ideas. They were both drunk, and together with Potter's two grown sons, they had proceeded to teach the Yankee boy a lesson. Afterward they had thrown him into the road. And Paul crawled to the middle of the bridge where he collapsed, his blood staining the fine old wood.

The blacks carried him into the house. Inga gave a hurt cry at sight of him. Then she and Dinah turned Honeybee over to the ministrations of Zada. The child slept while the women tended the injured man. Paul's face was a mass of bruises. A long cut crossed his forehead and ran the length of his tanned cheek.

"I'm gonna git my gold-eye needles an' some thread," Dinah said sturdily. "Gotta stitch that boy up!"

Inga held his unconscious face between her hands until Dinah had finished her work. Then two of the men carried him through the house and up the stairs to his room. He had not awakened once, and it was something to be thankful for.

Inga sat down at the table and burst into tears. How long, she wondered, would this harassment go on? Why would their neighbor take his venom out on an innocent boy? Why would he refuse to help a sick baby? Dinah laid a hand on Inga's shoulder, and she realized that she was shaking with anger.

If Theron were alive, Potter wouldn't have darcd!

But Inga could not afford to think about that right now. She needed all her energy to see that Honeybee got well.

That evening, as Inga sat by the child's crib, she was reminded of Dinah's saying, "Things is allus wuss at night. All we got to do is make it through till the mawnin'."

She had said that constantly throughout Theron's illness.

And he had died at midnight.

Inga felt a hand on her arm. "You got to res' awhile, Miz Inga. Zada an' me, we'll keep watch."

As soon as her head hit the pillow, Inga fell into an exhausted sleep. And in her dream Theron was standing before her in his burial clothes. His eyes were sorrowful as he reached to take the child she was clutching from her arms.

"No!" The cry was torn from her throat as she sat upright. She left her bed and hurried back to the kitchen, now turned into a sickroom. Dinah, at Honeybee's side, cast an eye at Inga and one at the clock.

She had been out of the room less than fifteen minutes.

Dinah started to remonstrate with her, then closed her mouth tightly. It was Inga's right to stay with Honeybee, as long as she could keep her senses about her. Nobody knew when Gabriel would blow his trumpet and send his sweet chariot down for this child; this night would give Inga something to remember. She would remember that she had tried.

But neither Dinah nor Zada had slept for thirty-six hours. At last Inga sent them to a pallet Dinah had spread on the floor, and she was left alone with the little one. Honeybee's face was white, her small body pared down to the bone from her struggle for life. Was she breathing?

Caught with sudden terror, Inga put an ear to the baby's chest. Suddenly a noise behind her caused her to whirl around.

Paul stood in the doorway, a bandage covering most of his bruised face, peering anxiously at Inga with one eye.

"Is the baby all right?"

Inga let out a shuddering breath. "Yes," she said. And suddenly she knew that what she had said was true. A glint of sunlight shining through the curtain heralded a new day.

"I just wanted you to know that I gave a good account of myself the other night," he said doggedly. "The other fellows don't look so good, either."

She smiled at her young brother, the bit of braggadocio he displayed only making her love him more.

"I'm sure you did."

"Inga?"

"Yes." She stared at him, noticing that the flesh around the bruises was turning crimson. Paul was blushing. He lowered his head, and when he spoke, his words were halting and hard to come by.

"Inga, I guess I've been acting a little high and mighty, but I haven't meant to be. I just want you to know that even if Honeybee is your child, it makes no difference in the way I feel about her. Sometimes I thought our papa was wrong about a lot of things. I guess I've been wrong too."

"She isn't mine, Paul. But thank you."

Inga went to him and kissed him on the cheek. He turned even redder, then made a move toward the baby's crib. "Can I hold her?"

"Of course."

He picked the child up in arms that were strong, though immature, then turned to face Inga. His voice was strong too, as he ordered her to bed, stating that he would take care of Honeybee.

Inga faltered. Then she smiled. Dinah and Zada were right here in the room if anything went wrong. But she didn't believe it would. After all, it was morning, the sun was shining in, and Paul had undergone a change of heart. This time with Honeybee was important to him; he needed it desperately.

It was Paul's apology to the little girl—and to Inga.

She hesitated for a moment, then smiled and left the room. She knew that she would be able to trust Paul to stand by her side—and Honeybee's—always.

She went to her bed, to sleep and to dream once more. This time, in her dream, Theron was dresed in his work clothes: slim blue trousers of denim cloth; and a faded blue shirt, the collar opened to show his tanned chest. One sleeve was pinned up to cover his missing arm. His black hair was rumpled, his skin golden, just as it had appeared under the sun of an autumn afternoon.

He was smiling at her, and the dream was very real. Inga was so pleased to see Theron, she didn't notice that he held something in his one arm; something that he was trying to give to her.

"Take this, Inga," he whispered. "Take it! It's yours." She looked down at his gift and saw that it was Honeybee. Theron had returned her, alive and well.

The dream shimmered, and Theron disappeared. Inga woke with tears on her cheeks. It was full day. The sun shining through her bedroom window cupped her face like a warm hand. She was now ready for whatever had occurred downstairs during her absence.

Inga went down to a kitchen dancing with refracted light from the crystal prisms she had hung in the windows. Dinah was humming at the stove, singing a hymn of joy over the ham and eggs and the biscuits. Outside, Inga could hear the pump handle going up and down in time to the melody as Zada fetched a pail of water.

And in a chair close to the stove sat Paul, with little Honeybee. The child was thin and white, her soft brown hair dull and lusterless. Her great gray eyes were solemn and quiet, but there was life in them now, a dim curiosity as she studied her Uncle Paul. As Inga came toward her the child lifted her arms.

"Minna."

And then her pale lips curved in a madonnalike smile as Inga gathered her into her arms.

49

The outbreak of diphtheria was confined to one child in the big house. Little Honeybee recuperated from her illness, but she was no longer the vivacious toddler she had once been. She was thin and grave, with great, misty gray eyes and a lingering cough that Inga did not like to hear.

She decided to have the little girl checked out by a doctor in Memphis. It was the first time Inga had left Sweethome since Theron's death. She took Paul and Dinah along, though Paul still bore the marks of his beating; Inga hurt every time she looked at him.

They set out in a small four-place wagon, Inga at the reins. Dinah was full of gloomy forebodings. Lately her worries had focused on her grandson, Boy. Dinah was certain that the skinny teenager wouldn't survive her absence.

In spite of Dinah's doomsaying, it turned out to be a marvelous journey. Paul and Dinah dropped Inga and the little one off at the doctor's office, then went to purchase some staples for Sweethome.

When they stopped back to pick up Inga and

the baby, Inga was as white as a sheet. Dinah leaned down to take the sleeping child from her arms, her brows drawn together in a frown.

"What's the mattah, Miz Inga? The doc fin' somethin' wrong?"

Inga shook her head and tried to smile. "Not really. He only said that she had been seriously ill and that the climate here is a little too damp for her. He suggested that I take her and go West."

"That's a dumb-fool idee," Dinah exploded. "Look what happen when he sont that Washburn woman West. She went an' died on her fambly an' lef' that poor Massa Ed with a bunch of little ones to raise by hisse'f."

"Yes," Inga admitted, "'but if it would help—"

"Naw-suh-ree-bob!" Dinah said firmly. "Onliest thing that'll help is time. But jes' in case, I'll have John set some buckets of lime aroun'. That'll draw off the damp."

Dinah sounded so sure of what she was saying that Inga forgot her concerns. After all, Dr. Hollingsworth hadn't said she *had* to take Honeybee to a different area. It had been only a suggestion.

She climbed into the wagon, and they started home, each talking of what they had learned while they were in Memphis. Dr. Hollingsworth had told Inga that there was a minor epidemic of diphtheria. He had lost six patients within a week. Inga had been a very lucky woman, with Honeybee pulling through as she did.

Paul was silent most of the way back. Finally Inga looked at him with concern.

"You haven't said anything, Paul. Did you enjoy your visit?"

Paul grimaced. "Not much. Inga, these people here really hate us, don't they?"

Inga's spirits had begun to brighten, and now they faded again. "Yes," she said, "I guess they do. What happened, Paul?"

"Nothing much."

Then he told her about his day. A clerk in one store had ignored him, leaving Paul standing while he waited on a fellow in a ragged Confederate uniform who came in after Paul. On the cobbled streets near the wharf he had been shouldered aside by bearded men, some of them maimed, yet hoping to start a fight with a fellow they regarded as an outsider, a Yankee.

"They certainly have a lot of guts," Paul admitted gloomily.

Recalling how Theron had felt when he first came home, Inga repeated her earlier words. "Yes, I guess they do."

It was evening when they approached Sweethome some days later. It had been a slow journey with frequent stops because of the ailing child. Dinah was fast asleep, sitting upright on the bench that served as a seat in the wagon. Paul held the baby, and once again Inga was at the reins.

She sighed with relief as they approached the opening among the trees that led to the small, arched bridge that spanned the creek. Sweethome lay just beyond. It was good to be back.

Then suddenly the horses reared.

As Inga fought them she caught sight of the men who had frightened them. Two riders had appeared out of the brush—one from each side of the road—to catch at their bridles as they shied away. When the wagon was finally brought to a dead halt, she stared at the intruders, finally recognizing them.

They were the two grown sons of Potter—her neighbor, her enemy!

Inga's mouth went dry.

"What do you want?" she asked. "Why have you stopped us? If there is some emergency—"

"No emergency, lady," the older boy said insolently, looking past Inga at Paul. "Just figgered we had us some unfinished business." He put a hand to a cheek that was swollen with a great, purpling bruise and managed a mocking smile that revealed several missing teeth.

Inga surveyed him helplessly, then turned toward his brother. He was in even worse shape, with one eye swollen shut and a bandaged ear. Paul had indeed given a good accounting of himself.

"Git down!" the older boy snarled at Paul. "By damn, we-all are goin' to l'arn you a lesson! Not fer what you done to us. You didn't hurt us none. But fer what you done to Pa, bustin' his nose thataway! C'mon, you yella-bellied Yankee son of a bitch! We gonna whip yer goddamn tail, then we gonna burn y'all out! Git down offa that wagon! Or," he said, sneering, "are you goin' t'hide behind yer sis's petticoats?"

Paul, his face white and his jaw set, handed the baby to Dinah. Then he half stood, preparing to climb down from the wagon. At that moment Inga came to life. Yanking the whip from its stock, she lashed first one Potter boy across the face, then the other. She finally laid the stinging lash across the backs of her startled horses, pulling hard to the right, praying that no one would be thrown from the wagon and that they wouldn't miss the bridge and go into the water.

They all stayed with the wagon. Honeybee was clamped so tightly in Dinah's arms that she screamed in terror, but she was secure. Paul, taken by surprise, almost lost his footing and had to hold on for dear life. The careening wagon caromed off the side of the bridge, losing a wheel, but the horses came to a stop at the end of the drive.

Inga put her head down to her knees, feeling faint. But only for a minute. Then she raised it again.

"Dinah, take Honeybee into the house. Paul, call all the men together. I must speak to them."

"I could have handled it, Inga," Paul said. "You should have let me—"

"Paul!" There was a dangerous note in her voice, and he backed away, suddenly more afraid of this new woman his sister had become than of the men who had beaten him once—and who would have done so again.

Paul ran for the old slave quarters, now converted into neat homes for a free people. Inga hurried into the house and took down a rifle that had hung, loaded and ready, above the kitchen door since the night of Weldon's wife's murder—the night Theron died.

Armed, Inga went out again, watching and waiting for the sound of horses' hooves on the little bridge. It was a sound that never came. Potter's sons were not brave ex-Confederates, such as Theron had been. Like Paul, they had been too young for the war. But unlike Paul, they were cowards—the kind that struck in the night.

And when they came, she would be ready.

Inga's men came running from their homes, carrying hoes, axes, anything they could grab that resembled a weapon. Though their eyes were filled with fear, they were prepared to defend this white woman who had given them jobs, a roof over their heads, and a share in the profits of Sweethome.

Inga explained what had happened and told of her fears that Sweethome would be burned out, destroying all their livelihoods. The blacks agreed with her that henceforth the plantation would be an armed camp, with men taking turns standing guard.

Leaving Paul to assign the guards, Inga went into the house. She found that Dinah had already put Honeybee to bed. The Negro woman was preparing supper, her face like a thundercloud as she sliced ham for sandwiches and stacked it on platters, along with pickles from the crock in the cellar and thick slices of crusty bread.

"This stuff an' a pitcher of milk. Thass all anybody's gonna git," she said huffily. "Meetin' up with them Potters done tuk all th' starch outta me! Ain' whompin' up nothin' fancy t'night."

She shook a warning finger at Inga.

"Mark my word, Miz Inga," she said grimly. "Some of our folkses here at Sweethome is gonna git hurted or kilt. And it ain' their fault."

"Is it mine?" Inga asked gently.

"No, ma'am. But, Lawd, I wish you was born here, like Massa Theron. Then mebbe them Potters would leave us alone."

Dinah frowned and changed the subject to something that was closer to her heart. "By th'

way, I been wonderin' where Boy's at. Ain' seen
him sence we got home, an' nobuddy seems tuh
know."

That night Boy was shot to death on the road.
Since Dinah, with her rigid sense of discipline,
was away, he had gone to visit one of his friends
and stayed over a couple of days to go fishing.

He had known nothing of the danger of riding
alone; nothing of the recent turn of events.

They fou..d Boy at dawn. He was lying on his
back, the Sunday-go-to-meeting clothing he had
been so proud of fluttering in the morning breeze.
Pinned to his breast was a placard, crudely
printed in a masculine hand.

It read, YANKEES, GO HOME.

50

The next day Inga stood once more near Theron's grave. A yawning hole awaited the interment of Boy's body. Due to the hot, humid weather, the funeral had to be conducted in haste. John had worked all night to finish the coffin. "Might as well start in on another'n, way things is goin'," he predicted sadly.

Inga flinched at his words.

Dinah, beside her, looked old and oddly shrunken. Inga remembered what she had said long ago, when Caleb died: "Everything goin' be awright, missie. Caleb goin' be fine. Goin' set on the Lawd's right hand an' sing with the angels."

Where had Dinah's faith gone? Why was it different with Boy?

As if she read Inga's thoughts, Dinah looked at her levelly. "Boy never had no chance to be growed up," she said. "He never had no wife, no kids, no mammy, 'cept me. An' he got tore away from livin' afore he was done."

"Ah, Dinah!"

Inga's cry of agony was silenced by Dinah's upraised hand. John had moved forward with his bible, to speak the last words over Boy's remains.

"The Lord giveth and the Lord taketh away. . . ."

No, Inga thought, the Lord giveth and the *war* taketh away. The war took Boy just as surely as it took Theron and Weldon's wife! The *damned* South!

John had closed his book, and now Dinah stepped forward with dignity to toss in her handful of earth. Boy's funeral service was over, and Inga had hardly heard a word of it. She had been standing here enveloped in anger, hating the war and all it stood for—ugly emotions for a funeral.

Now she had to get back to the house. Paul and an elderly crippled Negro, too lame to walk to the cemetery, were standing guard. They mustn't be left alone too long; it wasn't safe.

Inga turned to look for Dinah. She was holding onto Zada's arm and didn't seem to need Inga's help. Feeling strangely bereft, Inga hurried back to Sweethome.

That night she couldn't sleep. She kept seeing Boy, as he had been on that first day when he, Dinah, and Caleb had come back to Sweethome; he had been such a skinny little lad, with big, big eyes and a mischievous smile. And she kept seeing Dinah, an old and shrunken Dinah, staring at her with accusation in her face, as if somehow it was Inga's fault that Boy had died.

Wasn't it?

If she had not been here, Boy's life would not have been in danger.

And she had no right to be here.

She had had no right to move onto a burned-out plantation, appropriating it without thought of who it might belong to. She had no right to marry the owner of that plantation, no right to inherit it. She had learned from Paul that she was not free to wed, then or now. Yet she was asking her loyal black friends to protect Sweethome for her. Their lives would continue to be in jeopardy if they did so.

She thought of John's words; John, who had worked throughout the night, building Boy's coffin: "Might as well start in on another'n, way things is goin'." She put her hands to her ears to shut those words out, but she heard them over and over again.

Who would be next?

Oh, dear God! If only she could stop this shivering!

When she finally slept, she dreamed of Jenny.

The next day Dinah was back at work in the kitchen, refusing Inga's suggestion that she rest for a while. Work was good, the old woman told her curtly. And in every way possible, without coming straight out and saying so, Dinah indicated that she preferred to be alone.

Inga deferred to her wishes. Paul was not available to talk to, since he had been taking a night shift at guard. Now he was in his room, asleep. Inga played with Honeybee until it was time for the baby's nap, then sat quietly in Theron's den, trying not to think. It hurt too much.

When Dinah announced, rather formally, that guests had arrived, Inga went downstairs to find Ed Washburn. Her face lit up at sight of him.

She liked Ed. If he had been their neighbor instead of Potter, they would have had no problems. She greeted him warmly. Then he grinned a little sheepishly as he introduced the woman who was with him.

She was his new wife, Celia, a girl he had

gone to school with. She had been widowed last year, he said expansively. He had stepped in to console her, and she had hooked him, fair and square. They both laughed and exchanged loving glances. Then Celia came forward and embraced Inga.

"Y'all are jus' as pretty as Ed tole me," Celia said enthusiastically. "And this place is jus' plain scrumptious! It's 'xactly the kine of home we been lookin' for, what with Ed's kids an' all."

Inga liked the woman instinctively, just as she liked Ed. He was a lucky man, she thought. And it was a shame he had been unable to find a place like Sweethome. It would be a wonderful place to raise his children. He and his wife had both been born in the South. Clearly they belonged here, and Inga now knew she did not.

"Sweethome is for sale," Inga said. Then her jaw dropped in amazement at her own words.

Washburn's jaw dropped too. "Goddamn," he said, then, shooting a glance at Celia, he mumbled an apology. "Reckon you took me by surprise. Didn't figger you'd ever let this place go. And, to tell the truth, I ain't sure I can afford it."

For a moment Inga was shattered. Then she recovered her composure. She realized that her impulsive decision was the answer to all her problems. As much as she loved Sweethome, Theron was dead. She could not bring him back to life, and there was nothing for her here anymore. The news Paul had brought, that Olaf still lived, had cast a shadow on her love that would never be erased while Olaf was alive.

She drew a deep breath and tried to smile. "I don't think you can afford not to buy it," she said quietly. "Let's step into my husband's ... Theron's study and talk about it, shall we?"

As Inga led the way to the study she was surprised that she could remain upright. There was a terrible gnawing feeling in her middle, as if she were bleeding to death; as if something vital had been torn away.

But for now she had to think clearly. Part of the sale must hinge on the Negro employees being kept on, sharing in the profits as they had done since she came. With Southerners occupying Sweethome, at least they would be safe. There would be no more senseless killing, and one day the hatred between North and South would mellow and fade.

And Inga knew where she was going. The dream last night had told her.

They would go to Jenny. She and Honeybee and Paul; to Jenny, who would welcome them. Home, she realized, was not a place, it was a person. And Jenny was more than a daughter. She was Inga's best and only friend.

51

Several days later Inga stood beside Theron's grave. As far as she knew, it was for the last time. Ed Washburn had only been able to purchase a half interest in Sweethome. The rest was left in Inga's name, as a silent partner. In addition, Inga would receive enough from the profits each year to keep her comfortably for the rest of her life.

It was money that she did not deserve, she thought numbly. But Theron had left no other heirs. She had accepted it for the sake of Honeybee and Paul.

She knelt beside Theron's grave, her wide-brimmed hat casting lacy shadows across her face. For this final visit she had donned his favorite gown: a soft batiste strewn with faded yellow roses and fastened at the waist with yellow ribbon.

"I don't want to leave you," she whispered, "but I have to. Please understand."

But would he if he could?

Would he understand how she could desert this plantation he had fought for?

Or would he think she was selling out, giving

up, just letting go of Sweethome, the place he had always loved more than his life.

No, Inga thought. No, I can't do this!

She stood, choking on a sob, and looked around her. The meadow grass reached to her ankles, and bees droned among the wild roses on the fence behind the little graveyard. Cabbage moths flitted here and there, and a gigantic monarch butterfly poised itself on a dandelion's cushion of gold, opening and closing its wings.

Oh, Theron, I can't! Help me! she screamed inwardly.

As she twisted her head from side to side in an agony of pain, a sudden explosion of white light nearly blinded her. She caught her breath.

"Theron?"

Then she saw the light for what it was, the sun reflecting off an old tin that had been placed against one of the graves. She walked over to it and found that it had been freshly filled with flowers from Sweethome.

On the wooden cross that stood above it was burned a name: Boy.

And Inga knew what she had to do.

Eyes filled with tears, she knelt once more at Theron's graveside. Then, with a gentle hand, she smoothed the grass over the mound; the gesture of a mother covering her child. For that was what Theron had become toward the end. He had been a child when he came home from the war. Then he had been her lover. And finally a child once more.

The child in Theron might resent her leaving but not the man she remembered now, the man she loved.

Inga returned to the house, her hat hanging at

her side, its ribbon dragging on the ground. Ed Washburn came to meet her.

"I figger this must be mighty hard," he said huskily. "Mighty hard. When I had to leave Lizbet there, buried in the desert, I wished I was dead, too, so they'd lay me down beside her. Lizbet's lost out there, buried alongside the trail. Can't even find her grave. But there were the children, and now there's Celia . . ."

"Who is a very nice woman," Inga finished bravely. "I know you'll be happy here."

"I reckon what I'm tryin' to say is that Theron was a friend of mine. I'll tend his grave, same as I would Lizbet's. I just wanted you to know that. And if you're ever back this way, you'll be welcome to move right in. It's a big place. The kids even found a little summerhouse off in the woods back of the fields. Makes a fine place for them to play."

"Yes," Inga said in a faint voice. "Yes, it will. Now, if you'll excuse me, I must finish packing."

"Sure thing." Ed Washburn stood back. He knew he had sounded too hearty, too effusive, but he hadn't been able to help himself. Paul had told him of the happenings in the neighborhood, and it had made him very angry to think of this poor little woman being driven away.

Ed, too, had been a member of the Confederate army. He'd taken his lumps and hadn't shed any tears. Potter wouldn't dare try to bully one of his own kind. But Ed and Celia had already made a vow that there would be no friendship between the two houses.

Brotherhood be damned!

Inga packed for herself and Honeybee. Celia offered to help, but Inga shook her head. They would need only a few things on the riverboat they would take from Memphis, then they would buy heavier, coarser clothing when they joined the wagon train at Jefferson, Missouri.

Inga laid her gowns out on the bed. Most of them were too bright for a woman in mourning. And all of them held too many memories. That dress she had worn when she and Theron went to Shiloh. That one had been her wedding gown. And the soft batiste with the faded ribbons—it had been Theron's favorite.

"I'm leaving these things," she told Celia. "Perhaps you can use them."

Celia was pleased. She fingered the exquisite materials with admiration. She would never fit into one of them in a million years. But she would make the gowns over for Ed's girls. They would be tickled pink.

Finally everything was done. Paul had carried the bags down to the wagon. And still Inga hesitated, the baby in her arms. Though she hadn't said it aloud, she knew what she was waiting for.

She was waiting for Dinah!

She could not believe that all their years together, the work of rebuilding Sweethome, the grief they had shared, the fears meant nothing. Dinah had kept out of Inga's way, lately, but at least she could have come out to say good-bye.

Finally she could wait no longer. She took a last look at the room she had shared with Theron; the room where she had known both her greatest happiness and her greatest sorrow.

And then she went downstairs.

Celia and Ed were waiting to kiss her and little Honeybee good-bye. When Inga stepped out on the porch, she stopped short.

John and the rest of the hands were mounted. They surrounded the wagon, an escort to carry the people they loved beyond the Potters' reach. Their wives were standing beside the house, waiting to say good-bye. Inga moved along the line, reaching out and hugging each one, holding Honeybee out for them to squeeze. "Zada, Delta, Junie, Dahlia . . ."

She named them one by one as she said farewell.

But there was no Dinah.

Finally she turned to take her place on the wagon seat. And again she paused in shock. For there, sitting high and proud, with a face like a thundercloud, sat Dinah, dressed in her Sunday clothes with a fresh white apron to cover them, and a bandanna tied around her head.

"Y'all ain' goin' off an' leavin' me behind," she said, sniffling. "Give me mah chile!"

Inga handed Honeybee over, and the old woman squinched her eyes against threatening tears. Then the two women were rocking in each other's arms with Honeybee crushed between them. The child finally whimpered, and Dinah drew away.

"Jus' look what you went an' done," she grumbled. "Good thing I 'cided to come along. No tellin' what would happen to this baby."

"You know we're going a long, long way from here," Inga said softly. "To a place that is very different from what you're used to. We may never come back."

Dinah looked at the plantation that had always been her true home. On these lands she had buried those she loved. Now she faced an unknown future. She took a deep breath.

"Don' make me no never mind," she said, "I got nobuddy here."

And she didn't tell Inga that she had had a dream last night. A dream in which Massa Theron told her what to do. For Dinah already knew, herself, that leaving Sweethome was the right decision.

52

Several weeks after Ed Washburn, his new wife, and three children had moved into Sweet-home, they had a visitor. Washburn's jaw dropped in surprise. At first he thought it was Inga, that she had changed her mind and decided to take him up on his offer. But she looked . . . different somehow. He blinked in the morning light, seeing that it wasn't Inga, after all, but someone who closely resembled her. This woman was dressed richly but not in the manner of a lady.

Celia, entering the room after he opened the door, was equally stunned.

But they were no more surprised than was Kirsten. She had expected Inga or Dinah to answer the door and had decided to play the part of prodigal daughter.

"Who are you?" Kirsten asked coldly when she found her tongue. "And where's my mother! Where's Jenny? Theron?"

Ed's look of puzzlement lightened. "You're Kirsten, aren't you? I'm Ed Washburn, and this is my wife, Celia. We've never met, but Theron was a great friend of mine, God rest his soul. Just as your mother and sister were," he added hastily. "Won't you come in?"

Kirsten looked around the great front room. The carpet Theron had brought in to cover the parquet floors was littered with toys. And some of the furnishings had been changed. The room did not reflect Inga's style at all.

Suddenly she realized that the man had spoken of the members of her family in the past tense. She went white.

"What is going on here?" she asked, her voice strident with fear. "And what can you possibly mean, inviting me into my own house!" She brushed past Ed Washburn's rather rotund little figure.

"Mama? Where are you? It's me, Kirsten! I'm home! Dinah? Jenny?"

Celia gave her husband a stricken look and went after the girl, putting her arms around her to restrain her. Kirsten's eyes still darted from side to side in shocked disbelief.

This was not her mother's house!

Finally the sense of what the woman was saying penetrated to Kirsten's brain. Theron was dead. Inga's brother, Paul, had come to visit her. Driven off by unfriendly neighbors, Inga had sold out to them. Inga, the baby, Paul, and Dinah had all gone to New Mexico to join Jenny.

Kirsten was dazed, trying to absorb all their information at once. Celia led her to a chair. For the first time she noticed Kirsten's bandaged hand.

"Oh, my dear," she said in a shocked voice. "How did this happen?"

"It was the storm," Kirsten said vaguely. "A window broke." Celia peered at the pupils of her eyes. The girl appeared to be at the verge of collapse.

"You need a nice hot cup of tea," she said in a brisk voice. "Ed, stable her horse, put her buggy away, then bring in her things while I fix it." She bustled into the kitchen.

Kirsten sank back in the chair in disbelief. Theron was dead! The news shook her to the core, affecting her more than one would think.

She thought back to the time when she had wished to win him for herself and was jealous of his attraction to her mother. Twisting her mouth wryly, Kirsten had to acknowledge that all the way here she had considered renewing her efforts in that direction again, despite the fact that Theron and Inga had married.

It wouldn't have worked, anyway. Kirsten hadn't had any idea that Theron and Inga might have a baby. Theron would have been too damned self-righteous, under those circumstances, to have an affair.

Theron was dead. Inga, Paul, Dinah, and the baby had gone to Jenny in New Mexico.

That would mean that Jenny had married Jesse. Kirsten's lip curled. She was probably all settled in, becoming a tidy little housewife if she knew Jenny.

And Paul?

Kirsten remembered the thin fourteen-year-old in Minnesota who had helped support his family by trapping. It was he who aided her in escaping from her grandfather's farm after the old man discovered that she was pregnant.

What had Paul told Inga about the time Kirsten had spent there? Had he told her that her husband was not dead, after all? Did that have anything to do with Theron's death?

And why would Dinah ever leave Sweethome?

"Here is your tea," Celia said. "I stirred a little honey into it, to settle your nerves."

Kirsten wanted to tell her that some brandy would have helped more, but she smiled wanly and thanked her hostess, already calculating how she might remain here a short time while she pulled her wits together. She was short of money, and she hadn't even admitted to herself how much she had counted on seeing the members of her family.

Kirsten had stayed in the church until the storm was over. Then she went directly to the docks, taking passage on a riverboat that was going to Memphis.

She had remained hidden in her cabin until sailing time, venturing out only before daylight or after dark. Even now her blood ran cold as she remembered meeting a man who was sure he knew her.

No, she had never lived in New Orleans. She had just visited there. Now she was going home to Min-ne-so-ta. She used the thick Swedish accent she had all but forgotten. Though the man appeared perplexed, he believed her.

She slipped off the boat at Memphis, rented a buggy, and came to Sweethome.

And it was home no longer.

Kirsten set her cup down carefully and put her hands over her eyes. It didn't take much pretending, and soon some very real tears leaked through her fingers. Celia was devastated.

Which was Kirsten's old bedroom? Well, luckily it was not in use at this moment. But the bed was freshly made up, since they had washed all the linens this week. Kirsten was to go right up. She would send a maid with hot water so that she might freshen up after her journey. Then Kirsten must rest until lunchtime.

Kirsten went upstairs, smiling at how easily the Washburns had been taken in. Then she saw her room, and the smile turned into a frown.

She had once thought it beautiful, but it was a disappointment after the glamorous room she had recently shared with Nick. And it most definitely wasn't a match for Slim Morley's sumptuous quarters. She had not remembered the room as being so small, with its soft blue walls, its carpet of a darker shade. There was no canopy over the bed—she had forgotten that too.

Kirsten shuddered. The room looked so sticky-sweet, so virginal, it gave her claustrophobia.

She did remember one thing, however. From her window she had a view of Eden, across the road. And Matthew Weldon, if he stepped out onto his upper gallery at night, also had a view.

She recalled the way she had drawn the blue velvet draperies to make a frame for herself and had sat by the window in her nightgown, her neckline opened to show a bit of pearly flesh, hoping he would see.

And he certainly had!

Perhaps she would try that tonight! She would show Matthew what he had missed, marrying his stupid Martha! The thought of coming home from Minnesota, certain that Matthew would want her and the baby, still burned in her memory.

"Damn," Kirsten whispered. "Oh, damn!"

Then she laughed a little bitterly, wondering why she even cared.

Of course, Matthew Weldon had been the first man she ever slept with, and she was bound to think of him romantically. But since those days, she had had some expert lovers who knew how to please a woman. Maybe Matthew would turn out to be like this room she had once recalled with such fondness: a bit crude, not as charming as she remembered, a bit clumsy.

Maybe, just maybe, she would find out before she left this place for good.

Kirsten lay down on the blue bed and slept the sleep of exhaustion. And she dreamed. She dreamed of Lydia, coming at her with a knife and falling backward with a look of shocked surprise; of Pete, painfully getting to his feet and coming toward her, his scarecrow body aflame.

"No," she screamed, cowering away from him. "No!"

Then Pete's face became Theron's. He looked at her with dead eyes and shook his head, echoing her words.

"*No.*"

When Kirsten woke, her face was white, blue shadows beneath her eyes. She looked at herself in the mirror, then dampened a length of blue ribbon to smudge them a bit more. It wouldn't hurt to enhance the color a little, and maybe she could gain a few more days to figure out the best thing to do. Somehow she had to get hold of some money. The next step was to choose a destination. And it had to be done before anybody thought of looking for her here.

Finally, pasting a brave little smile on her face, Kirsten went downstairs to Celia's motherly arms.

53

Ed Washburn was a happy man, not much given to worry or meditation. He had spent his life believing that one should ignore what couldn't be helped and tend to the things that could.

But lately he had been unable to sleep.

On this particular night, he rose at midnight and strapped on his pistol through force of habit. Going outside, he walked to the middle of the arched bridge, not knowing that this was Inga St. Germain's special worry spot. Folding his arms, he leaned on the railing and stared down into the murky water as he wondered what he could do about that girl.

Celia, of course, adored her. But Celia had a maternal streak a mile wide. All Kirsten had to do was look at her with those sad blue eyes and Celia melted like butter. Washburn tried to talk to his wife about Kirsten, but all he got in return was, "You're imagining things, Ed! Tell me one thing that's wrong with her!"

He had tried a light approach. "Well, for one thing, she's been here for three weeks! And she doesn't show any sign of leaving."

"Her mother still owns half of Sweethome," Celia pointed out.

"I know." Ed sighed. "But we made the deal with Inga, not with Kirsten. I guess my main reason is that I don't think she's good for our girls."

"Ed Washburn! I'll admit that sometimes her language slips, but so does yours! And her clothes are a little different, but after all, she's from New Orleans. They'd have the latest styles. And the poor child's been out there without her mother . . ."

"Did you ever stop to think that there might be a reason? That maybe they didn't get along?"

That brought on such an explosion that Celia had shared a room with Ed's oldest daughter for the last two days. Ed had also been called cruel, heartless, and selfish, three names that he had never thought applied to his behavior in any way.

Could he possibly be wrong?

He was chewing on a stem of grass, and now he shifted it in his mouth as he thought of Kirsten's actions since her arrival. She had gone to visit the graveyard the second day and had seemed slightly grieved over Theron's tomb, though not at all over Boy's. Then, after hearing that Matthew Weldon's wife had died and that Matthew, himself, had gone back East, Kirsten broke down and cried like a baby.

Why?

You're just a suspicious old fool, Washburn told himself. *A suspicious old fool!*

But the Negro workers didn't like her, either. And they had to have a reason.

Washburn had one reason he wouldn't even admit to himself; surely he must be wrong. A little over a week ago, somehow he had gotten the

notion that Kirsten was making a play for *him*!
A short, plump man, Washburn had no illusions
about his own charms. While Lizbet was alive,
he was faithful to her. Now he was faithful to
Celia, and he had made that plain to Kirsten.
He couldn't figure what the devil had gotten
into the girl.

One thing for sure: It would soon be too late
in the year to start for Santa Fe. If that was
what Kirsten had in mind.

Washburn suddenly noticed a flickering light
coming from across the way. Somebody had come
out of the upper gallery at Eden and was waving a lantern, as if signaling. Washburn turned
automatically toward Sweethome and stared at
its upstairs windows. He saw an answering light.

What the hell!

It was from a room at the front—the room
where Celia had put the girl!

Now the light had gone out. And the one across
the road moved from the upper gallery. He saw
it reappear on the lower floor, then it appeared
at the front of the house.

Whoever carried it was coming this way!

Instinctively he moved backward and toward
one side, behind a tulip tree that grew by the
bridge. He heard a thrashing in the brush that
lined the road and removed his pistol from its
holster.

Then he heard a door slam and the light sound
of running feet behind him. Someone was coming from Sweethome. It was Kirsten! Kirsten in
a gown so sheer, it was almost nonexistent. It
revealed every curve of her body in a shameless
manner.

And this was the girl he had taken into his
house! With his children!

He heard Kirsten's dancing footsteps and a man's heavy boots. They met in the middle of the bridge. Ed stepped out from the shadow of the tulip tree. He saw the girl throw her arms around the man's neck with a little breathless cry.

"Benjie! You did come! I didn't think you would! Did you bring the money?"

Washburn was dumbstruck. What he had taken to be a man was Benjie, the older Potter boy. But he was still much younger than Kirsten.

Benjie set his lantern down and reached into his pocket indecisively. Then he withdrew his hand and shook his head.

"You gotta gimme what you promised me first. I went to a helluva lot of trouble to get that money. Stole it off of Pa. He'll beat hell outta me if he finds it out."

"Oh, Benjie! You're so brave! I do love you! And I'll do whatever you want."

Kirsten stood on tiptoe, kissing the hulking boy on the mouth. His hands roved wildly over her body. Ed Washburn was sick to his stomach. He walked quietly to the edge of the bridge, his pistol raised to waist level.

"All right," he said wearily. "That's enough. Potter, go home!" He jerked his head in the direction of his own house, "Kirsten, go to your room and stay there, or by God, I'll lock you in!"

Beneath a mop of strawlike hair, Benjie's brutish, freckled face was as red as fire. Now the boy turned on Ed, his big shoulders hunched forward, fists like hams doubled at his sides as he snarled and backed up at the same time. "I don't have to leave! You can't tell me what to do! I'll tell my pa!"

"You do that," Washburn said calmly, "and I'll have something to tell him. About the money you stole, for instance. And how his boys' hatin' Yankees don't extend to their women folk. Now git!"

Benjie took to his heels.

"Benjie, wait!"

Kirsten's cry followed him, but it didn't stop him. She turned accusing eyes on Ed Washburn. "You—you funny-looking little fat man! See what you've done? There went my stake to get out of this damned place and make something of myself. It's all your fault!"

Washburn had been icily calm until now, but suddenly he was shaking with anger. "That son of a bitch was partly responsible for Mrs. Weldon's death and for Theron's. Along with his dad and his brother, he ran your mother away from Sweethome with their vi'lence and their lies! They killed Boy, sure as shootin'! And now, here's Inga St. Germain's daughter dealin' with trash! I got too much respect for your folks to let you get away with it!"

"It was only for the money," Kirsten said faintly.

"We got a name around here for wimmen that sell their love for money," Washburn said grimly, "and it ain't pretty."

"I didn't know what else to do. I can't stay here."

Washburn thought a minute, then came to a quick decision. He looked at her with steady, angry eyes.

"In the mornin' we'll start for Memphis together," he said. "When we get there, we'll go to my bank and withdraw just enough for your passage by riverboat to Saint Louis. And since it's getting late in the year, I'll give you enough for food and travel by stagecoach along the trail to Santa Fe as well. And by God, it'll be a one-way trip!"

Kirsten opened her mouth to speak, but Washburn held out his hand. "I want something in return, Miss Kirsten. The happenings of this night are to be kept from Celia. My wife is a good woman, and she dunno that there is any another kind. Now you go back to your room, git some decent nightclothes on, and make damn sure you stay in your own bed."

Kirsten tossed her head, but she obeyed. She had done as she planned to do with Matthew Weldon: seated herself before the window in tantalizing poses until she attracted Benjie's attention and roused his interest. There had been an interchange of notes; a deal had been made.

And Ed Washburn had interfered.

It had probably been for the best. She would get more out of Washburn than she would have gotten from Benjie, though she wasn't too interested in going to the New Mexico Territory. She wondered how many New Mexicans spoke English, and if they gambled. Perhaps there would be an opportunity to start a gaming parlor down there.

Then she forgot about the gaming parlor, her mind on something else. She couldn't help wondering what it would have been like with a boy so big . . .

And so young.

Ed Washburn was true to his promise. The next morning Kirsten packed her things and said good-bye to a weeping Celia. "Promise you'll come visit if you ever return," she said, holding Kirsten against her matronly bosom.

"I will," Kirsten lied. "I certainly will." She said good-bye to Washburn's children, giving each of them a trinket from her luggage; a bit of ribbon, some scented soap, a comb set with paste jewels. Then she hugged them, promising to return.

Secretly she hoped she would never have to see these grubby little brats, their silly, sugary stepmother, or this damned place again.

As they rode off toward Memphis, Celia fondly watched Ed and Kirsten go. The night before, her husband told her why the girl stayed so long without mentioning a departure date. The poor child had just confessed to him that she had no money. He had wakened Celia at midnight, asking her if they could tighten their belts a little until their crop was in, so that he could lend Kirsten enough to get to her mother.

And all this time she had thought he was being stingy. Some folks might not think Ed was much to look at, but as far as Celia was concerned, he was a real man!

What she didn't know was that he was man enough to be scared out of his wits. And he would be terrified until this girl was off his hands and on her way.

54

Ed Washburn drew a small amount of money from his bank, then, on second thought, added a little more. Kirsten's clothes looked like they could be worn at a—a whorehouse.

And they probably had, he thought sourly.

But at least Kirsten ought to have a few decent things—for Inga's sake, if nothing else.

Ed sighed, thinking of his Celia, with her one good Sunday gown and her two everyday ones. He ought to be making purchases for her, but he couldn't afford it. Maybe when the crops were in . . .

Washburn went to the docks where he purchased a ticket on a riverboat leaving for St. Louis in two days. Then he separated the rest of the money. "Here," he told the girl. "This packet will be for your stagecoach fare and for food along the way. The rest you can spend for clothing, and"—his face reddened—"*necessaries*. You're not to go to your mother unless you are dressed proper-like."

Ed paid for a room in a small, sedate hotel for women, giving Kirsten instructions to remain there until her boat sailed. Then, satisfied that he had done all that was required of him, he left Memphis and went home to his Celia.

Kirsten counted the money he had left her, and her lip curled in scorn. What did he think she would buy with this? Calico rags, like the ones Celia wore? She wouldn't be caught dead in gowns like that! Yet some of her own had seen better days. She needed a whole new wardrobe!

Why hadn't she taken more time to pack?

Her mind dwelled lovingly on the amber street dress she had created and modeled for Slim Morley. True, it was designed to be provocative. But Inga would never have noticed. Kirsten sighed.

Well, she would just have to see what she could do with what she had. And her first stop would be Miz Fannie's place of business. Miz Fannie's girls would know of the best places to make her purchases.

Neither Miz Fannie nor her sister was at home, but several of her girls volunteered to go shopping with Kirsten. In the late evening Kirsten left the giggling crew and returned to her hotel to survey the purchases she had made.

There were velvets, satins, and silks in crimson, rose, azure, and royal blue with dainty hand-embroidered underthings to wear beneath them. Nothing she had bought would fit Ed Washburn's definition of proper apparel.

And except for a riverboat ticket and a few dollars in her purse, Kirsten was dead broke.

Maybe, she thought, she could cash the ticket in. There would be enough to hold her over for a while, until she could find work. But Memphis was too close to Sweethome, and Washburn knew most of the people in town.

No, she had to go on.

Kirsten stood for a moment, one finger touching her chin as she stared at the gowns on the bed. Finally she snatched one up and held it against her, looking into the small, wavy mirror above the dresser. Her lips curved in satisfaction.

It would do.

A few minutes later the desk clerk at the hotel glanced up and gasped at the apparition coming down the stairs. Kirsten had donned the crimson gown. It left a great expanse of her shoulders bare, and she had fastened a scarlet ribbon about her throat, as if to conceal that fact. She wore a wide-brimmed hat, decorated with egret plumes, which matched the gown.

She was on her way to make some money.

Within the hour Kirsten presented herself at the most elite gambling house in Memphis. The man at the door was taken aback as she pushed past him.

"No, lady! This place is for men only. Wimmen don't come in here."

She took off her gloves and smiled sweetly. "Really? Well, one has."

"Look, missus. If you're huntin' your husband, he ain't here. I know all the clientele—"

"I have no husband," Kirsten said frostily, "nor am I looking for one. I understand this is a place to gamble. And I intend to do just that, if you'll step aside!"

"But, *lady*!"

Kirsten walked past him, through the foyer, and into the main room where male heads swiveled in amazement.

"Hello, boys," she said, smiling. "I'm looking for a game. Who's feeling lucky tonight?"

There was a moment's dead silence as they stared, then a general stampede as they left their tables and clamored to join her. She selected an affluent trio with expertise, and the others gathered around to watch; some with their eyes on the cards, the others crowding close to see the magnificent view the neckline of the crimson dress afforded.

And Kirsten won.

She won steadily all night and finally bet all she had in one desperate move.

And lost, to a trio of aces.

"I saw that," one of the onlookers shouted drunkenly. "Goldurn it, ol' Bart had an ace up his sleeve! He was cheatin' "

The man called Bart was also a little bit tipsy. He rose, his fists doubled belligerently, his face shoved into the onlooker's face.

"Say that again!"

"You was cheatin'!"

Bart swung a hamlike fist, and the other man went down. Someone else struck Bart and was sent crashing against the wall. Soon all of the club's patrons had joined in the melee.

Kirsten scooped up all the money on the table and dumped it into her purse. Then she looked around for a way out.

A big, burly man gripped her arm, protectively, placing his body before her. His face was filled with concern. "A girl like you doesn't belong in a mess like this. You'd better leave. Let me help you."

Kirsten smiled up at him, fluttering her lashes. "Oh, thank you," she breathed.

And in gentlemanly fashion, he escorted Kirsten and the money she had taken out the doorway.

Kirsten stood on tiptoe to kiss his cheek, and then she ran. She ran back to the hotel where she counted the rewards of her evening.

Now Kirsten not only had several brand-new gowns, she also had enough money to take her all the way to the New Mexico Territory, and then some.

She went to bed and fell into a dreamless sleep.

55

Jenny was no longer in the New Mexico territory, as Inga and Kirsten thought. She, Daniel, Ugly Woman, and the children were at last on their way to join Cochise.

"I want to fight beside my people," Daniel said. "Will you go with me, Jen-nee?"

At first something in Jenny held back. Then she realized that her mother and Theron had been the only people of her own race who had been kind to her. Her grandfather was a fanatic, her real father despised her. Rebel outlaws had tried to rape her when she had been little more than a girl. Then there was Sam—and Jesse!

Yes, Jesse—who had not kept his promises to a girl who had trusted him with her life. Nor had he kept the promises he had made to a woman he married.

Her only loving friendships had been shared with the blacks at Sweethome and the Indians of New Mexico.

"Yes," she said. "I will go."

"And you understand," he said gently, "that we may be fighting for a lost cause. The white people could roll over my people, swallow us up—there are too many of them, and they are accustomed to taking. We can only try."

"We can only try," she repeated. But her voice lacked the ring of conviction. Would she ever be able to shoot a white man under any conditions? Evidently Daniel thought she could, because he was constantly training her to do just that. She would close her eyes tightly as she pulled the trigger and miss by a mile. He had no idea that when it came to putting meat on the table, she was a dead shot.

It was just the thought of shooting at humans that put her off.

On the day of departure Daniel and Jenny had dismantled their hogan. The hours they had spent there were too precious to be tainted by another presence. And, as Daniel had said, the white people would come. They would view the hogan with curiosity, perhaps even laugh at it, as they built their fine homes that kept the weather out but could not keep love in.

After they had taken down the hogan they went to the cliff dwelling, to pack all the food they could carry for the journey and to say goodbye to Kwass'ini.

They had left a message for Jesse at the cilff dwelling, a message only he would be able to understand.

Last but not least, they had filled water skins at the spring. These must be refilled at every stop, since there would be little water on the trail they were taking.

Then they finally left the area, Ugly Woman and the lame So'tso riding double on the horse Jenny had brought back from Santa Fe, the others taking turns on Daniel's mount with little Ee'yah before them.

They were exceedingly cautious until they crossed the Arizona border riding parallel to the trail much of the time. It was too late in the year for wagon trains to set out for California, and they met up with no one. Soon, now, they should catch up with Cochise's group.

Jenny knew she would be sorry to have the journey end. It had been idyllic, with warm, balmy days and cold nights when she and Daniel cuddled close for warmth, loving each other even more as they turned to each other for comfort.

Now, watching Daniel as he took his turn at riding, with little Ee'yah on the saddle in front of him, Jenny thought how well this rugged country suited her husband. In the summer it would be a burning inferno, all reds with purple shadows. But now the landscape around them was misty with the rose and lavender of early dawn. As she clambered among the rose-red rocks leading down to the desert floor, which led to the painted mountains beyond, she shivered with the beauty of it. Daniel glanced down at her.

"Cold?"

Her great eyes were warm as she smiled up at him. "No, just happy!"

Then she said, "Daniel, look!" She pointed ahead and a little to one side. There, clearly visible, was a lone wagon, one wheel at a slant.

"Looks like they're having trouble," Daniel said. "Greenhorn, probably, or he wouldn't be trying to cross the mountains this time of year."

"Can't you help them? There might be children in the wagon."

Daniel hesitated a minute, then smiled. He had no fight with family men. His fight was against a corrupt government that attempted to enslave his kind.

"Here, Jen-nee."

He handed little Ee'yah down from his saddle and galloped toward the wagon. Ugly Woman did not understand what he was doing, and she whipped up the horse she shared with So'tso. Jenny, Bit'so, and little Ee'yah were left behind. And suddenly Jenny had an odd feeling about that wagon.

She sat down among the rocks, pulling Bit'so and Ee'yah close.

Though Daniel did not know it, the three men in the damaged wagon were not family men. In fact, they were far from it. The owner of the vehicle was Jim Jellico—Lucky Jim, they called him in New York, since the police had never been able to pin him with a crime. He headed up every vice available in the city, from extorting money from immigrants to shanghaiing unsuspecting men who stopped off at his saloon for drink.

With him was the Duke, a well-read gentlemanly type who made his profit from houses of ill-repute, and Slugger Sandler, a huge man with cauliflower ears, Jim Jellico's bodyguard. And they were not here because they wanted to be but because they had to be.

Jim Jellico's luck had run out. He, the Duke, and Slugger had robbed a bank, and two people had walked in, recognizing them. They killed one, but the other got away. Now they were wanted for robbery and murder, and their only hope was to get to California before the snow, then maybe take a ship to the Hawaiian Islands.

And now the goddamn vehicle had broken down!

It was Slugger, trying to fit the wheel back onto the wagon, who alerted the others.

"*Indians!*" he cried.

Swearing, the two men burst from the wagon where they had been counting their ill-gotten goods. They were not at all knowledgeable about the frontier, and this looked like an Indian attack.

"Could be it ain't," Slugger said.

"What the hell difference does it make? It's better to be safe than sorry!"

Jellico showed his teeth in an ugly grin as he lifted his gun. He snapped off a shot, and the lead horse went down, its legs thrashing. The horse rolled over on its rider, who lay still.

The Duke fired then, almost simultaneously, his one bullet penetrating the bodies of the woman and child who brought up the rear.

The horse paused, confused, as Ugly Woman and So'tso slid to the ground.

Her face pale and hard, Jenny stood among the rocks. She forgot her qualms about shooting whites as she aimed her rifle straight and true.

Lucky Jim Jellico was lucky for this one last time. He didn't know what hit him when he took her bullet squarely between the eyes. Slugger Sandler heard only the *spang* of the first bullet. He was next, hitting the ground like a fallen tree.

The Duke panicked, certain that they had been attacked by an entire tribe. He recalled the horror stories he had read about the Indians; how they hung their victims over a slow fire, watching them jackknife as their brains roasted.

He would not be taken alive!

He lifted his pistol to his forehead with shaking hands, squeezed his eyes shut, and pulled the trigger.

Jenny threw her rifle to the ground and began to run.

When she reached Daniel, he sat up, groggily, shaking his head to clear it. Her eyes went over him quickly. He had only been stunned by the fall. There were no bullet wounds.

"Thank God," she breathed. And then she ran on.

Ugly Woman and So'tso had not been so lucky. Little So'tso was dead. The same bullet that had gone through her heart had penetrated Ugly Woman's stomach. Ugly Woman was dying. She was obviously in great pain. Jenny knelt beside her, holding her hand, until the lovely eyes glazed over and she lay still.

Ugly Woman hadn't been as close a friend as Tsis'na. She had been quieter, more stolid in her ways. But Jenny had grown to love her, just as she had loved Tsi'dii and little So'tso. Now they were gone—all of them!

She heard the sharp crack of a gun and raised her eyes to see Daniel standing over the body of his horse. His face was pale as he lowered his pistol to his side. He was still a little dazed, but he did what he had to do. He had put the animal out of its misery.

Jenny wanted to go to Daniel. He would need her. Then she saw Bit'so. Knowing that she had the responsibility of Ee'yah, the child had carried the heavy toddler through the rocks and out onto the desert floor. Now she stood looking at So'tso's body. The little girl lay like a blood-stained rag that had been tossed away.

"*Shi dei'zhi?*" Bit'so asked hesitantly, her lip quivering.

My younger sister!

So'tso was Bit'so's only sister, all she had left of a laughing, happy family of brothers, sisters, and cousins. And they were all dead at the hands of the white man! Jenny's eyes were pools of black anger as she drew the child to her.

"So'tso has been avenged," she whispered harshly. "Do not cry."

That night Jenny spread her blanket apart from Daniel's. There was no room in her heart for love.

56

Daniel could not sleep. He had buried the dead, but he knew the spirits of Ugly Woman and So'tso would haunt him forever.

They had died because he had been thinking like a white man, going to the aid of the stranded travelers, forgetting that they might see him as an Indian.

He glanced at Jen-nee. She lay on her back, but her eyes were open, reflecting silver in the moonlight.

He wondered what she was thinking. Perhaps that she had brought the woman and child through all kinds of perils, only to see them die as a result of his carelessness.

Or that she, too, might now be lying dead, her blood slowly sinking into the sand.

Jenny wasn't thinking of any of these things. She was thinking only of the men she had shot. And that she felt nothing.

It was a long night.

The next day they took three of the horses that had been hitched to the wagon and traveled on. Their one remaining animal was laden with what they found in the wagon. Bank bags filled with money indicated that the dead men were criminals, but that made no difference to Jenny. She had killed them and she didn't care. She couldn't seem to care about anything.

She rode in silence, her eyes dull and unresponsive to Daniel's or the children's conversation. She was like a squaw: docile, obedient.

I do not know this Jenny, Daniel thought. *I should never have brought her to this*!

He was to remember the thought that night.

He spread his blankets far from the firelight and led Jenny to them. She went quietly, submitting to his lovemaking as if it were something to be endured.

But in the night he heard her crying.

Two days later they came upon an Indian encampment. This time Daniel rode forward and left Jenny, Bit'so, and Ee'yah to wait. He was gone for nearly two days, and when he returned, he was not alone. Riding forward, he looked down at Jen-nee—a long and searching look.

"Cochise has accepted life on the reservation," he said quietly. "Others of us are heading for Mexico to continue the fight. There is no place for women and children. You can find your way home?"

Jenny nodded, dazed. "Yes, but—"

"Then go. I release you from your vows."

He rode away, then turned to look at the small figure staring after him. He rode back again and dismounted.

"I once made a vow in a strange church, to a god who was not my god," he said quietly. "I regretted it. Our marriage was never a true one. Go home, Jen-nee. Go home to your Jesse, who loves you."

"He has a wife," she whispered.

"And she is dead." Daniel said stolidly, his eyes on her face. "Good-bye, my Jen-nee."

She was crying now, shocked out of the stupor she had been immersed in for these last days. She came toward him, her arms outstretched. But he mounted in one agile movement and was off in a cloud of dust, racing ahead of his new companions.

It wouldn't do for them to see the tears that streaked his bronze cheeks. Tomorrow he would be happy about the action he had taken in sending Jen-nee away, back to a life of peace and gentleness. The two people he loved would be together.

And he would be with his people, his people whose sun was setting, while Jesse's and Jenny's was high on the eastern horizon.

57

Inga arrived in Santa Fe on a bright blue day in the fall. It was warm in the sunshine, but there was a snap to the air that presaged the coming winter. Inga and Dinah, after years spent in the lowlands of Tennessee, were enervated by the seven-thousand-foot altitude. Paul was in slightly better shape, and little Honeybee, who had regained her sparkling spirits on the journey, was irrepressible.

The atmosphere was exotic, unlike anything Inga had ever seen before. There were Indians everywhere, stoic in their colorful garments. As the small caravan with which they had traveled entered the town, there was a frightful din. Mules brayed as they pulled carts with creaking wheels. Men cursed in Spanish and in English. And beautiful señoritas lounged in arched doorways, low-cut blouses slipping from amber shoulders. Their dark eyes were inviting above spread, lacy fans.

Inga laughed as Paul's head swiveled to stare at them, and the back of his neck turned crimson with embarrassment. She had a feeling he would find this world quite different from his native Minnesota.

"Minna, see!"

Honeybee was pointing toward the hotel where the leader of their wagon train suggested they stay. After their rather desolate journey, the place looked rather grand. Inga smiled down at Honeybee and hugged her.

This was the end of the trail. Here there would be food, rest, and a bath, and tomorrow they would travel on to find Jenny.

They checked in and found the rooms sparsely furnished but strangely beautiful: whitewashed walls and high beds with crudely carved and painted headboards. Hot water was brought, and Inga bathed and dressed. Leaving Honeybee with Dinah, she returned to the desk to question the clerk.

"Is there a way to send a message to the Whitman-Norwood ranch?" she asked the man behind the counter.

The clerk was well acquainted with Sam, Whitman had supplied liquor for the hotel bar for a long time. "Ain't no such place no more," he said apologetically, "Sam's dead. Kilt in an Injun raid."

The woman before him seemed stunned. The fellow looked her over. He wouldn't have thought Sam would even know a female of this caliber.

Inga found her voice at last. "Mr. Norwood and his wife . . . wife." she whispered. "They are safe and well?"

The clerk took off his narrow wire-rimmed glasses and polished them on his sleeve. "I reckon he's awright. He's here in town. Went back to work last week. He was some tore up when that little wife of his died and left him with a kid."

He put his glasses back on, then his expression changed to one of alarm.

"Missus? Missus! What the hell—"

He came around the counter and took the arm of the woman who had gone dead white. For a moment she swayed against him, as if she were going to faint.

"Consuela," he shouted. "Consuela! Gitcher butt out here! Bring me some whiskey!"

Inga braced herself and spoke through stiff, frozen lips.

"Tell me," she said, "where I can find Mr. Norwood."

In his office at the post, Jesse Norwood shoved aside his papers and rested his head in his hands. He could no longer lose himself in his work. He supposed it was because he had come back to work too soon.

Lately all he could think about was what a mess he had made of his life. He had lied to himself when he married Elena, telling himself that he could make it work; that his love for Jenny had been deep affection for an enchanting child; that this, his marriage, his commission, was his big chance.

He still had the commission. The wife he had cheated out of true love was dead. The child she had given him was sickly and not expected to live.

When it died, he would be truly alone.

He even blamed himself for the loss of Daniel, his Indian scout, his friend. If he hadn't taken leave, Daniel never would have deserted. He should have known that Daniel couldn't stomach Gomez.

He lifted his head impatiently as his aide opened the office door. "You have a visitor, Colonel. A lady," the young man said.

It was probably an angry wife who had learned of her husband's high-jinks at the Exchange Hotel, he thought wearily. She would probably demand that they be sent back East.

"Send her in."

"*Mrs. Saint Germain!*"

Jesse came instantly to his feet. The woman swayed before him; the healthy color he remembered had faded into a greenish pallor. Instantly he was around the desk, seating her in a chair.

"You've heard about Jenny, that she's gone," he said. "Oh, God, I'm sorry! I'm so sorry!"

Inga looked up at him with an unfocused expression. "Then what the clerk said was right. Jenny's—Jenny's dead—"

"Oh, no," he burst out. "No!"

Inga's blue eyes widened with a faint dawning of hope. "Then what—where—?"

Jesse groaned.

It was all going to come out in the open now. How could he explain his behavior to Jenny's mother when he couldn't even explain it to himself? He sought some way to gain a little time before breaking this woman's heart.

"Jenny's with friends," he said. "I can't explain now, but I may be able to find a clue to her whereabouts. It will take a few days. You and your husband must be patient."

"My husband is dead."

The news stunned Jesse. He had always regarded Theron as an adversary—and someone to pattern himself after. He felt suddenly lost, rootless.

"I will find her," he said again.

Inga found herself outside his office door, dazed and bewildered. Jenny was alive! But what had happened between Jenny and Jesse? Why was she staying with friends, and who were they?

This was all her fault! She should have known better than to allow her daughter to go so far away! Lovely Jenny, her heart filled with love and her head stuffed with dreams.

A small wind sprang up, whirling its way across the square, carrying dust and trash before it. Inga shrank inside her coat and hurried her steps, praying that Jesse's journey would be swift and that Jenny would return with him.

Jesse, as he had promised, left Santa Fe within the hour.

The sight of Jenny's mother had brought back more than he cared to remember.

58

As Jesse rode toward the Place of the Old Ones he relived those final days in the little shack on Belle Terrain. The rickety structure had once been his home. His family had lived there and worked for the people who owned the plantation.

He returned from the war to find Belle Terrain burned down, only the shack still standing. His parents were dead, his brothers and sisters scattered to the winds. But it was peaceful there.

He decided to stay for a little while, to try to pull himself together until he could decide what to do.

And he had found Jenny, with her great, steadfast eyes, her sunny nature; Jenny, who had been only a little girl but who had had the strength and courage to defy both Inga and St. Germain on Jesse's behalf, all for the sake of a boy that even Sweethome's black cook, Dinah, regarded as white trash, an overgrown lout who could neither read nor write.

Jenny taught him a little. The rest he had learned from Sam, who was well-read as a young man, despite his crude language and rough exterior in later years. And along with that learning came driving ambition—a need to prove himself.

Sam's rape of the Indians provided the reason. Elena's father, a Spanish *grandee* who didn't realize that Jesse once had been considered to be of a very low class, provided the tools that Jesse needed to counteract the actions of people like Sam. They included a commission issued straight from Washington.

And the hand of his beautiful daughter.

All these things had been Jesse's excuses for what he had done to Jenny.

He somehow managed to change his thinking. He tried to remember Jenny as being a child, telling himself that she would find someone else, someone St. Germain considered good enough for her. He tried to erase her from his mind, and until she had come to the New Mexico Territory, he had almost succeeded. He managed to forget her gentle sweetness, her impish beauty, her steadfast faith in him.

But that did not excuse the thing he had done. He had loved Jenny once. How the hell could he have left her here in the wilderness, at the mercy of the wild things.

Or any renegade white man who came along.

Jesse had almost reached the cliff dwelling. He realized that he had ridden more slowly these last hours. Maybe it was because he was afraid of what he might find when he reached his destination. It was growing dark, and he still had several hours of riding ahead of him. There was no point in going on tonight.

Jesse sighed, then dismounted to build a small fire. He put some stew on to boil; then, after he had eaten, he sat by that fire for a long time, seeing Jenny's laughing features in the flames. At last he banked the coals so that they would be in readiness for the morning and rolled up in his blankets. Though he was exhausted, stiff, and sore from the long journey, he could not sleep. He spent most of the night staring at the stars that glittered overhead.

The eyes of the night, Jenny would have called them.

Jesse rose at dawn, uncertain of whether he had slept at all. The air was chilly, but sweet and soft with mist. At the edge of the trees a deer watched him, curious and unafraid. Finally it became startled and fled, its graceful leaps giving it the appearance of being free from earthly ties.

Jesse's mouth went dry and his throat hurt as he thought of Jenny.

The cliff dwelling was closer than he remembered. The morning dew still sparkled on the grass as he approached it. He looked upward at the structure hidden in the face of the cliff, noting how vines had grown over the entrance; how the branches of trees with scarlet-and-amber leaves almost concealed it.

It was quiet.

There was no one there!

What in the name of God was he going to tell Jenny's mother?

Jesse gave a soft halloo, then dismounted from his horse. He was pretty sure the Indians had come for them, as they had promised, but he had to be certain. He climbed the side of the cliff and stepped over the wall, half afraid of what he might find as he drew a great, shuddering breath.

There was no odor of death.

One by one, he checked all the signs of their departure. The ashes were cold and scattered. There had not been a cook fire here for many weeks. Their supplies were gone. But then, they might have been stolen. . . .

Here!

He exclaimed aloud as he found the message Jenny had left for him. A huge heart scratched in charcoal on the floor of the dwelling, well out of the rain.

In the center of the heart was a button from a red dress, a dress he had once recognized and loved. Beside it was a button from a soldier's uniform.

"I'll be damned!"

Jesse closed his eyes, remembering the slate on which Jenny had given him writing lessons; recalling how he had left it behind when he fled the shack at Belle Terrain, determined to make something of himself. He had left the slate centered in the middle of the table they had used.

There had been a drawing of a heart chalked onto it, a heart with Jesse's name drawn in crude, sprawling letters.

It seemed a very long time ago. He had been so proud of being able to print his name. And he had been aching with love; a love that began in the little shack on Belle Terrain; that he, himself, had ended in New Mexico.

Jesse opened his eyes and picked up the red button. It seemed to burn in the palm of his hand as his fist closed over it in a convulsive movement. Then he picked up the second button, turning it over and studying it. It was brass, as with all military buttons, but he immediately knew whose it was.

Daniel's, of course!

Daniel and Jenny!

So Daniel had lied to him. He had known that Jenny was here all the time.

He remembered how the scout had stayed here, long after his wound was healed; how uncommunicative he had been upon his return. Everything about the man shouted that he was in love. But if Jesse had thought about it at all, he had figured that the object of Daniel's affections was Ugly Woman. With her air of calm and serenity she was a pretty girl, in spite of her clubfoot.

Jesse felt a gnawing pang of jealousy. He raised his eyes to the surrounding area where the trees, in their bright fall colors, stood out clearly from the mist. Across the grassy declivity he saw a squirrel scrabble up a tree with acorns for its winter hoard; he saw a bird that would soon be winging its way south to Mexico. A rabbit scurried into the brush, peeping out, only the tips of its ears showing.

These things would be a part of Jenny's life from now on.

Jesse put the red button in his pocket and started down the side of the cliff. Halfway down, he had second thoughts. He scaled the steep incline once more and laid the button back in its former place with grudging fingers. He was taking something that wasn't his to take.

Jenny was Daniel's now. Jesse owned no part of her. He had sold all rights to the girl he loved when he married Elena.

Now he had to go back and tell Jenny's mother that Jenny was gone; that she was very likely married to an Indian. Inga, most probably, would never see her daughter again.

And he would have to tell her somehow that in this situation, Colonel Jesse Norwood had played a very important part.

59

Jesse shaved and changed along the trail. He was determined to tell Inga about Jenny's disappearance and to confess his part in it as soon as possible. Otherwise, he knew that he wouldn't be able to face the brokenhearted woman. He would have to play the coward and run away.

When he reached Santa Fe, he still hadn't decided what to say or how to say it.

Instead he sent an aide with a message, asking Mrs. St. Germain to come to his home.

He had something important to tell her.

When Inga appeared at the adobe mansion with its roof of Spanish tile, she had Dinah in tow. Dinah had not approved of Jesse at Belle Terrain, her angry expression said that she did not approve of him now.

It was not an auspicious beginning.

Jesse invited them into a house that had become slightly cluttered and ill-kept. It was obvious that this was a home without a mistress. A smell of grease and chili had permeated the drapes. And there was another scent, a familiar one, but one that Inga could not place immediately.

That mystery was solved when little Juana entered the room, carrying what looked like a doll. And then Inga knew what the odor was. It was the aura that surrounds a desperately sick child. She recalled Honeybee's terrible bout with diphtheria.

"This is my daughter," Jesse said heavily.

With a small, pitying sound, Inga moved to take the baby. But Dinah was already ahead of her. Cradling the tiny thing against her massive bosom, she fixed Juana with glowering expression.

"Whut you been feedin' this chile?"

"She doesn't speak English," Jesse said, his face very red. "Mashed frijoles, I think."

Dinah uttered a squawk of fury that set Juana to trembling.

"We goin' intuh that kitchen an' see whut we find," she said firmly. She marched out, and Juana, after an anguished look at Jesse, followed.

Jesse sighed.

It was time to tell his story.

He told Inga how he had traded his memories of Jenny for marriage to Elena. That Jenny had been ... away, staying with friends, when he saw her again, for the first time since he came to the New Mexico Territory.

He had known then that Jenny was his true love, and he had come home to ask Elena to release him from their marriage contract.

He had found Elena sick and pregnant. And he could not leave her. She was on the road to recovery when the baby was born prematurely. Then ...

Colonel Jesse Norwood turned his back and uttered a harsh, sobbing sound. In a few minutes he pulled himself together and turned to face Inga.

"I'm sorry," he said hoarsely.

"You haven't told me about Jenny," Inga said.

"I—I have reason to think that Jenny may be married and in another state." Averting his eyes from Inga's sudden pallor, he rushed on.

"I'll find her for you, I promise."

His gray eyes welled with tears, and Inga moved toward him, putting a compassionate hand on his arm. He was still little more than a boy, she thought. A boy who had been through a war, and had lost his wife, who was left with a baby that might not live.

As for Jesse, when he looked at Inga, he suddenly saw not the proud mistress of Sweethome, whom he had considered her to be, but a ministering angel. His own mother had been overworked, worn down into a harsh bitterness before her death. He had never known real tenderness. He knew he could not let this woman leave before Jenny was found. His face was pleading.

"Mrs. St. Germain—Inga—would you care to move in here for a short time? It's a large house."

Move into the home of a man who had jilted her daughter? Who had let Jenny come out here, not knowing that he had a wife? Dear God, how could he even consider such a thing!

"I am sorry, Colonel Norwood," Inga began stiffly. "It would be quite impossible."

"You hesh yoh mouth, Miz Inga!"

Inga whirled to see Dinah in the doorway, still with the baby in her arms. The old woman glowered at her.

"This yere chile needs you. As much as Honeybee do, mebbe more. Without nobody knows how to keep care of her, she gonna die."

"But, Dinah!"

"Don' 'but, Dinah' me! You don' stay here, I'm gonna. Somebuddy gotta nuss this little tyke."

"Please, Mrs. St. Germain!"

Inga hesitated. Her mind went back to a Christmas dinner at Sweethome. Jesse had been invited, and only too late did Inga realize that Theron had been using the occasion as a wedge, to show Jenny that Jesse was an ill-bred, mannerless boor.

The dinner had ended when Jesse spilled a glass of water in Inga's lap. He had left the house.

And he had said good-bye to Jenny.

Inga had been at fault then too—at fault for not seeing what Theron was doing. Jesse had gone away hurt, with a low sense of self-esteem. And he had forgotten Jenny in an effort to better himself.

The baby cried, a thin little mewling sound, and Inga felt the cry pierce her heart.

This might have been Jenny's child. The fact that it wasn't made little difference now. It was a baby and it was sick.

Inga capitulated.

Late that afternoon the entourage from the Exchange Hotel moved into Jesse Norwood's home. To Inga's surprise it was a happy occasion. Dinah took over the household, Paul had a case of hero-worship for Jesse, and, best of all, Honeybee fell in love with a little sister she had never seen.

60

Ugly Woman and So'tso were dead. Jenny had killed two men. Daniel Strongbow had left her. And Jesse Norwood no longer had a wife.

Jenny's mind was already too full to cope with all it had been forced to accept. So she refused to think, concentrating fiercely on what she had to do. First of all, she must get two small Indian children to safety.

It was only intolerable at night when the sun went down and a blue chill settled over the desert sands. Jenny would lie shivering in her blankets, holding the children close, remembering Daniel's warmth against her. Sometimes a few soundless tears would slip from beneath her lashes. But in the morning she led the remnants of her small family stolidly to the north and east.

Once they were lost for a time.

"Look at the sun," Bit'so said, pointing. "It will tell us the way."

"I have been looking at it." Jenny sighed, nearing her breaking point. "But I know this is not the way we came! The sun should be there!" She waved toward a spot on the horizon.

"You are thinking of the summer sun. Now the winter sun shines on the sky world. It is this way. Let me show you."

The little girl took the lead, and soon they were passing places they recognized. They saw the wagon with its broken wheel, careened in the sand. They paused for a moment beside the graves of Ugly Woman and So'tso. An icy wind had sprung up, and they stood there shivering, their garments fluttering around them in the wind. Then they moved on to the spot where the murderers of the woman and child had been buried in a common grave.

At last everything righted in Jenny's mind. She had been forced to kill them. It was a thing she had had to do, just as Daniel had done what he had to do.

He could not go back to face a desertion charge. And he would not accept life on a reservation now that he had freed himself from all commitments to the white man. Instead, Daniel had chosen a life of danger.

He had left Jenny behind, not because he didn't love her, but because he loved her too much. And he had paid her the compliment of believing that she was competent to care for herself and these children, until they reached Santa Fe and Jesse.

But that was where Daniel had erred. Jenny had no intention of returning to civilization. She was heading toward the Place of the Old Ones.

She was going home.

They left the place of the dead, leading their horses up the rocky, red ridge that rimmed the sand. Skirting Silver City and the little mining town of Alto, they made their way upward into the early snows. And at last, on a morning as brittle and fragile as glass, they clambered up the hillside toward the dark mouth of the dwelling.

It was all just as they had left it. Jenny stood staring at the dwelling for a moment, surveying the heart she had drawn with a charred stick, the red button from the dress that Jesse would remember, the military button from Daniel's coat.

Her eyes welled with tears. Her marriage had been a brief idyll, and now it was over. Even the hogan that Daniel had built for their wedding night was gone. Except for this childish message before her, and the fact that Ugly Woman and So'tso had been killed, it might never have taken place.

But there was no time now to reminisce. Firewood must be gathered, a kettle set to boil. The animals had to be unloaded and released to find what forage they could beneath the snow. And then their stores had to be counted out and divided, they would have to last until spring.

No matter what, Jenny must keep busy. Too busy to mourn Daniel. Or to dream of Jesse, who was now free.

It was a terrible winter. Snow followed snow. Even the animals left the forested slopes, heading south in search of food. The horses, without oats or grass for grazing, soon became gaunt. The trees below the cave dwelling were stripped of all edible bark.

One day Jenny recklessly began to dole out her precious seeds to the horses. She must keep their mounts alive at all costs.

But her care only prolonged the inevitable.

One of the horses died in January. In spite of Jenny's revulsion toward doing it, the animal was butchered and cut into strips that Bit'so smoked over a fire. Jenny and the children were now hollow-eyed and bone-thin, their food almost completely gone, when the second horse went down, struggling in a February snow.

Jenny put a merciful bullet through its head. It, too, was cut up for food.

That night Jenny sat up late, taking stock of her position. Their horses were gone. The seeds for the spring planting had been for naught, and except for the meat from the horses, they were almost destitute.

Her eyes roved to a corner of the dwelling where the bank bags Daniel had taken from the wagon were stacked. There was money there. More than she had ever seen in her lifetime. If she could only get to Santa Fe, she would be able to purchase all they needed.

But how could she accomplish that, in this weather, dragging two children along?

The next morning she awoke, looked at the world around her, and came to a decision. A warm sun had miraculously appeared, and the icicles at the cave's mouth sent down a steady rain, like tears.

If the weather held, Jenny might be able to leave tomorrow. Could Bit'so care for Ee'yah until she returned?

The little girl nodded gravely when asked, and Jenny hugged her in an agony of love. She spent the afternoon carrying firewood for those she would leave behind. The next morning she left early, carrying one of the money bags, fighting back the urge to run.

It would be a long walk to Santa Fe.

Jenny was only to remember the first few days. After that, everything was a blur. Sometimes Daniel walked beside her. Sometimes Jesse. And at other times she was a little girl, walking the roads of Tennessee with her mother and sister, searching for a place that had been deserted by its owners during the war.

Two days out of Santa Fe it began to snow again. Jenny stumbled on blindly, her instincts telling her that she must not stop to rest or she would never rise again. She wondered for a moment at the heavy weight she was carrying, then dropped the money bag she held cradled in her arms. The snow sifted over it as she made her way, again by instinct, to the only place she knew.

Jesse would help her.

At the arched doorway of Jesse Norwood's home Jenny scrabbled at the door with freezing fingers. Then she sank to the steps where the snow, falling steadily, covered her dark hair with a mantle of white.

61

Jesse Norwood could not sleep. He sat before a dying fire, a pipe in his mouth. He had pulled off his shirt, and his enormous shoulders were bared. Inga, Dinah, and Honeybee had long since gone to bed; Paul and he had sat up late discussing a partnership. Sam Whitman's ranch belonged to Jesse now, and Paul wanted to work it on shares.

Jesse couldn't think of a better partner, nor a more honest and dependable one.

He sighed heavily. The coming of these people into his life had brought him a great deal of contentment. He was no longer so lonely, and his little daughter, Ellen, was thriving at last.

He was a happy man—almost.

His mind was on two women, out there in the cold. Elena had hated the winters, yet snow was now falling on her grave in the churchyard. There was nothing anyone could do to warm her, ever again.

And Jenny?

Had Jenny found what she wanted? Was she someplace safe and warm? Or was she following her mounted husband on foot, through this weather, her head bent against the elements like a squaw.

Jesse felt his anger rise against Daniel, and then he was angry with himself. Daniel had treated Jenny better than Jesse ever had.

He rubbed his eyes and stood, knocking out his pipe against the adobe fireplace. Both Jenny and Elena seemed to be haunting him tonight. It was time to go to bed.

He started for the stairs, then paused as the knocker at the front door sounded above the fury of the storm. A crease appeared between his sandy brows. Surely he wasn't being called out on a military mission on a night like this.

He threw open the front door, and the fire in the fireplace flamed up in the sudden draft. A gust of snow hit him in the face and took his breath away.

So did the vision that entered the room. For a moment Jesse thought he was seeing an angel. The lovely blond woman was swatched in furs from head to toe; she was bejeweled and spangled with snowflakes. Her eyes took in the massive chest before her, liking what they saw. An elusive dimple flickered at the corner of her mouth as Jesse stared at the woman, unable to find his voice.

"I'm Kirsten, Inga St. Germain's daughter, Jenny's sister," she said sweetly. "They told me at the hotel that Mama was here. I just got in and couldn't wait until morning. You must be Jesse! I don't believe we've met."

Kirsten, of course! Now he could see the resemblance to Inga.

"Come in," Jesse said heartily. "I'll have Juana

call your mother. She will be so pleased. Here, let me get your luggage."

He went out on the steps, drawing a suddden breath as the wind struck his bare torso. Then, as he bent to pick up his visitor's portmanteau, his eyes fell on an object partially covered with snow.

It was human—an Indian! And his visitor had to step over it to get to the door. He looked at Kirsten, in the doorway, with startled eyes.

"A drunk," she said deprecatingly. "You don't need to apologize. We have lots of them in N'Awlins. . . ."

Her voice trailed off as Jesse scooped the still figure up in his arms and carried it past Kirsten. He set it down on a couch and reached for his shirt to brush the snow away.

"It's a woman," he said, "and she's still alive."

Then he froze.

When he spoke again, it was to release a strangled cry that echoed through the house and brought Inga and Dinah to the head of the stairs.

"It's Jenny! I've found Jenny! My God, help me!"

Within seconds it seemed that the room was filled with people. They stood over Jenny, all talking at once.

Kirsten waited to one side. Maybe, she thought sourly, after a while someone would notice that *she* was here.

62

Jenny wasn't surprised to see Inga, Kirsten, and Jesse through her haze of feverish exhaustion.

After all, hadn't they walked with her from the Place of the Old Ones? But there had been someone else too. Her face twisted as she searched for a name.

"*Daniel!*" she cried suddenly.

Jesse flinched at the name, then sat upright as he finally made sense of what had appeared to be incoherent babbling.

"*Bit'so, Ee'yah, Old Ones. Hurry!*" Jenny's pale fingers plucked at the coverlet as she cried out, her head twisting on the pillow.

Jesse rose abruptly. "Stay with her," he said to no one in particular, his eyes fiercely determined.

Then Jesse left the house, saddled his horse, and loaded another with supplies. He rode out into a white world.

When he reached the cliff dwelling, it was empty, though the ashes of a small fire were filled with embers. Searching, he found the two children huddled in the storage room, hiding from the strange man they had watched approach. Both of them were a little feverish, and they attacked the food he brought with the appetite of wolves.

They had not eaten for three days. After they ate, they slept. And after they slept, they ate again.

Then Jesse wrapped them in blankets and began the long trek home. As they rode, Bit'so talked. She told Jesse how Daniel and Jenny had gotten married and of the incident in the Arizona desert in which Ugly Woman and So'tso had lost their lives.

She explained that Jenny had saved the rest of them. Then Daniel decided to go to Mexico with some of Cochise's men. He set Jenny free and sent them away.

She did not see that Jesse's fists were clenched, white-knuckled on his reins as he thought of all that Jenny had endured.

And it was all his fault.

When they finally reached Santa Fe, Jenny was asleep. Dinah was horrified at the sight of the little urchins and sent Inga and Kirsten out to purchase clothing while she scrubbed them down to the skin. Jenny awoke to see a solemn-faced little brown boy in a plaid shirt and blue jeans, and a dusky, slightly miserable-looking girl with tight braids and full skirts.

It took her a moment to recognize them. Then Jenny gave a glad cry. She held out her arms, and they came into them.

Those listening outside heard her weeping, a thing she hadn't even done when she heard of Theron's death. Dinah rubbed her wet eyes with a black fist.

"Can't stan' aroun' here all day," she said

sourly. "Somebody gotta take keer of Miss Honeybee an' Miss Ellen."

That afternoon, Jesse entered Jenny's room. She looked up at him with eyes still swollen from crying, and he took her hand. It fluttered like a little bird in his own big, warm one.

"Jenny, you know about Elena?"

She nodded her head against her pillow.

"And I know about Daniel."

Jenny turned her face away, and his grip tightened on her fingers.

"Jenny, I'm going away for a while. And when I come back, I have something to ask you. Will you listen?"

Again she nodded. But her eyes were filled with confusion.

Jesse bent to kiss her on the forehead. It was a chaste kiss but one that seemed to burn there forever. Then he was gone.

To Jenny, waiting, it would seem as if he were gone forever.

63

Spring brushed the landscape with a faint green. It soon deepened into summer. Then Jesse returned; Paul was with him. They both walked into the courtyard to find Jenny, in a yellow-checked gingham morning gown, playing in the courtyard with Bit'so, Ee'yah, and Honeybee. Small Ellen was watching, giggling and clapping her hands. Jesse looked on for a while, smiling, and then strode forward.

Jenny saw him at last. His hair was golden in the sunlight, his eyes startlingly gray in a tanned face. He was not in uniform but wearing a faded gray shirt and worn trousers.

He looked like the Jesse she had once loved.

Her dark hair loosened and falling around her shoulders in disarray, Jenny ran toward him with a glad cry. Then she stopped herself just in time. Jesse looked at her, a mysterious smile quivering around his lips.

"Hello, Jenny."

Then he and Paul greeted the children and went into the house to tell the others that they were home.

At dinner that evening Jesse made an announcement. He had stopped by to see Paul, who had almost finished rebuilding the ranch house. "We're going back there in the morning, and I want Jenny to come with us, since she's seen the place in its original state." Jesse paused, and looked at Jenny. "Providing, of course, that you're willing," he added, his face reddening.

Jenny nodded solemnly.

She had forgotten how far it was, she thought disconsolately as they rode. She felt left out, almost forgotten, as Jesse and Paul rode ahead of her, discussing their plans to build up the area. Once, she lagged so far behind that they were almost out of sight. And neither noticed.

Jenny knew that her feelings were on edge. She told herself that she had finally come to terms with Jesse's marriage to Elena. Like Daniel, Jesse had done what he thought he had to do.

But she knew she still loved him, more than life itself. She had never stopped loving him, not even while she had lain in Daniel's arms.

Then they reached the ranch.

The structure on the hill above them was no longer gray and unpainted but was now gleaming, pristine white. Several rooms had been added on, forming two wings, and a veranda ran around the front and one side.

It was beautiful.

To her surprise the men shook hands, and Paul rode his mount on up the hill. Jesse looked at Jenny.

"Come," he said gently.

They rode some distance away, to a spot where a stream sparkled briefly in a hidden glade, and Jenny was surprised to see a second house, a smaller one, its frame covered with hand-hewn shakes. It blended perfectly into the scenery. The meadow before it was filled with wildflowers. Behind it rose a mountain, still capped with snow.

Jenny looked at the house with awe. "Who lives here?"

Again Jesse said, "Come."

Mystified, she followed him. He entered the house without knocking, and she followed him. Then she stood completely still, staring in disbelief at the interior. Jesse went to start a fire, already laid in the fireplace. The room was an exact replica of the big room at Belle Terrain. The wood cook stove, the shelves—everything was perfectly restored.

Jesse reached for an old red woolen shirt that hung behind the door.

"I thought maybe if we could go back—" he said humbly.

Jenny burst into tears.

He pulled her down to the rug in front of the fireplace. "Remember how I got chilled when my leg was hurt? How you held me and warmed me?"

"Yes," she whispered.

He wrapped his arms more tightly around her.

"Then warm me now."

It was later, much later, when he revealed his plans. They would be married. Then, if Jenny approved, he would resign his commission and they would live here, on the ranch, where their children could grow up in a healthy atmosphere. He anticipated her next question and put a finger to her lips.

"And that includes Ee'yah and Bit'so." He smiled. "Paul, your mother, Dinah, and Honeybee will all be nearby."

"And Kirsten?"

A furrow appeared between his brows. "Kirsten is talking about buying my house in Santa Fe. I think she will find it much too large. But let's forget about everyone else for now! God, Jenny! I love you."

She lifted her mouth to his, and he found it just as sweet as it had been all those years ago. The two came together again in the way of a woman and a man.

In Santa Fe, Inga waited to hear the results of Jesse's surprise for Jenny. And Kirsten wandered from room to room, considering the changes she would make. How easily this place could be transformed into another French Rose. And now she had the wherewithal to do it.

She thought of the money bag she had found not too far from Jenny's body on that winter night long ago. It was hidden now, in the far back of a drawer in Kirsten's bedroom.

Daniel was making his way with his men through the blue mountains of Mexico. He paused for a moment to send a message to the gods. He prayed that Jenny was safe in Santa Fe, that she had found her man.

And he prayed that she would be happy.

About the Author

Aola Vandergriff, born in Le Mars, Iowa, spent her formative years in Oklahoma City, OK. Her credits include a book of poetry, more than 2500 short stories and articles, and 18 novels published worldwide and in several translations. Home is the adobe hacienda which is located in a haunted canyon above the village of La Luz, near Alamogordo, New Mexico. Though she travels extensively to research her novels, she is active in political and civic affairs. She is the mother of six children.